THE TIN GOD

THE TIN GOD

A Tom Harper Mystery

Chris Nickson

Severn House Large Print
London & New York

This first large print edition published 2019
in Great Britain and the USA by
SEVERN HOUSE PUBLISHERS LTD of
Eardley House, 4 Uxbridge Street, London W8 7SY.
First world regular print edition published 2018 by
Severn House Publishers Ltd.

British Library Cataloguing in Publication Data
A CIP catalogue record for this title is available from the British Library.

ISBN-13: 9780727829542

Severn House Publishers support the Forest Stewardship Council™
[FSC™], the leading international forest certification organisation. All
our titles that are printed on FSC certified paper carry the FSC logo.

MIX
Paper from
responsible sources
FSC
www.fsc.org   FSC® C013056

Typeset by Palimpsest Book Production Ltd.,
Falkirk, Stirlingshire, Scotland.
Printed and bound in Great Britain by
T J International, Padstow, Cornwall.

'She was warned. She was given an explanation. Nevertheless, she persisted.'

Spoken to Senator Elizabeth Warren in the U.S. Senate, 2017

To the late MP, Jo Cox, Catherine Buckton, Mary Gawthorpe, and all the women who keep persisting after warnings, explanations, and violence.

One

Tom Harper stared in the mirror.

'What do you think?' he asked doubtfully.

He felt ridiculous in the swallowtail coat and stiff, starched shirt. But the invitation had been clear: it was an official dinner, formal dress required. The fourth occasion this year and the suit wasn't any more comfortable now than the first time he'd worn it. He'd never expected that rank would include parading round like a butler.

'Let's have a gander at you,' Annabelle said and he turned for inspection. 'Like a real police superintendent,' she told him with a nod. 'Just one thing.' A few deft movements and she adjusted the bow tie. 'Never met a man who could do a dicky bow properly. Now you're the real dog's dinner.'

She brought her face close to his. For a moment he expected a kiss. But her eyes narrowed and she whispered, 'I've had another letter. Came in the second post. May Bolland's got one, too.'

His face hardened. He'd expected some outrage when Annabelle announced she was running to be elected to the Board of Poor Law Guardians. A few comments. Plenty of objections. He was even willing to dismiss one anonymous, rambling letter as the work of a crank. But two of them? He wasn't going to ignore that.

1

'What did it say?'

She turned her head away. 'What you'd expect.'

'The same person?' he asked and she nodded. 'What did you do with it?'

'I burned it.' Her voice was tight.

'What?' He pulled back in disbelief. 'Why? It's evidence.'

'Little eyes,' she hissed. 'You know Mary's reading has come on leaps and bounds since she started school. Safer out of the way.'

He breathed slowly, pushing down his anger. For a long time he said nothing. What could he do? It was dust now. Maybe Mrs Bolland had kept hers; he'd send Ash round to see her in the morning.

'Button me up and we'd better get a move on.' Deftly, she changed the subject. 'That hackney's already been waiting for five minutes.'

Annabelle was wearing a new gown, very demure, dark blue silk, with no bustle, high at the neck with lace trim and full leg-of-mutton sleeves, the pale silk shawl he'd bought her draped over her shoulders. Her hair was elaborately swept up and pinned. She looked every bit as lovely as the first day he'd seen her.

There were calls and whistles as they walked through the Victoria pub downstairs. Her pub. She laughed and twirled around the room, enjoying the attention. He was happy to keep in the background, to try and slink out without being noticed. People didn't dress like this in Sheepscar. They owned work clothes and a good suit for funerals; that was it.

2

'What is this do, anyway?' she asked as the cab jounced along North Street.

'The Lord Mayor's Fund,' he replied. 'Charity.'

The Mayor's office had finally become the Lord Mayor's office that summer, Leeds honoured by Queen Victoria to mark her Diamond Jubilee. Sixty years on the throne, Harper thought, going back to well before he was a twinkle in anyone's eye, before his parents had even met. There had been parties and civic events around the city all summer, all carried off with hardly any problems, as if everyone simply wanted to celebrate the occasion with plenty of joy.

The chief constable had been pleased, and even happier once the crime figures came out: down everywhere. The biggest drop was in Harper's division. God only knew why; he didn't have an explanation. He'd praised his men then held his tongue, not wanting to tempt fate.

Annabelle's elbow poked him in the ribs. 'You're miles away.'

'Sorry.'

'Is this a sit-down do tonight?'

'Three courses, then the speeches.'

She groaned and he turned to smile at her.

'We'll have plenty more of these once you're elected.'

'If I'm elected,' she warned. 'Don't be cocky.'

She was one of seven women who were standing to become Poor Law Guardians, their election costs paid by the Suffrage Society and the Women's Co-op Guild. The campaign was no more than a few days old, but already the Tories and the Liberals were deriding the women for trying to rise above their natural station. The Independent Labour Party had its eye on the positions as stepping stones for their ambitious young men. And the newspapers had their knives out, pointedly advising people to vote for the gentlemen. He'd arrived home two days earlier to find her pacing furiously around the living room, ready to spit fire, with the editorial in her hand.

'Listen to this,' Annabelle told him. 'Apparently they think men "don't possess the domestic embarrassments of women". What does that mean? I could swing for the lot of them.'

'Who wrote that?'

'Gerald Hotchkiss.'

Of course. A journalist who praised political balance, as long as it leaned far to the right, and believed a woman's place was firmly behind the front door. He'd savaged the police a few times, as well. One of those hacks who loved to manufacture outrage.

She threw the newspaper on to a chair. But he could hear the hurt behind her words. Whatever she'd hoped, this election wasn't going to be a fair fight.

The first letter arrived the same day. Second post, franked at the main post office in town, no signature or return address. It was a screed explaining that women should be guided by their husbands, live modestly, and look to the welfare of their own families. Religious, condescending, with everything written in a neat, practised hand. Senseless and rambling, Harper judged when he read it, but no real threat. All the women running for the Board had received one. He'd placed it in his desk drawer at Millgarth and forgotten about it. But another . . . Now he was going to do something.

'Take a look at that,' Harper said and tossed the letter across the desk. Inspector Ash raised an eyebrow as he read, then passed it on to Detective Sergeant Fowler.

'Looks like he's not all there, if you ask me, sir,' Ash said. 'I notice he didn't bother to sign it. Anything on the envelope?'

'Nothing helpful.' He sat back in the chair. For more than two years this had been his office, but the ghost of Kendall, the old superintendent, still seemed to linger; sometimes he even believed he could smell the shag tobacco the man used to stuff in his pipe. 'All the women candidates running to be on the Board of Guardians received one.'

'I see. That was Mrs Harper's, I take it?'

'There was another yesterday. She burned it.'

'Whoever wrote this was educated,' Fowler said as he studied the letter. 'All the lines are even, everything spelled properly.' He grinned. 'Of course, that's doesn't mean he's not completely barmy.'

He pushed the spectacles back up his nose. The sergeant had been recommended by a copper from Wakefield. He was moving back to Leeds to be closer to his ill mother. Harper had taken a chance on the man. Over the last twelve months it had paid off handsomely.

Fowler didn't look like a policeman, more like

a distracted clerk or a young professor. Twenty-five, hair already receding, he barely made the height requirement and couldn't have weighed more than eleven stone. But he had one of the quickest minds Harper had ever met. He and Ash had clicked immediately, turning into a very fruitful partnership. One big, one smaller, they seemed to work intuitively together, each knowing what the other would do without needing to speak.

'Mrs Bolland, one of the other candidates, received a second letter, too.' He gave them the address. 'Go and see her. I doubt we'll be able to track down the sender, but at least we can put out the word that we're looking into it. That might scare him off.'

'Yes, sir.' Ash stood. 'How's Mrs Harper's campaign going?'

'Early days yet.'

She'd only held one small meeting so far, in a church hall just up Roundhay Road from the Victoria. Soon enough she'd be going full tilt; their bedroom was already filled with piles of leaflets ready to be delivered and posters to plaster on the walls all over Sheepscar Ward.

'I'm sure she'll win, sir.'

He smiled. 'From your lips to God's ears.'

Once they'd gone he turned back to the rota for November, trying to recall when he'd once believed that coppering meant solving crimes.

Billy Reed drew back the curtains, pushed up the window sash, and breathed in clean, sharp salt air. After so many years of soot and dirt in Leeds, every day of this seemed like a tonic. He heard Elizabeth moving around downstairs, then smelt the frying bacon.

They'd been in Whitby since July, all settled now into the terraced house at number five, Silver Street. The pair of them, and her two younger children, Edward and Victoria. The older ones had stayed in Leeds, both in lodgings, with work, friends and lives of their own.

Moving had been a big decision, an upheaval. He'd come to love Whitby on his first visit, after he'd left the army, just home from the wars in Afghanistan and troubled in his mind. The water, the beach, the quiet of the place had brought him some peace. Since then he'd always had a yearning to live here. But when he'd seen the advertisement for inspector of police in the town, he'd hesitated. After all, he was an inspector with the Fire Brigade in Leeds, moving across from the police. He already had rank and responsibility.

'Why not write and apply?' Elizabeth urged him. 'The worst they can say is no.'

'We're fine here. I'm doing well enough. And you have the bakeries.'

She stared at him. 'Billy, do you think we'd be happy there?'

'Yes,' Reed answered after a moment. 'I do.'

'Then sit down and write to them.'

It had taken time. First the application, then an interview. Elizabeth travelled with him on the train and inspected the town while he was questioned by the watch committee. Another wait until the answer arrived, offering him the

7

position. After that, life became a scramble of arrangements. In the end, he'd gone on ahead while she finished up the sale of the bakeries, packed the rest of their possessions, and said goodbye to all the friends they'd made.

He had no regrets. He liked his job, but it was time for a move, for something new. And this was certainly different. Through the bedroom window he could make out the shouts of the fishermen on the piers as they unloaded their catch, and hear the gulls screeching. That wasn't something he'd ever known in Leeds.

'You'd better come and get it while it's hot,' Elizabeth shouted up the stairs.

The children were already eating, ready to hurry off to their jobs. Soon enough, Elizabeth would march down Flowergate, over the bridge and along Church Street to the shop she'd leased, ready to open her tearoom and confectioner's in the New Year. She'd made the bakeries in Leeds turn a fair profit, and she wasn't one to be content as a lady of leisure. She relished work; she needed something to spark her.

'It's right by the market,' she pointed out to him, 'so I'll pick up some regulars from there. And all those folk going to the abbey in holiday season will pass right by the door.'

She'd developed a good eye, he knew that, and she'd already managed to cultivate a few friends in town, like Mrs Botham, who had her own bakery and tearoom up on Skinner Street and knew Whitby like the back of her hand. A formidable woman, Reed thought, but she and Elizabeth could natter on for hours.

8

Reed had settled quickly into the rhythm of his job. During the summer he'd mostly dealt with complaints from visitors and broken up occasional fights once the pubs closed. If things carried on like that, it was going to be an easy life.

He strolled over to the police station on Spring Hill and went through the log with Brown, the sergeant, before setting off in the pony and trap. Sandsend and Staithes today. Both of them poor fishing villages, hardly any trouble to the law, but he still needed to put in a monthly appearance. Show the flag. He covered a large area, all the way down to Robin Hood's Bay, and inland as far as Sleights, but on a day like this, with the sun shining and a gentle breeze blowing off the water, no job could be better.

No, Reed thought with a smile as the horse clopped along the road, no regrets at all.

Two

'I saw Mrs Bolland.' Ash settled on to the chair in the superintendent's office. 'She'd kept the letter.' He ran his tongue round the inside of his mouth. 'It left her scared.'

'What does it say?' Harper put down the pen and sat back.

'Read it for yourself, sir.' The inspector pulled a folded sheet of notepaper from his inside pocket.

A woman's place is in the home, tending to her family and being a graceful loving presence. It is not to shriek in the hustings like a harridan or to display herself in front of the public like a painted whore.

The Good Lord created His order for a purpose. Man has the reason, the wisdom, and the judgement. He is intended to use it, to exercise his will over women, not to be challenged by them, the weaker element. Eve was persuaded to eat the apple and tempted Adam, and since that time it has been her duty to pay for the sin.

It is time for you to withdraw your candidacy. Should you fail to do so, if you continue to talk and challenge men for what rightly belongs to them, we shall feel justified in taking whatever means necessary to silence you for breaking God's profound will.

'A death threat this time. No wonder it frightened her.'

'Yes, sir. Funny what these types come up with in the name of religion, isn't it? It was all love thy neighbour back when I was at Sunday school.' Ash gave a wry smile.

Harper took the first letter from his drawer and compared them.

'The same handwriting. Twice means he's a problem, especially with words like these. We're going to follow up on this and make sure nothing happens to her.' He thought about Annabelle. 'To any of them. Where's Fowler?'

10

'I sent him off to talk to the other women, to see if they'd had anything like this.'

'Odds are that they have. That "we" in there makes me wonder, too.'

'I noticed that, sir.' Ash pursed his lips. 'If I had to guess, though, I'd say it's a man acting on his own.'

'I agree. Still . . .'

'Better safe than sorry, sir.'

'Exactly.' A death threat. He could see why Annabelle had destroyed the letter. Not to keep it away from Mary; she could manage that by hiding it in a pile or on the mantelpiece. No; she was frightened. It was hard to believe that words scribbled on a page could terrify her. She always seemed so strong, so fearless. But this election campaign was already putting a strain on her and it had hardly begun. 'No signature again. Handy, isn't it? He can just pop it in the post, then sit back and stay anonymous behind the paper.'

'Any ideas for catching him, sir?'

'None,' Harper said with a sigh. 'We'll just stay on our guard and hope he doesn't have any bigger ideas.'

'How was your dinner the other night, sir?' The inspector smiled slyly. 'Big affair, from all I hear.'

'Big?' Harper snorted. 'Pointless, more like. Tasteless food that was barely warm by the time it reached the table, followed by an hour of mumbled speeches.'

'The perks of rank, eh, sir?' Ash's eyes twinkled with amusement.

'You'd better be careful, or I'll start sending you in my place.'

'My Nancy would probably enjoy it.' He grinned, slapped his hands down on his knees and stood. 'I'll go out and ask a few questions. Who knows, maybe we'll be lucky and our gentleman writer isn't as discreet as he should be.'

'If you really believe that, I'd better check out of the window for a herd of pigs flying over the market,' Harper told him.

'Stranger things have probably happened, sir.'

'Not in Leeds, they haven't.'

'Was your letter like this?' he asked. Mary was tucked up in bed, exhausted by a day of school and an evening of telling them every scrap of learning that had gone into her head since morning. Harper was weary from concentrating, trying to make out all she said with his poor hearing.

Annabelle read it. 'Word for word,' she said, quickly folded it and thrust it back at him.

'Ash and Fowler are after him.'

'Doesn't help if you don't know who you're chasing,' she said. They were in the bedroom. He sat by the dressing table while she counted election leaflets into rough bundles, ready to be delivered in the morning. She raised her head. 'I'm not a fool, Tom. There's not enough in there for you to find him.'

'We can ask around. And I'll make sure there's a copper at the meetings.'

Annabelle stopped her work and stared at him. 'Would you do that for the male candidates?'

'Yes,' he told her. 'If I believed things might get rowdy.'

12

'Don't you think it's wrong that women should need special protection? We're in England, for God's sake. A civilized country.'

'Of course it's wrong,' he agreed. 'But when there are men like this poison pen writer, it's better than something bad happening.' He let the idea hang in the air. 'To anyone.'

Her gaze gradually softened to a curling, twinkling smile.

'Well, if you think looking after me is so important, Superintendent, perhaps you could offer me some very close guarding of my body.'

He grinned and bowed. 'My pleasure, madam.'

'They all received identical letters,' Fowler said. He pushed the glasses back up his nose and produced the papers from his pocket. 'Three had burned them. But it's the exact same wording and the handwriting as Mrs Bolland's.'

'And like the one my wife received,' Harper confirmed. 'What do you two have on your plates at the moment?' he asked Ash.

'Next to nothing, sir. We've been too successful, that's the problem.' He smiled. 'They're all too scared to commit crimes these days.'

'Don't get over-confident,' the superintendent warned. 'We could be up to our ears tomorrow. But while you have the chance, spend some time with this. Do you have a list of where and when these women are holding meetings?'

'I do,' Fowler said. 'There are four tonight.'

'Make sure there's a uniform at every one of them. And I want him visible.'

That should deter any troublemakers, he

thought. If it didn't, the weeks until the election were going to be long and difficult.

'Mr Ash and I have been talking, sir,' the sergeant began. 'We thought perhaps we could each go to a meeting. You know, stay quiet and keep an eye out for anything suspicious.'

'A very good idea. Not my wife's, though,' he added. 'I'll take care of that.'

He'd grown used to the routine of running a division, of being responsible for everything from men on the beat to the number of pencils in the store cupboard. But it still chafed. So much of the work was empty detail and routine; a competent clerk could have managed it in a couple of hours.

Official meetings were the worst; every month, all the division heads got together with the chief constable. So far they'd never managed to resolve a single thing. Then there was the annual questioning by the Watch Committee, the council members who oversaw the force. Several of them had no love for him. They thought he was a lucky upstart from the lower classes. But he'd managed to fox them. The crime figures kept falling, and he stayed well within his budget. He hadn't walked away with their praise, but he'd been happy to see that his success galled them.

Small, worthless victories. Had he really been reduced to that? Sometimes two or three days passed when he barely left Millgarth. It felt as if an age had gone by since he'd been a real detective. That was one reason he was looking forward to tonight. He smiled. Standing at the back of the hall, watching the faces and the bodies, thinking, assessing, alert for any danger. At least he could feel like he was doing some real work.

On the stroke of five, Harper pulled on his mackintosh and hat and glanced out of the window. Blue skies, a few high clouds, and a lemon sun: a perfect late autumn afternoon. Saturday, and a day away from this place ahead of him. Not free, though; he'd promised Annabelle he'd spend tomorrow walking round Sheepscar, delivering leaflets for her campaign.

Ash sat at his desk in the detectives' office, writing up a report.

'Did you find anything yet?'

'Not a dicky bird, sir.' He sighed and scratched his chin. 'You weren't banking on it, were you?'

'No.' He shook his head. 'If there's any trouble tonight, make sure you let me know.'

'I will, sir. Let's hope it's peaceful, eh?'

It was warm enough to walk back out to the Victoria. Even if the air was filled with all the soot and smoke of industry, so strong he could taste it on his tongue, it still felt good to breathe it into his lungs after a day in a stuffy office.

'Do you think I look all right, Tom?' Annabelle stood in front of the mirror. She was wearing a plain dress of dark blue wool. It was cut high, to the base of her throat, modest and serious, a cameo brooch at her neck. Her hair was up in some style he couldn't name but had probably taken an hour to engineer so it looked nonchalant.

15

'I think you look grand,' he told her. 'Like a member of the Poor Law Board.' He nudged Mary, who was sitting on his lap, staring in awe at her mother.

'Da's right. You're a bobby dazzler, Mam,' she said. 'I'd vote for you.'

'That'll do for me.' Annabelle picked up her daughter and twirled her in the air. 'You're absolutely sure?'

'Positive,' Harper replied. He pulled the watch from his waistcoat. 'We'd better get going. That meeting starts in three-quarters of an hour.' It wasn't that far – the hall at St Clement's, just up Chapeltown Road – but he knew she'd want to arrive early, to prepare herself, and put leaflets on all the chairs. Ellen would bring Mary shortly before the event began.

It was a fine evening for a stroll, Indian summer, still some sun and a note of warmth in the air. The factories had shut down until Monday morning, the constant hums and drones and bangs of the machinery all silenced. The chimney-stacks rose like a forest, stretching off to the horizon, the dirt leaving its mark on every surface around Leeds.

Annabelle took his arm as they walked. He'd put on his best suit, the fine dove-grey worsted she'd had Moses Cohen tailor for him seven years before. It was still smart, but growing uncomfortably tight around the waist.

'It's going to be fine, isn't it?' she asked.

'Of course it is.' He glanced over at her. 'It's not like you to be so nervous. You usually dive right in.'

16

'This is something new, that's all,' she replied after a moment. 'And if I fail, well, it'll be obvious, won't it? I'd be letting everyone down who's helping.' She nodded at the hall, just visible behind the church, its low outline stark against the gasometers. 'All of them who turn up tonight. If anyone does.'

'You'll do well.' He kissed her cheek and grinned. 'Trust me, I'm a policeman.'

'I thought you lot were only good for telling the time.'

The words had hardly left her mouth when he heard the low roar. It grew louder, then a deep, violent explosion ripped out of the ground. A column of smoke plumed up from the hall, throwing wood and roof tiles and bricks high into the air.

'Christ.' They stared for a second, not knowing what to say. He didn't have the words for this. 'Stay here,' he told her, then changed his mind. 'No. Go home.'

Before he'd finished speaking Tom Harper was running towards the blast.

Three

Rubble, broken glass and splintered wood littered the ground. He hurdled over them. The sound of the blast seemed to echo through his head. Three of the windows in St Clement's had been blown out, he noticed as he passed.

Already people were appearing on the door-steps of the houses close by. A few grim-faced men were dashing towards the scene. One of them tried to stop him.

'Tha'd better not get too close, mister. Could be dangerous.'

'Police,' Harper told him as he dodged by.

The air was choking with smoke and the smell of cordite. Tiny fragments of paper kept falling like a shower of blossoms. Half the hall had gone; the rest looked in danger of toppling.

'Was there anyone in here?' he shouted.

'Caretaker, most likely,' a man answered, already shifting bricks and stones. Harper joined him, then others arrived. Together, they heaved at a large block of concrete until it began to move and they could push it aside.

By then, it seemed as if every man and boy in the neighbourhood was there; the ground was thick with them. Some formed a chain to clear spaces. Others used spades, shovelling away all they could.

'Over here,' a voice called and the superintendent slid between groups towards the sound. Two men were looking down, not saying a word.

They'd uncovered the top half of a man's body. His legs were still trapped under the rubble, but there was no hurry to free him. He was already dead.

'Do you know him?' Harper asked.

'That's Roy Harkness,' one of the men answered. He brought a pipe from his waistcoat pocket and lit it with shaking hands. 'Caretaker here. He was probably getting everything ready.

There was supposed to be some political meeting tonight.'

He looked at the one who'd spoken.

'I'm Superintendent Harper with Leeds City Police. Is there a telephone nearby?'

'The doctor up the road has one.'

'Go there. Tell him to ring Millgarth Station. Say I want some officers here.' He paused and looked around the scene. 'Have them get a message out to check all the other places where there are meetings tonight. We need the fire brigade, too. Got that?'

The man nodded and dashed off.

Harper knelt by the body, trying to take in everything around him. Harkness's skull had been crushed; he never had a chance. The stink of gunpowder lay heavy all around. It looked as if someone had planted a bomb.

'Tom.' He turned his head and saw Annabelle staring down. Her mouth was open in horror. 'Is he . . .?'

'Yes.' He stood and wrapped her in his arms, feeling the shivers rack her body. 'If it helps, he wouldn't have felt anything,' he whispered. 'The force is on its way.'

'What happened?' she asked, unable to turn away from the body. 'Do you know?'

'Not yet.' It wasn't a complete lie. He still needed confirmation. 'Why don't you go home?'

She had no colour in her face, and her hands were trembling, but she shook her head.

'Who was he?'

'His name's Roy Harkness. He was the caretaker.'

'Does he have a family?' she asked. 'Where does he live?'

When he didn't answer, she raised her voice and asked again.

'Over there.' An old man pointed to the house at the end of the terrace. 'His daughter lives with him. I think she must be off somewhere. I haven't seen her since Monday.'

'Poor man,' she said quietly. 'Poor, poor man. God, Tom, if this had happened an hour later . . .'

He'd already considered that. The hall would have been full of people. Dozens might have died. She started to shake again and her teeth began to chatter. He took off his jacket and draped it around her shoulders.

'You should go back to the Victoria,' he told her softly. 'There's nothing you can do here. You've had a bad shock.'

'I can help the women make some tea for you lot.' She tried to make her voice bright, in control, but the words came out brittle and fragile.

'Yes. We could do with some.' He smiled at her. Maybe it would be good for her to do something, to take her mind off all this. He knew the sight would haunt her for a long time.

By the time the arson investigator finished his examination it was full dark, an autumn chill growing in the air.

'You're right on the money, sir,' Inspector Binns said. He'd replaced Billy Reed during the summer, but this was the first time Harper had met him. 'Definitely a bomb, under the stage here. You can make out the radius of the blast on the ground, that black circle. Without the fuse, though, I can't tell if it was meant to go off later, or if it was a warning.'

'A warning?' Harper asked in astonishment. 'What do you mean?'

'A threat, maybe,' Binns corrected himself. 'You know, set off the bomb when the hall was empty. I'll come back and search properly in the morning, but we might never know.'

'Was there anything at any of the other places?'

Binns shook his head. 'All clean.'

The coppers had already been and gone. They'd taken statements from those at the site, not that anyone had much to tell. Tomorrow he'd make sure the uniforms were back, going house-to-house for witnesses. Harkness's body had been freed and taken to the police surgeon for the post-mortem.

Annabelle had finally left, still pale and quiet. One of the local women had walked back with her.

A warning. A threat. He let the idea play in his mind as he strode down Chapeltown Road to the Victoria. This had moved far beyond letters penned in an educated hand. It didn't matter what the bomber intended. The result had been murder.

She was in the living room, sitting in the dark. The grate was empty, neatly swept; it was still too warm at night to need a fire. He placed his hands on her shoulders and kneaded them lightly.

'Where's Mary?' he asked.

21

'She's spending the night up in Ellen's room. I thought it was best.' Her voice was raw. He could hear her hesitation. 'Tom, was it my fault?'

'Yours?' At first he wasn't sure he'd heard her properly. 'How could it be your fault?'

'If I wasn't standing for election. If I hadn't been holding that meeting there. Would that poor man still be alive?'

What could he tell her, he wondered. She knew the answer every bit as well as he did. There could only be one reason for placing a bomb in that hall.

'What are you going to do?' he asked.

Annabelle reached up, taking tight hold of his hands.

'I've been sitting here wondering about it,' she said quietly. He noticed an empty gin glass on the table beside her chair. 'Whoever did this, he wants to terrify me, doesn't he? He wants me so frightened that I'll stop. Not just me. All the women who are running.'

'Yes,' Harper agreed quietly. 'He does.'

'I can't,' she said slowly. 'If I give up, I've let him win. And I really believe I can do something that makes a difference to people if I'm elected. But I can't stop thinking about that poor man.' She turned her head to look at him helplessly. 'How do you do it? How do you cope with seeing that all the time without going mad?'

'You get used to it.' It sounded like a hollow answer, but it was true. Death was part of the job; if you couldn't take it, you left. 'And it's not that often.'

'It's still . . .' Her voice trailed off into silence.

'Come on,' he said softly. 'Let's go to bed. I'll be working tomorrow after all.'

'Yes.' A new resolution entered her voice. 'And I have a meeting tomorrow night.'

They had the letters spread on the desk, going over them again for the smallest clue. He was due to meet Binns in an hour, to go through the scene of the blast once more.

'There are threats in these,' Ash said finally. 'But we're looking at them after the fact. We couldn't know how serious they were when we read them.'

'No hint of what or where, though,' Fowler added. 'The bomber might not even be the same man who wrote these, sir. Have you considered that?'

'I have, but it would be too much of a coincidence,' the superintendent said. 'How many could actually set off a bomb? How many would even know how to make one?'

'Can't be more than a handful,' Ash replied.

'Dig through Records. See if you can find any, then go and talk to them. Drag some more names out of them.'

'Yes, sir.'

They left the office, and Harper picked up the telephone on his desk. He'd finally become used to the instrument, though he still didn't care for it. But it saved time, he had to admit that.

'Carlton Barracks, please,' he told the operator. He was transferred through a series of clerks, to an NCO, all the way to the adjutant. Then, after five dull minutes of waiting: 'Colonel Mackenzie-Smith. I'm the CO here.'

23

The voice was crisp, every word carefully enunciated.

'It's Superintendent Harper, A Division, Leeds City Police. Have you read about last night's bomb?'

It had happened early enough to be the headline in the Sunday papers. By now everyone should know.

'I have.' The soldier's voice was loud; even with his hearing, he had no trouble making out each word. 'What can we do for you?'

'Do you have any men trained to find and defuse explosives?'

Inspector Reed spent the morning strolling around Whitby. He was constantly discovering new places, delighted to notice a sign saying Arguments Yard above a tiny passage that ran down some stone steps to a small court of run-down cottages above the water, or the grand beauty of the ruined abbey as he approached from the road and saw it rise on the headland.

It would be a year or more before he had a real grip on the place. For the moment he relied on his sergeant and the constable for knowledge. Their families went back generations in the town. It seemed as if they were related to half the population, from fishermen to gentry.

He made his way back from West Pier after the balm of watching the waves crash against the shore. It always calmed him to look at nature, to see the birds ride high, then dive with their sure eyes before rising up with a fish.

Boats bobbed against the jetties and men sat

on crates, making repairs to their nets. The air was raucous with the squawk of gulls. He felt at peace with the world. Up on the hill, church bells rang for the Sunday service.

A group of men had gathered on one of the quays, five of them talking rapidly to each other. Most were local, their faces vaguely familiar. Fishermen by the look of them, weathered and rough, with their tall heavy boots, thick jumpers and beards. Men who made their living out on the water every day. But one was wearing a dark suit and a bowler hat, side whiskers neatly curling along the line of his jaw. He knew that man's face, and it wasn't from Whitby.

Back at the station on Spring Hill, Reed asked Sergeant Brown. His face curled into a slow smile.

'You must mean John Millgate, sir.'

John Millgate. The name opened the floodgates. Terrier John, they'd called him when Billy Reed worked in Leeds CID, because his sharp nose and sleek, pomaded hair made him look like a Jack Russell. He'd been in jail five or six times, and probably lucky to get away without a sentence every bit as often.

'How long has he lived here?'

Brown pursed his lips. 'Must be a bit over three years now. Turned up in the spring and I doubt he's spent two nights away from Whitby since then. He has a bob or two, mind. He bought hissen a house on John Street.'

'What does he do?'

'Nothing,' the sergeant answered. 'Least, not as far as I can tell. A gentleman of leisure, if you

25

like, sir. Very interested in the fishing, though. You'll often find him down on the quay or having a drink with the men from the boats. He's good pals with Cud Colley and a couple of the others there.'

Terrier John with plenty of money in his pocket? That didn't square with the man he remembered. Back then he'd always been scuffling for a florin. He tried to recall any big, unsolved crimes from three years ago in Leeds. Reed had been in the fire brigade then, but anything large enough to set a man up for life should have stuck in his mind.

Nothing.

He'd keep an eye on the Terrier. Something was strange there.

'That's all I can tell you, sir,' Binns said.

They'd finished their examination of the ground. The fire inspector had pointed out the details. No doubt at all that it was a bomb; they'd even found a few fragments of the tin that held it. But still no fuse.

'If you had to guess, what would you say?' Harper asked. 'A warning, or to go off during the meeting?'

Binns rubbed his chin. 'Put me on the spot, sir, and I'll go with a warning. But that's only because I can't imagine anyone wanting to blow up people. I don't know what that sort of man would be like, and I'm not sure I want to.'

With a crisp salute, he returned to the debris.

Still no answers, the superintendent thought as he gazed at the scene. All this destruction, a death,

26

because a man was afraid of women in politics. This wasn't Westminster. It wasn't even the council. Women could only run for the School Board and to be Poor Law Guardians. Why would that frighten someone enough to do this?

'Thank you for coming.' Harper shook the man's hand.

'Glad to help, sir.' The man stood straight, uncomfortable in his scratchy dress uniform, thick moustache bristling on his upper lip. He was around thirty, with sandy hair and fine lines around a pair of very clear blue eyes. 'I'm Sergeant Buckley, Royal Engineers. Here like you requested.'

The men with him remained at attention, as if they were still on parade. In their pipeclay and polished brass, they seemed an awkward group, none of them much past twenty-one. They carried full haversacks on their backs, eyes moving around the detectives' office at Millgarth with curiosity. And wariness on a couple of faces, he thought.

'I'm sure you read about what happened last night.'

'Indeed, sir. Terrible business.'

'There are meetings tonight at several halls. About an hour before they start, I'd like your men to check each one for bombs.'

Buckley nodded as if it was a request he heard every day. 'Easily done, sir. If we come across one, we'll defuse it.' He glanced over his shoulder. 'Right, lads?'

'Yes, sir,' they shouted as one.

The superintendent nodded at Ash and Fowler. 'My men will take care of the details with you.'

'Glad to be of assistance, sir.' Buckley grinned. 'And this lot would prefer a little action to an evening dubbing their boots again.'

A few hours later he and Buckley were standing outside the brick building off Lovell Road. It was neatly kept, the Sunday school for the Baptist chapel next door.

'Ready?'

'And keen as mustard.' The sergeant saluted.

He liked the man. He'd taken him back to the Victoria and fed him a hearty meal while Buckley told them stories from all the parts of the Empire he'd seen. Mary had been entranced by the magic tricks the man could do, pestering him until he showed her how to make a coin vanish and reappear in someone's ear. Harper knew he'd have to put up with her doing it endlessly now, but it was a tiny price to pay for safety.

It took half an hour before the sergeant emerged, beaming and brushing the dust from his uniform.

'Nothing dangerous in there. I'd wager a month's pay on it.'

'Thank you,' Harper told him, surprised at the flood of relief through his body. 'And your men will be available to keep checking the halls for the next few weeks?'

'Glad to. Good practice for them, sir.'

He slipped two florins from his pocket and passed them to Buckley.

'Make sure your lads know I appreciate it.'

'I'm certain they'll keep drinking your health all evening, sir.'

28

Four

Annabelle stood nervously outside the hall, hands fidgeting with her reticule.

'Are you sure it's safe?'

'Sergeant Buckley's gone over it from top to bottom.' Harper gave her a reassuring smile. 'All you have to do is persuade them to vote for you.'

'Leaving me the easy job, eh?'

'They'll love you.' He squeezed her arm gently.

'How many are in there?'

'About fifty.' The hall wasn't even half full. Not too surprising, really, between the Sabbath today and what happened the night before. People would be wary. They'd be scared. But they'd forget soon enough; folk had short memories.

The superintendent had watched them arrive in dribs and drabs. The older ones, the churchgoers, the earnest and the curious. Not a troublemaker among them. But he still stationed himself just inside the door, not far from the uniform assigned here, ready for anything.

No other speakers tonight. Not even anyone to introduce her. Just a leaflet on each seat and a painted banner behind her: Vote Annabelle Harper for Poor Law Guardian.

The soft hum of speech halted as she climbed the three steps to the stage. The heels of her button boots clicked sharply on the wood. She faced them and smiled.

'Thank you for coming.' She paused and took a breath. 'I'm here to ask for you to vote me on to the Board of Poor Law Guardians. You know, the ones who decide how much relief someone should get or if they have to go to the workhouse. Now, I'm sure you've all heard what happened last night. A man died because of a meeting. A meeting! He didn't even have anything to do with it. And all because someone was so scared of a woman talking to people and standing for something that he believed he had to plant a bomb to try and stop her.' She pursed her lips and shook her head. 'I saw it go off. I was no more than two hundred yards away, and it was awful.' She paused long enough to stare around all the faces in the audience. 'I'll tell you this. I'm not going to stop. The bomber isn't going to win. Last night I kept thinking: this isn't Leeds. This isn't the place I know.' Annabelle took a deep breath. 'Pound to a penny it's not the Leeds you know, either. We might not always like what people say, but we give them a chance to speak.

'And we look after our poor. You know plenty of them. So do I. It's not hard to find poverty round Sheepscar: you just have to stick your head out the door.' A few chuckles of recognition came from the crowd. 'I'm sick of the well-to-do saying that folk have a choice about being poor and telling them to pull themselves up by their boot-straps. Well, there are plenty whose boots don't have straps. More who don't even have boots.' He heard the passion rising in her words. The traces of fear and hesitation had left her face. 'Do you really believe anyone wants to go into

30

the workhouse or get relief? I've lived round here all my life and I know they'd rather have a wage. There are those who can't work. Of course there are, and it's not their fault. I want to make sure we treat them with some dignity. For God's sake, they're human beings, the same as you and me. The same as them with big houses up in Roundhay who think they can look down on the world. We're supposed to be the richest country in the world. That's what they've been telling us all year while we've been celebrating the Queen's Diamond Jubilee. Surely we can afford a little to look after our poor, instead of it vanishing into some London coffer.' Annabelle stopped, as if she'd just heard the fury in her voice. She started again, on a quieter note. 'You might have heard that there are seven women running to be Poor Law Guardians in this election. We think a woman's touch would be a good thing. We know families, we know what it costs to live every day, right down to the last farthing.' She spotted a woman nodding and smiled. 'You know exactly what I mean, don't you? And we know how close poverty walks behind us all. We can look up the hill to Burmantofts and see the shadow of the workhouse. It's always there.' Another small reflection. 'You know what I really want to do? I want to help the poor, not vilify them. They're not outcasts. They haven't sinned. They're us. And that's why I'd appreciate your vote, so I can do that. Thank you.'

They applauded and roared, and Harper joined them. She'd done superbly up there. It wasn't the speech she'd rehearsed. This was better. It came from deep inside her, and they seemed to sense that.

There were questions, mostly sympathetic, but some from people with little love for the poor. He watched her answer every one of them with respect. She'd walk out of here certain of quite a few votes.

Once it was all over, with another round of clapping and Annabelle beaming with pleasure, he helped some of the men put away the chairs while she talked with three of the women. Recruiting volunteers for the campaign, most likely.

'You went down a treat,' he said as they walked to the Victoria.

'It's a start. Once I found my stride I felt fine.'

'They believed you.'

She gave him a sidelong glance. 'Course they did. Every one of them knows someone who's had relief or gone into the workhouse. They dread it because they could be next. It's not words, Tom. It's real to them.'

Better to change tack away from the earnest, he decided.

'Did you find some campaign help?'

'Two of them offered to come and deliver leaflets tomorrow.' She skipped a couple of steps, then put her arm through his. 'We're on the way, aren't we? Come on, if we hurry we can see Mary before her bedtime.'

He'd been dreading the knock on the door, news of some disaster at one of the meetings. But he had a clear eight hours' sleep, woken by the smell

32

of eggs and sausages from the kitchen. Then the dash of feet rushing across the floor and a small body landing next to him on the bed.

'Are you awake, Da?' Mary bellowed into his ear. 'Me mam says breakfast is almost ready.'

For a moment he lay still, then suddenly rolled over, grabbing her and tickling until she screamed with pleasure and wriggled away. In the doorway she turned. 'Mam says if you're late she's going to give your food to the tinker.'

Where had she learned *that*? He hadn't heard it since he was a boy. Of course. School. She was picking up all sorts there. And learning as if knowledge was a meal she couldn't devour quickly enough, always hungry for more. A prodigy, her teacher called her with a mix of pride and horror. Ready to march off to Roundhay Road Primary every morning and wanting all the things the day could bring her.

The food was on the table, a cup of tea already poured. Annabelle took off her pinafore and sat, picking up her knife and fork.

'Comfortable shoes today,' she said. 'I'm going to be on my feet delivering leaflets.'

'Winifred Brady says Mam could get elected without doing a thing,' Mary said.

'Don't you believe everything Winifred Brady tells you.' She rolled her eyes. 'There's plenty of work involved. And time.'

Harper hid his grin behind a piece of fried bread. Families. He was a lucky man.

Monday morning and he'd barely had time to hang up his coat and see the pile of papers waiting

33

for him when the telephone started with its insistent ringing. Harper picked up the receiver, careful to hold it against his good ear. A few clicks, then someone was speaking to him.

'Inspector Binns here, sir. The arson investigator.' Flat and metallic, the voice could have been almost anyone.

'Yes, Inspector. Did you manage to find that fuse?'

'No, sir, and I doubt we will. But one of my men did come across something. I'm not sure what it means, though.'

'What is it?'

'A piece of paper. Heavily scorched at one edge, so it wasn't too far from the blast. But it had been placed to preserve it. Deliberately, I'd say.'

Harper recalled all the fragments tumbling like dandruff.

'There was plenty of paper.'

'Hymn books and the like, sir. I checked. This has writing on it. I asked the vicar. He didn't recognize it.'

'What sort of writing?' He felt the prickle along his spine, the sense of something changing.

'It'll probably be easier if I have one of my lads bring it over to you.'

'Thank you.'

'I hope it helps, sir.'

Harper looked at it again. Larger than he'd imagined, perhaps five inches by three, like a page torn from a notebook, heavily blackened along the rough edge. But it was the writing that interested him. Ink, on one side of the page, smudged but faintly legible.

He took the anonymous letters from his desk and laid them on the blotter, this fragment alongside. The same hand. Blurred and blotched as it was, he could tell. It was there in the loop under the 'g' and the flourish that completed an 'e'.

They were after one man.

He called for Ash and the inspector came in, Fowler right behind him.

'What do you make of that?'

'Exactly the same, isn't it?' Ash said slowly after he'd examined them. 'Where did this come from, sir?'

'The bombing. Can you make out what he's written?'

The pair passed it between them, trying to puzzle out words from the faint blobs of blue ink.

'I can't be certain,' Fowler said hesitantly, 'but it looks like a song. I think that's "die" right there, and "morrow" below it. Looks like that second line could be "she died on the morrow". Nobody says "morrow".'

Harper had made some of the words out, too. But he'd never considered they might be part of a lyric.

'If this really is a song, you should probably go and talk to Frank Kidson,' Ash suggested. 'He'd probably know it. Might even know the writing.'

Kidson . . . Kidson. The name sounded familiar, but he couldn't quite place it.

'He writes a column in the *Mercury*, sir,' Fowler

prompted. 'About folk songs and the like. Supposed to be an expert.'

That was the one. Harper had never read his pieces. Who cared about old songs? But for once, the knowledge could be useful.

'Good thinking,' he agreed. 'I'll find him later. Did either of you hear of any problems last night?'

Everything had been quiet, no more than a pair of drunks arrested for fighting after one of the speakers had finished.

'We have plenty of meetings between now and the election. The army's going to check every location each time. There'll be a bobby on hand. But I'd like the two of you to keep attending them as well. Go here and there. See if a few faces tend to crop up regularly or if anyone we know makes a habit of politics. In the meantime, keep digging for information.'

Dinnertime had passed before he managed to leave Millgarth. He had to go through the weekly disciplinary roll, with Sergeant Tollman marching in the constables who'd broken the rules. Fines, suspensions for one or two days; it was all standard fare. Only one whose record meant he'd probably be dismissed from the force, and he'd had it coming for years.

He found Frank Kidson's address on Burley Road in the City Directory. A very comfortable neighbourhood, Harper thought as he walked, even with plenty of industry at the bottom of the valley. The house looked trim enough, although the lintels and door frames needed a lick of paint.

The windows shone in the weak sunlight. There was money here. Respectability.

At first he took the young woman who answered the door for a servant. But she was too well-dressed, too precise in her speech.

'I'm Superintendent Harper with Leeds City Police.' He raised his hat. 'I'm hoping to consult Mr Kidson about something. He might be able to help us.'

Her eyes widened in surprise.

'Goodness, you'd better come in,' she said. 'I'm Ethel Kidson.' The woman blushed. 'Not really. My proper name is Emma, but Uncle calls me Ethel. Please, come through.'

She led the way to a back parlour that looked out over the garden. A few roses were still in bloom, splashes of pink and yellow against the rear wall. A man was seated at the table, pen in his hand, writing furiously, as if the words needed to gallop out of him. Books were piled every-where, many more even than Annabelle had at home. All the shelves on the walls were full, and others were stacked around the floor.

The furniture was old, probably expensive when it was bought. Now it seemed worn and shabby; Harper spotted two threadbare patches on the rug. But he had the sense that the people who lived here didn't set much stock by their surroundings.

'Uncle,' the woman said, but he didn't seem to hear. She smiled her apology and Harper grinned. Finally she shook the man's shoulder. 'Uncle, there's a policeman here to see you.'

Kidson looked up quickly, blinking with surprise

behind his spectacles. His hair was dark and wild, standing on end as if he often pushed a hand through it as he worked. A thick beard, and bright, intelligent eyes. He was dressed in a dark woollen suit, sober tie, with a turnover celluloid collar on his shirt. Somewhere in his forties, the superintendent guessed; certainly much older than the woman.

'Forgive me,' he said, standing and extending a hand. 'I'm trying to complete something.' He cocked his head to one side. 'What would the police want here?' He glanced at his niece. 'We haven't done anything wrong, have we, Ethel?'

'It's your knowledge I'm after, sir.' He began to explain, but Kidson quickly interrupted him.

'You think it's a song? Do you have the paper with you, Mr . . .?'

'Harper, sir. Superintendent Harper.' He took it from his jacket, carefully wrapped in tissue.

The man studied it for a minute, turning it over and back.

'Well, I don't know the writing, but that's definitely a song, you're right about that.' He strode quickly to a bookcase and pulled down a thin volume. 'What makes it especially curious is that it's in here. My book.' He marked the page with a slip of paper. 'The song's called *Barbara Allen*. But it's quite well known. Famous, I suppose, if any old songs really are. The lines are "*And he did die on one good day/ And she did die on the morrow*."' He pursed his lips. 'I wonder why someone would write down the words to that?'

'We found the paper where a bomb had gone off.'

38

Harper saw Ethel Kidson exhale slowly.

'I'll go and see to some tea.'

'She's invaluable to me,' the man said with pride after she'd gone. 'Keeps everything in order here, and she goes with me when I travel to collect songs. A remarkable memory for the tunes.' He paused. 'The chap who wrote that . . .'

'We're trying to find him. He almost certainly set off the bomb.'

'I see.' He clicked a fingernail against his teeth. 'He could have copied it from the book, of course. I doubt he was a song-hunter. I'd probably know him otherwise. There aren't too many of us.' He gave a wry smile. 'Just as well, Ethel would say. But I'm not sure how I can help you, Superintendent.'

'You already have, sir.' He was about to leave when Miss Kidson returned, the servant walking behind her, carrying a tea tray.

'Please stay,' she said. 'We don't have too many visitors who aren't involved with music.'

Just long enough to be polite, he decided, and a quarter of an hour later he replaced his cup in the saucer and stood.

'Thank you again.'

'Take a copy of Uncle's book,' Miss Kidson insisted. 'This way you'll have the words of the song.' Before he could refuse, she'd picked one from a pile and placed it in his hand.

'If you think of anything useful, please drop me a note at Millgarth,' Harper said.

'Of course,' Kidson agreed. 'Tell me, Superintendent, do you know any songs?'

'Songs?'

39

'Old songs. Maybe your parents sang them.'

'No, sir, I don't,' he answered, and saw the disappointment in the man's eyes. 'You should talk to my wife. She has plenty of old Irish songs she remembers from her parents.'

'Perhaps I will,' the man said thoughtfully. 'Perhaps I will.'

Five

Kidson and his niece made a curious pair, Harper thought as he sat on the tram into town. But they seemed perfectly content with their life full of old songs. He looked at the book with its brown leather binding. *Traditional Tunes: A Collection of Ballad Airs, Edited with Notes by Frank Kidson*. Inside, he found a few pieces he remembered from his childhood: *Geordie*, that old Mr Bell at the end of Noble Street used to bellow when he was drunk, or *The Grey Mare* that his Aunt Edna would always perform at family gatherings. He'd completely forgotten about them; he'd certainly never imagined they were part of history.

There seemed to be nothing special about the words of the song the bomber had written down, other than it mentioned a woman's death. The morrow. Was that a clue? It couldn't be. A day and a half had passed since the bomb. Well, it might not bring them much closer to identifying him, but it was two steps in the right direction.

* * *

40

'Is it good?' Annabelle nodded at the book. He had it open on the table as they ate, the way she did so often.

'Folk songs,' Harper replied. 'A lead to the bomber.'

She raised an eyebrow, then glanced over at the clock. 'You can tell me later. I need to go downstairs. Dan's poorly, so I said I'd look after the bar tonight.'

'I thought you were going out knocking on doors this evening.'

'Needs must,' she told him. 'I still have a pub to run.' Annabelle kissed him, nuzzled her daughter on the top of her head, and was gone.

'Da, do you have to learn all those songs?' Mary asked. 'There must be *hundreds* of them in there.'

'No,' he laughed. 'I only have to look at them. I don't even have to sing. Do you know why that's good?'

'Because you don't have to know them all by heart?'

He leaned close to her and whispered: 'Because I have a terrible voice.'

Before he left Millgarth for the day, he'd compared notes with Ash and Fowler. The sergeant had spent some time with Tollman, going through years of records and trying to come up with suspects. The inspector had been out asking questions, talking to his touts.

But between them, it was a poor harvest. And it barely looked better after he told them what he'd learned from Kidson. Harper listed the points on his fingers.

'We know our suspect is an educated man who hates women in politics. Either that or he fears them. He has the knowledge to make a bomb and he's ruthless enough to set it off. On top of that, he's interested in folk songs, at least ones that seem to mention women dying. But,' he added cautiously and held up *Traditional Tunes*, 'he could have found it in this. It's Kidson's book. Not a fat lot to go on, is it?'

'Since we've had no luck so far with the first two things, maybe we should look at the song angle,' Ash suggested. 'After all, there can't be many people interested in that.'

'Do you know any?'

'One or two I could ask,' he replied after a moment and turned to Fowler. 'What about Walter Summerfield? He likes a good sing in the pubs, doesn't he?'

'If you can call that singing. I've heard cats that were more in tune.'

'I recall him telling me someone had come around once, wanting to know if he remembered any old songs. Paid him a tanner for each one.'

Fowler began to laugh and pushed his glasses back up his nose. 'Knowing Walt, he probably made half of them up on the spot.'

'Talk to him,' Harper said. 'And any more you can come up with. We need names. I want this man in court before he can do more damage.'

On the way out, Tollman had called him over to the desk.

'This came for you today, sir. Your name on it, not just Superintendent. Looks a bit like Mr Reed's writing, and it's a Whitby postmark.'

'Thank you.' He slipped it into his pocket without a glance.

He played sums with Mary, then spelling, until it was time for bed. She was like a sponge, soaking everything into her brain. When he was her age he had gladly left his learning at the school gate; more of it was the last thing he wanted. The lessons themselves had often seemed too much. He read her a story from *The Blue Fairy Book*, glad that some part of her still seemed young enough to enjoy it.

Once she was asleep, he settled before the fire with a fresh cup of tea, took out the letter and slit it open.

Dear Tom,

I hope you are all well and that the job is going smoothly. I feel like we landed on our feet when we moved here. I like the job and it's not too strenuous. Elizabeth is opening a tea shop in town. There are already a few, but she thinks she can do well. She sends her best wishes to everyone.

I'm writing because I saw someone we both know here. Terrier John. Do you remember him? John Millgate is his real name. Been here for three years. Evidently he arrived with money in his pocket. He still appears to have plenty of it and owns a respectable house.

I seem to recall he was always scraping just to make ends meet in Leeds, so he's come into something somehow. Was there a crime where you never managed to recover the money or arrest anyone? I've been racking my brains, but I can't think of any, although it could be after I moved to the brigade.

I'd appreciate any information you can give. As far as I know, he's not involved in anything here, or so my sergeant says.

Wishing you all the best,
Billy

Terrier John. He hadn't heard the name in a long, long time. There had been crimes they'd never solved, but none where the thieves had made off with much. Certainly not enough to leave a man wealthy. He'd dig into that tomorrow.

He folded the letter and left it on the side table; Annabelle would be glad of a little news about Elizabeth.

'Any luck with that Summerfield man?' Harper asked.

'He's seventy if he's a day, sir,' Ash replied. 'And not the least interested in politics. Took us a while to finally track him down in the Horse and Trumpet.'

'But he did come up with something interesting,' Fowler continued. 'Seems that someone was going round the pubs a while back, asking about old songs.'

'Not Kidson?'

'Definitely not. Summerfield knows him.'

44

'Did he get a name?'

'Not that he recalls,' Ash said. 'Only a vague description. Man in his forties, well-dressed, short hair going grey.'

'But . . .' Fowler picked up the thread with a grin, 'he did give the man the names of some other singers. Didn't find any of them last night, but I'll go out again this evening.'

'Very good.' They had the first decent sniff of their man, like hounds raising their heads as they picked up a fox's scent. 'I'll want everything you can find out about him tonight. We have a start now. Keep looking, and tell me as soon as you find anything. Ash, I need a word with you.'

Once they were alone, the door closed, he said, 'Terrier John. Do you remember him?'

The inspector chuckled and rubbed his moustache. 'I ran him in once or twice when I was on the beat. He never knew when to give up, did he?'

'It seems he's turned up in Whitby.'

'Has he, now?' His eyes narrowed. 'Mr Reed spot him, did he?'

'He sent me a letter. Evidently Terrier's been there about three years.' He paused. 'And he arrived with money. Living like a gentleman, no job, bought himself a house. What do you make of that?'

'He must have some sort of fiddle going on,' Ash said. 'Bound to. Terrier never turned an honest penny in his life. He wouldn't even know what one looked like. And I doubt he had a rich uncle to leave him a legacy.'

'Billy Reed asked about any unsolved crimes here before the time John showed up in Whitby. Ones where we never recovered the money.'

The inspector pursed his lips. 'Nothing springs to mind.'

'No,' Harper agreed. 'But go back and see. We might have forgotten it. You might ask a few questions, too. Just in passing.' He grinned. 'We don't want anyone thinking we're nosing around.'

'I'll be very circumspect, sir.' When the superintendent raised an eyebrow, Ash said: 'Nancy's all in favour of us widening our vocabularies. I don't even ask why any more.'

'Women, eh?'

'God bless them all. No more reports of trouble on the campaigns, at least.'

'There will be. We need to keep alert and stop it before it becomes serious. I'll breathe easier once we have this bomber behind bars.'

'I'm going to pop in at a couple of meetings tonight. The uniforms will be out keeping watch, too.'

'And the army's going to check every hall,' Harper said. 'I know we're doing all we can, but—'

'But it's your missus out there, too, and some lunatic on the loose.'

'Exactly.'

'We'll find him, sir.'

'Let's make it soon. Before anyone else dies.'

'I'm jiggered.' Annabelle sank into the easy chair and took off her button boots. 'That's better,' she said with a sigh. 'They've been killing me for the last hour.'

'You've got a hole in your stocking, Mam,' Mary said.

'I'm surprised I have any feet left, the amount of walking I've done.'

Harper poured her a cup of tea from the pot on the table. She grinned as she took it from his hand.

'I always knew there was a reason I married you.'

'Rough afternoon?'

It was coming on dusk, the air hazy with the hint of darkness. The supper plates had been cleared away, and Mary was lying on the rug, looking at a picture book.

'I feel like I've traipsed round half the streets in Sheepscar. I swear there were a few I've never even seen before.'

'A good reception?'

'Very,' Annabelle said thoughtfully. 'Some who weren't convinced, but I don't expect to win them all. It's encouraging, though.' She leaned back against the antimacassar and closed her eyes. 'I'm just glad there isn't a meeting tonight.'

'You can read to me,' Mary said.

'I'll do that,' Harper said. 'Go on, get ready for bed and I'll be in to tell you a story.'

'Thank you,' Annabelle said when they were alone. She leaned back and closed her eyes. 'I don't think I can move.'

'You need to soak those feet.'

'I will,' she said. 'No news?'

'A hint of this and that. But nothing definite.'

47

She nodded. 'I saw the letter from Billy. Elizabeth opening a tea shop. Very grand, isn't it?'

'She'll probably do well.'

'I'm sure of it. She's got her head screwed on right, that one. I was thinking, we should go and see them next summer. Maybe make a little holiday of it, two or three days. Mary would love it. I've never been to Whitby.'

'That's not a bad idea,' Harper agreed.

'Could you be a love and see if there's another cup in the pot? And I don't suppose you fancy filling a bowl with warm water?'

'What did your last one die of?'

She opened one eye and stared at him. 'The same thing you will if you're not careful.'

Six

No reports of trouble at the meetings. Good.

'Any suspicious characters?' he asked Ash.

'It was mostly women and older folk. No one you'd look at twice, sir.'

'What did you discover in the pubs?' Harper asked the sergeant.

'It seems our friend has been about a bit, asking about songs,' Fowler answered. 'I came across three people who talked to him. Funny thing, though, sir, he's only interested in ones about death and dying.'

'Did you come up with a name?'

'I did,' he answered slowly. 'And a better description.'

'Go on,' the superintendent told him. 'What's wrong?'

'He claims he's called Randall Stonebrook. I checked the City Directory. Nobody by that name.'

'I suppose that would have made it too easy for us.' He sighed.

'He's about five feet nine, sandy hair starting to turn grey on the temples. Middle forties at the most. A local accent, but educated. Decent clothes.'

'That's more exact than we usually get.' Still not a great deal, but something.

'Three different people and they all agreed. I think that might be a first.'

Harper chuckled. Usually witnesses wildly contradicted each other.

'Get that circulated to the bobbies on the beat. One of them might recognize him.'

'And if they spot him?'

'Drag him in for questioning.'

No reply from Leeds, but Reed hadn't really expected anything yet. They'd need time to dig around and ask a few questions. Tom had probably given the job to Ash. But he'd hear something, he was certain of that.

He'd started keeping a cautious eye on Terrier John. The man was definitely living like the gentry. A couple of servants, not out and about until after ten. But after that he spent the morning down near the fish market, smoking his pipe and chatting to the skippers and hands. Home for his dinner and a quiet afternoon, then around the public houses in the evening.

49

Maybe he felt more comfortable with people like them, Reed thought. Back in Leeds, John had passed his time with labourers and thieves. The explanation could be as simple as that. But in his gut, he knew something was wrong.

Reed sat with the Excise officer in the Customs office overlooking the harbour. They met once a month, seeing where their interests overlapped and making sure nothing slipped through the cracks.

'Does the name John Millgate mean anything to you?' Reed asked.

'Should it?' Harry Pepper puffed at his pipe. He'd worked on the boats when he was young, and he had a fisherman's physique, broad and heavy, with large, callused hands.

'He was known as Terrier John when he lived in Leeds. Been here three years, according to my sergeant. Spends a lot of time by the boats.'

'And you think he might be up to something?' Pepper smiled.

'It would be his style. You're the one who knows the people here.'

'A few of them. The rest keep their distance now I work for the Crown.'

'They smuggle?'

Pepper shrugged. 'There's always been a bit of it. Always will be. Nothing like it was a few years ago, mind. It was a war back then. They'd shoot us if we tried to arrest them. It was worst down at Robin Hood's Bay, like an industry there.' He made a note on a pad. 'Leave it with me. I'll let you know.'

Elizabeth was still at the shop, supervising the

50

carpenter who was fitting the counter. She turned as Reed rapped lightly on the window, then smiled.

'Hello, Billy love, this is a surprise.'

'There's not much on. I thought you might fancy a walk. It's a grand afternoon. We probably won't have many more of them this year.'

She glanced doubtfully over her shoulder at the man working quietly, then nodded.

'Why not?'

Along Church Street, then holding her arm and guiding her up the steep cobbled hill of the Donkey Road to the abbey. In the churchyard they stopped, gazing down over the town. It never failed to lighten his heart, seeing everything laid out before him, the hills and the houses rising away from the water, the piers and the sea.

'Are you glad we moved?' he asked.

'I am,' Elizabeth told him. 'I was scared at first, but I think it's going to be one of the best things we've done.' She smiled at him. 'Apart from when we met, of course.'

The late-night banging on the door. Harper thought he'd left that behind when he was promoted. But it persisted, until he was groping his way down the stairs in his dressing gown and pulling back the bolts on the pub door.

A constable, a new face he didn't recognize, so young he must have barely finished his training.

'Beg pardon, sir, but they need you at the station.' He touched his cap in an embarrassed attempt at a salute.

51

The superintendent tried to rub the sleep out of his eyes.

'What's happened?' It had to be important to drag him out at . . . 'What time is it?'

'Struck midnight not long ago, sir. I'm not right sure what's going on. Something to do with a woman, I know that. They just sent me down here to fetch you.'

'You can go back. Say I'll be there as soon as I can.'

Annabelle stirred as he dressed, but she didn't wake. Very quietly, he slipped out and started walking along the empty street. His footsteps rang off the buildings, the only sound in the dark.

'Right,' he asked the night sergeant, 'what's so urgent?'

'Detectives' office, sir. The inspector and the sergeant are there.'

There was a woman with them, sitting with her face hidden in her hands. Good clothing, covered in dust, a tear on the shoulder of her gown. Harper raised an eyebrow, and Ash tilted his head: out in the corridor.

'That's Mrs Pease, sir,' he said quietly once he'd closed the door. He waited for the name to sink in.

'She's the candidate for the Poor Law Guardians in Hunslet,' Harper said.

'Yes.' The inspector's face was hard. 'She stayed late after a meeting and was on her way home when a man grabbed her. Hand over her mouth, she didn't even have chance to scream. Dragged her to a railway arch. Hit her a bit and told her that if she didn't withdraw from the election he'd beat her properly.' He paused. His mouth tightened. 'And he threatened to rape her.'

'How is she?'

'Terrified, sir. Hardly stopped shaking yet. After he'd gone she managed to find a copper. He helped her. Luckily, she found a bright one. He knows what's been going on, the threats. He whistled up a hackney and brought her here.'

'She needs to go to the infirmary.'

Ash shook his head. 'I already tried. She refused. Says she's fine, just needs a few minutes to collect herself.'

'Have you questioned her?'

'Not yet. I thought it might be better if you did it, what with your wife being a candidate.'

Harper nodded. That made sense. She might be willing to tell him a little more.

'Right. Bring a couple of mugs of tea, then you and Fowler clear out for a while.'

'Yes, sir.'

He brought a chair round and sat opposite her. The woman didn't look up when he placed the tea on the desk.

'I'm a copper,' he began gently. 'Tom Harper. I'm Annabelle Harper's husband.'

That made her stir, uncovering her face and looking up at him.

'You're safe here,' he continued. 'I promise.'

She nodded and tried to swallow. An older woman, plenty of grey in her hair. Small, probably only five feet, and thin as a rope. But her could sense her determination struggling against the fear and the pain.

'He . . .' she began. 'He . . .'

'Just take your time,' he told her. She started to shake and he brought an old blanket from the cupboard, draping it round her shoulders like a shawl. She drew it tight around her, huddling into it as if it was armour.

It took a while to emerge, filling out the story she'd garbled to the copper on the beat. Mrs Pease turned her head to show the bruise on her cheek, and rolled up her sleeve to display the marks on her arm.

The tears came after that. Shame, humiliation, anger. He brought a handkerchief from his pocket and passed it to her, listening without speaking. Better to let her go at her own pace, to take the path she needed.

Finally, he had it all. The demand that she withdraw her candidacy, the threat of rape if she didn't. She gulped at the last of the tea.

'Can you tell me what he looked like?' Harper asked softly.

'Not too big. Average. But he was strong. It was dark . . . I was too scared.' She hung her head.

'It doesn't matter,' he assured her. 'Is there anything you remember about him?'

'His shoes,' she replied after a second. 'They were very shiny. I could see the lights in them. And he spoke well.'

'Spoke well? What do you mean?'

'Enunciated his words.'

'I see.' That fitted with their man. Educated. He waited, but there was nothing more. Finally, Harper said: 'The police will have someone guarding you all the time, Mrs Pease. What does your husband do?'

'I'm a widow. Bert died a few years ago.'

'Do you have anyone you can stay with?'

'My sister,' she answered. She looked at him again. 'Why?'

'It's probably a good idea to be there for a few days.'

Realization dawned in her eyes and her mouth opened in horror.

'Do you think he knows where I live?'

'I'm not sure,' the superintendent said, 'and I don't want to take chances. Like I said, we're going to keep a bobby with you from now on.'

'I'm not going to let him stop me.' She set her jaw firmly. 'You tell your missus that.'

'I will,' he said with a gentle smile. The questions were building in his mind. What about the other women? What if the man went after more of them? 'You go and try to get some sleep. I'll have someone escort you to your sister's.'

'That bomb,' Mrs Pease said sadly, 'and now this.'

'I know.'

'He must be a very frightened man.'

'Yes,' Harper agreed. 'I think he is.'

'Well, he's not going to win.' She spoke with quiet, dignified determination. 'We've fought hard to get this far.'

She stood, looking a little frail but refusing to hold on to anything. With a nod, holding her head high, she walked out of the detectives' room. Ash would look after her. He'd organize the cover.

What would the man do next? How could they keep all the other women safe?

Harper glanced at the clock. Five minutes past two. Late, or early, depending which shift you worked. Pitch black beyond the window. He knew what he had to do first thing in the morning.

'I've got to go and see her,' Annabelle said. They were standing in the kitchen, drinking tea and talking quietly; Mary was still sleeping. 'I can't believe it. Poor woman.'

She wasn't dressed yet, and her long hair still hung loose. He'd worked through the night then walked home, coming softly into the Victoria, up the stairs, and woken her in whispers. He wanted her to hear it all from him, before the rumour-mongers started their exaggerations. The reality was bad enough. But no worse, he reflected, than a dead caretaker in a church hall.

'I need to go back soon,' Harper said.

She nodded. 'I'd better get madam up so she isn't late. She loves to make sure everything's prepared in the morning.' Annabelle pressed her lips together. 'I'm glad you came home again. Thank you for telling me yourself.'

'We'll catch him.' But he wasn't certain if he was trying to reassure her or himself.

'Everything in place?'

'Yes, sir,' Ash replied. 'I took her over to her sister's. There's a bobby on her door now. Round the clock.'

'We need to work with Hunslet on this, it's their manor. Fowler, you take care of that.'

56

'Yes, sir.'

'Make sure you let me know what's going on.'

'Of course.' Then he was gone.

'What do you want me doing, sir?' Ash asked.

'I'm not sure yet.' The superintendent picked up a pen and twirled it slowly in his fingers. 'I thought we had him pegged. Educated, knowledgeable, curious, happy to keep a distance from his actions. Now he gets violent. What do you make of that?'

'It changes the picture. You saw Mrs Pease, though. She's small, and not so young any more. I wonder if that's why he chose her, thinking she might be easier to intimidate.'

There was some logic in that, especially as she said her attacker wasn't a big man.

'If he thinks he succeeded, he's going to get a shock.'

'I have the idea he doesn't really understand women, sir. Or particularly like them.'

The tone of the letters, the assault . . . even the bomb fitted, in a curious way. A man who liked technical things, who kept his emotions at a distance.

'Never married, do you think?' Harper asked.

'It's a fair guess.'

It added to the picture, another tiny brushstroke in the portrait.

'That's something. Let's see what you can do with it. By the way, anything on Terrier John yet?'

'I've been going through old reports with Sergeant Tollman, but so far we haven't come up with anything hopeful. He's been in Whitby for three years, you said, sir?'

'That's what Billy Reed wrote.'

'I'll keep digging, then. But I don't see how we'd have missed anything big.'

'Nor do I,' Harper agreed. 'But he didn't magic the money up out of nowhere and he doesn't have the nous to print it himself.'

'I could widen the search. Try all over the West Riding. That might bring us something.'

'It's worth a shot. But don't spend too much time on it. I need you out there searching for our bomber.'

Ash grinned. 'Don't you worry about that, sir. Think of the Terrier as my hobby for those empty moments.'

Seven

He had plenty of work to keep himself busy. Reports to read, another to write, rotas and schedules and memoranda to sign. But Harper ignored them all, put on his hat and overcoat and walked over Crown Point Bridge into Hunslet.

Leeds was busy, alive, bustling with people and traffic. Horses trotted with their loads. Even to his poor ears, the city was noisier than it had ever been. Every day it grew louder and brassier. And bigger. Places that had been fields when he was a boy were covered with houses and factories now. Walk through town and you were lucky if you could find a tree or a spot of grass.

Dick Grayson had taken charge of the Hunslet

58

division the year before. He was older, cautious and thorough; this would be his final promotion before retirement. But he was a good, honest copper, a man who'd seen a lot and been willing to learn from it all.

'Very bad business,' he said gravely. He wore a formal frock coat and high wing collar, grey hair blossoming into broad mutton-chop sideboards. 'We had your sergeant here, working with our lot. It must have you thinking, your wife a candidate and all.'

'It does.'

'I've got men out searching where it happened.' He pulled a watch from his waistcoat. 'Been there a couple of hours, if you want to go and take a look.'

'I will. Thank you.'

'How seriously should we take this man, Tom?'

'With threatening letters, a bomb, a dead body, and a woman assaulted?' Harper asked in disbelief. Grayson reddened.

'Sorry. Stupid question. But having a man guarding Mrs Pease all the time is going to stretch us. Are you going to do it for all the women? Seven of them, isn't it?'

'I have an appointment with the chief about it this afternoon. But I think we need to do it. If we don't and something happens, the press will maul us. And they should.'

'The devil and the deep blue sea.'

'Something like that.' He stood, ready to leave.

'Talk to Walsh out there,' Grayson advised. 'He's young, but quick as anything. Give him ten years and he'll be after your job.'

* * *

59

It was easy to pick out Walsh. He was one of three constables, the others both older, but they deferred to him. Harper introduced himself and the men all snapped to attention.

The railway line ran over a low viaduct, most of the arches below converted into workshops. But the closest one was empty, dark, the brick walls damp and dank to the touch.

'It happened here,' Walsh explained. 'He dragged her off the street. No one would be able to see them.'

'How long has this been empty?'

'A year or so, sir. It used to be a painter and decorator's yard, but the old fella who had it died.'

'Our man knows the area, then,' the superintendent said thoughtfully as he looked around.

'At least he must have taken a good wander round in the daylight, sir.'

He could hear the smallest trace of an Irish accent in Walsh's voice. It was pleasant, giving a soft musicality to the words.

'Have you found anything yet? Paper with writing on it.'

'It's mostly wrappers from this and that, sir.' Walsh gestured to a small pile in the corner. 'But there was one that had been written on, I think.' He squatted, quickly sorting through everything, then held out a torn piece of notepaper. 'Here we are. It doesn't make any sense, though: *Six pretty maids I drowned here* then *And the seventh thou shall be*. The paper's torn. It sounds gruesome, if you ask me.'

He took it from the constable's fingers and

60

stared at the handwriting, feeling the tingle in his spine. It looked all too familiar; he'd swear on a stack of bibles that it was the same as the other note and the letters. No surprise, but the confirmation he needed.

'Good work,' he said. 'Is there anything else?'

'Not in here. We've been up and down the street, but no one remembers anything. Mind you,' he added with a wry grin, 'the knocker-up comes by early when you're on the morning shift, so you can hardly blame them.'

'I remember that.'

'Aye, so do I,' Walsh said. 'Better off on the force, if you ask me, sir.'

Harper started to move away, nodding to the constable to join him. Grayson was right; the young man impressed him. He was thinking the whole time, looking, questioning and remembering. It was what a copper should be doing. But most didn't.

'Tell me, Mr Walsh, have you ever thought about moving into plain clothes?'

The constable let out a low whistle. 'Well now, I'd be a liar if I said no, sir.'

'How long have you been on the force?'

'I started two years ago in August, sir.'

Grayson should have made him a detective by now, Harper thought. Perhaps he'd simply wanted to keep an intelligent man on the beat.

'If you decide you'd like to give it a crack, come and see me.'

'I'll do that, sir. And thank you. We'll keep looking here, but if I'm honest, I don't think there's anything to find.'

The superintendent held up the piece of paper. 'This helps me.'

'It's becoming a bloody awful business.'

The walls of the chief constable's office were lined with portraits of his predecessors, grand-looking men in uniform, serious expressions fixed forever on their faces. A picture of the Queen, stout, unhappy, hung behind him, overlooking it all. Colin Crossley sat behind a large desk, dressed in a lounge suit, shirt with a turnover celluloid collar, his hands very clean and nails manicured, looking more like a successful businessman than the person who ran the police force in one of England's largest cities.

'It is, sir,' Harper agreed.

'How do we keep these people safe? Not just the candidates, but those who come to hear them speak? We can't have them too fearful to show up.'

Crossley was an astute man. He'd been in the army and he'd been in the police. He'd earned his rank, not just a pen pusher or someone who looked dignified in gold braid.

'We have a twenty-four-hour guard on Mrs Pease now. We could do that for the others – if they'd let us. I know my wife would say no.'

'Why would she?' He reached into a humidor, selected a cigar, clipped off the tip, then lit a match, making sure the end caught evenly as he puffed smoke.

'She'd feel hemmed in. Some of the others might, too.'

'Surely it's better than the alternative,' Crossley

wondered. 'But that would be taxing on us, given the men we have right now. Recruitment's down at the moment. I'd be reluctant to have good bobbies standing around all day, and the poor ones wouldn't be worth a damn.'

He knew the job, but the man was also a politician. A good one. Crossley would never have been appointed otherwise, and he certainly wouldn't have lasted in the position; the watch committee would have savaged him like a pack of wolves. He needed to keep an eye on how things would look to the council, the press, and the public.

'I say we offer it, sir. Let them make the choice.'

The chief considered the idea, then nodded.

'We'll do that. But what about the other half of the equation? How can we make people feel they'll be safe at meetings? That there won't be another bomb?'

'I've had soldiers checking the halls beforehand. In uniform, so people can see them.'

'Good,' Crossley nodded. 'What else?'

'I've posted coppers at the women's meetings.'

'The only problem . . .' the chief constable began.

'I know, sir. The male candidates are going to start complaining.' He frowned. 'I don't see any way around that. Plenty of them hate the idea of women running for office, as it is. They'll say we're giving them special treatment.'

'And we are, but it's for a damned good reason,' Crossley said. 'I'll tell them that if they bring it up. I'm not so certain about women in office myself, but they have the legal right, so it's up

63

to us to make sure they can run.' He held up a hand. 'I'm sure your view is a lot more radical than mine, Tom. How's your investigation coming along? Do you have any suspects yet?'

Harper brought the chief up to date, the man listening closely.

'So we have no name and just a fairly general description? From the sound of it, he could be almost anyone you see on the tram. And if he's working alone, how are you going to find him?'

'I wish I knew, sir. Keep plugging away and asking questions. If he's this determined, he'll try something else. With men at the meetings and watching the women, we should be able to catch him in the act.'

'As long as it's before anything else happens.' He took the cigar from his mouth and stared at it. 'But you can't guarantee that, can you?'

'You know I can't, sir.' It seemed like a ridiculous question. There were always so many things that might happen, and Crossley knew it.

'Let's just hope that luck is on our side for once. Who have you put on the case?'

'Ash and Fowler.'

'The first team.'

'I'm working on it, too.'

'I assumed nothing less, Superintendent.' The chief nodded and smiled. 'After all, you have a vested interest.'

'That I do, sir.'

'I'm not having a bobby following me around,' Annabelle warned.

'I never believed you would,' Harper told her.

'It's there for the women who want them. We'll still have a copper at every meeting and we'll keep checking the halls.'

She nodded. 'That's fine. And I like having you there when I speak. *You*. But that's it. If people saw me with a bobby behind me they'd start wondering.'

He needed to move her off the topic if he could. 'How did the campaigning go today?'

'I only spent this afternoon on it. I went over to see Catherine Pease this morning. She's not giving up.'

'That's what she told me, too.'

'Nothing on whoever did it?'

'Not yet.'

Annabelle glanced at the clock.

'I'd better get myself scrubbed up for the meeting tonight. Don't want to stand in front of them looking like a mucky pup.'

There was no question of Mary coming. Not now, with all the trouble. She'd stay upstairs at the Victoria, with Ellen. It wasn't far to go, easy walking distance; that was one advantage to living in the ward. That and the fact that everyone knew and respected her. Simply strolling down the street, Annabelle had to stop every few yards to say hello, to ask after a husband, a mother, a wife, the children. It wasn't politics, it was simply the way she was with them all.

She'd win the election hands down, Harper thought, watching as she listened to a young woman with a threadbare shawl around her shoulders. None of the other candidates stood a chance round here.

At home he'd paged through Kidson's book until he found the words from the piece of paper Walsh had discovered in the railway arch. A song called *The Outlandish Knight*. More women dying. The man behind this was leaving his clues. He'd discuss it with Ash and Fowler in the morning. Maybe one of them might have a bright idea.

Eight

'I'm sorry to disturb you at home, sir,' Sergeant Brown said as he stood on Reed's doorstep. The last echo of the church bell from St Hilda's still hung in the darkness, nine o'clock at night.

'What's happened?' He was settled for the evening, waistcoat unbuttoned, tie and collar removed.

'We've had a spot of bother on the beach between here and Sandsend.' He frowned. 'One man badly wounded, and another not looking too happy, though he'll live. I brought the pony and trap and some lanterns. The tide's out for hours yet.'

'Let me get my coat.'

'You might want a muffler, too, sir. There's a sea fret forming. It's going to be chilly.' Brown paused. 'The Excise and the Coast Guard are already there. This was their do. It was an Excise man who wounded the two fellas.'

Smuggling, Reed thought. It couldn't be

66

anything else. 'Who are they? Do we know them?'

'Probably. We got a telegraph message from Sandsend. Constable Johnson didn't know what to do so he sent for me. I thought you ought to be involved, sir.'

'Good man.'

Soon enough the cart was rumbling along the road. There was a sliver of moon, just enough to give some light, the clouds shifting slowly overhead.

'If it was an Excise job, I don't see why they want us,' Reed said.

'Probably because of the shooting, sir. And it's our patch. Politics and that.' He pulled back on the reins. 'It's near here. There's a track goes down. We'd better light some lanterns first.'

Brown was as surefooted as the goats Reed had seen on the mountainsides in Afghanistan. The inspector moved warily, taking his time. His foot slipped here and there, sending small showers of scree tumbling along the hillside as he held his breath.

Down on the beach a series of lights illuminated a boat, one of the small local cobles, pulled high on the sand, still loaded with something, oars stowed on board. A member of the Coast Guard stood by it in his uniform, rifle at his side.

Harry Pepper was talking to one of his men.

'Billy,' he said as Reed approached.

'What happened?'

'We had a tip that someone was bringing contraband ashore tonight. Caught them as they were pulling on to the beach, but they decided to put

67

up a fight. One of them is on his way to hospital in Scarborough, and we winged another in the arm. But I thought it best to let you boys know.' He smiled and lit his pipe.

'Who were the smugglers?'

'Nobody local. They must have come from the ship to meet someone up here. We got in first.' Pepper glanced out to sea. 'Coast Guard is out there. With luck, they'll catch 'em.'

'Who do you suspect locally?'

'All of them,' he laughed. 'It's a good way to make a little extra money. We'll sweat the ones we caught and try to find some names. My bet's on the Shaws.' Reed gave him a questioning look. 'Family from Robin Hood's Bay. Anything from there up to Staithes, they probably have a hand in it.'

'When you question the men, see if Terrier John's name brings any response, will you?' Reed said.

'Still on about that? I can ask.'

'News?' Harper asked.

'The meetings all went off without incident, sir,' Ash said. 'That's something.'

'Hunslet are having no luck tracing that man,' Fowler told him.

The superintendent rubbed his chin. 'What's the population of Leeds?' he asked.

'Three hundred thousand,' the sergeant replied without hesitation. 'Probably closer to three hundred and fifty these days.' He shrugged when the others stared at him. 'I read it, that's all.'

'Let's say half of those are men, that's a hundred

and fifty thousand,' Harper calculated. 'Call it two-thirds adult, one hundred thousand. Not so many in their forties, we'll go with fifteen thousand of them. Educated narrows it down even further. We're down to two or three thousand. At most.'

'Are you trying to cheer us up, sir?' Ash wondered.

'I'm trying to be realistic,' Harper said. 'He seems to be working alone. The odds are against us. He does keep leaving us clues, though.' He explained about the new fragment of folk song. 'Does that strike any sparks?'

'Could be worth having another word with Kidson and his niece,' Fowler said. 'They might have managed to turn up something. Really, sir, they look like our best bet at the moment.' It was a bright, close morning, the Indian summer stretching on; even with the window open, the room felt stuffy.

Harper nodded; he'd planned on going there again today.

'Whoever's behind this only has a limited time. The elections are in less than five weeks.'

'He's already made a good start, sir,' Ash pointed out. 'How many of the women are taking police protection?'

'Four. The male candidates will squawk, but the chief is going to take care of that. Any other suggestions for safety?'

'I don't know what else we can do, sir.'

'There is one thing.' The superintendent gave a dark scowl. 'Catch this bugger.'

* * *

'Oh,' Ethel Kidson said as she opened the door. 'Superintendent. Come in, please.'

He'd walked out to Burley Road from Millgarth. The day was pleasant, too warm for a coat, and who knew if there'd be any more this year? It gave him time to let his mind wander, to shape his thoughts and try to make some sense from them. But by the time he reached the house he'd had no revelations. All they had were scraps of this and that. Fragments of knowledge.

The hallway smelt of beeswax and dust, the banister and newels of the stairway gleaming, as if the maid had just gone over them. But the Turkish rug covering the floorboards was faded, half its fringe gone. In the parlour Kidson was seated at the table, the chaos of books and papers exactly the same as it had been before.

'Uncle, Mr Harper's back. The policeman.'

The man looked up, eyes dark and quizzical as he stood and extended his hand.

'You're always very welcome here, of course, but I thought we'd answered your questions. And I'm afraid we haven't found anything.'

'Just one or two more questions, if you don't mind, sir.'

'Of course.' Kidson glanced at Ethel. 'Whatever we can do.'

'Does this mean anything?'

Harper brought the piece of paper from the Hunslet arch out of his waistcoat pocket and handed it over. The man squinted, then passed it to his niece.

'*The Outlandish Knight*,' he said with surprise. 'It's in my book, Superintendent.'

70

'I saw it. We found this yesterday, sir. This was at the scene of an assault on a woman.'

Kidson ran a hand through his hair, leaving it standing on end. 'I really don't understand it. Do you, Ethel?'

'No. It's definitely nobody we know. None of them would . . . at least I don't think so.' She blushed, then hardened her face into a frown.

'What other songs in the book mention dead women, sir? I only found a very few.'

'There are plenty of them out there,' Kidson replied. 'I printed some songs I collected in Yorkshire, but most of them have their origins elsewhere.'

'Could you make me a list of the pieces in the book that include dead and dying women, sir? It would save me poring through everything.'

'Of course,' he said, as if he should have thought of it himself. 'It won't take long. The woman who was attacked, how is she?'

'Shaken but fine. No damage.'

'Good.' He sighed. 'I feel a sense of responsibility for all this.'

'It's hardly your fault, sir,' Harper told him.

'I know, but . . . these are lovely songs, Superintendent. They've been around for a hundred years, often much longer. Someone leaving them as clues to crimes, it just seems to . . . tarnish them.'

'I don't know about that.' It seemed far-fetched. Yet there had to be a reason for it, something he didn't see yet.

'I'd like to help, if I may.' Kidson looked at

71

his niece. 'We both would. This is our field. We know it well. I'm respected, if I might say so.'

He had nothing to lose by accepting the offer. As the man said, folk songs were their world. They knew all the people. Maybe they'd have luck in places he didn't even know existed.

'Gladly,' he said, gazing from one face to the other. 'I'm happy for whatever I can get.'

'That's settled.' Kidson rubbed his hands together. 'We'll start work later today.' His eyes were twinkling with anticipation. 'This is going to be a very different type of song hunt.'

'I just hope it's a fruitful one.'

'We'll do our best,' Ethel Kidson said.

He was preparing to leave for the day, drying the pen nib on an old rag and pushing the signed papers to the corner of his desk, when there was a knock on the door. Always one more thing, Harper thought.

'Come in.' He sat down again.

Constable Walsh. The officer he'd met in Hunslet the day before. He'd wondered how long it would be before the man turned up, but this was quicker than he imagined.

'Good afternoon, Constable.'

Walsh stood at attention, eyes straight ahead.

'Relax,' Harper told him. 'Sit yourself down.' He waited until the man had settled himself on the chair. 'I take it you're interested in the job.'

'I am, sir. I talked it over with the wife last night. I told her, it's too good a chance to turn down.'

'There's no more money in it.'

'I know, sir. But for the future . . .'

He was ambitious. Good, as long as it didn't get the better of him. Harper had seen that happen before.

'When I saw you in the railway arch, you were giving orders to the other constables. Directing them.' He saw Walsh give a soft smile. 'Tell me, can you take orders as well as you give them?'

'I can, sir. I want to learn.'

'You'd be working under a couple of the best coppers I've ever met. You have potential. Listen, understand, and it might develop. But if you start thinking you're God's gift I'll kick you out so fast you'll be on the far side of Leeds Bridge before you know it.'

'Yes, sir.' Walsh grinned broadly, showing off a set of brown, stained teeth.

'I want you to talk to Superintendent Grayson. Have him sign the official request. If he's willing do that, you'll be welcome here.'

'Thank you, sir. I won't let you down.'

'I know,' Harper told him. 'I wouldn't give you the chance.'

Finally he was home, after a jolting ride on the tram that left his back aching. The brakes squealed at every stop, metal on metal, the sound grating against his poor hearing. Harper was glad to walk through the doors of the Victoria and see Dan behind the bar.

The pub was busy with thirsty men enjoying a pint or two after work. The air mixed the smells of the forge, the chemical plant, the tannery and God knew what else as he passed through.

73

Upstairs, though, the only scent was Annabelle's perfume. She was kneeling on the floor in her best frock as she and Mary went through the girl's arithmetic.

'The teacher said I got this wrong, but she didn't tell me how.'

'Let's take a look. You've got three numbers. Try counting it out on your fingers.'

Mary did as her mother said, slowly and deliberately. Harper stood by the door, watching, smiling. Just before the end, the girl looked up, eyes wide with realization.

'Now do you see it?' Annabelle asked.

'Yes, Mam.' The girl set her jaw, disappointed at herself.

'You got everything else right.'

'I know. But I wanted to get it all.'

No rest for the wicked. A quick meal of cold pie and a cup of tea, then off to tonight's meeting.

'She wants to be perfect,' Harper said.

'Then she's going to get a rude awakening one of these days,' Annabelle said.

'You know what she's like. She'll keep trying.' Like mother, like daughter, he thought. Neither of them would ever give up.

'Then we'd better hope she grows out of this. I feel sorry for her teacher.'

He laughed as they crossed Roundhay Road. Mary was a handful, no doubt about it.

'It's the funeral tomorrow,' Annabelle said quietly.

'Funeral?'

'Mr Harkness. The caretaker at the church.'

The bomb. He should have remembered.

'Are you going?'

'Yes,' she replied with a sad nod. 'I have to. If it hadn't been for my meeting . . .'

'I told you. You can't blame yourself for someone else's madness.'

'Is that what it is, do you think, Tom? Madness?'

'In a way, perhaps.'

The soldier was standing outside the hall, smart in his uniform, chatting to an old man in a battered suit; the caretaker here, of course. As soon as he spotted the superintendent, the Engineer snapped to attention.

'Evening, sir, ma'am. I've given it a good going over. Clean as a whistle, inside and out.'

'Thank you.'

The man marched off as if he was on the parade ground, back still straight.

'Ten to one he'll start slouching as soon as he's round the corner,' the caretaker said with a liquid, wheezy laugh. 'You must be Mrs Harper, luv.'

Nine

'It was a good crowd,' Harper said as they strolled home. There was the start of a chill in the night. The gaslights gave their small, shimmering glow in the darkness. He felt Annabelle still bubbling with excitement beside him as he tried to stay aware of the other people on the street. No one who seemed like a threat. No men of average height with greying hair.

'Good? They were wonderful, Tom. All those questions. They were interested. Really interested.'

'You answered them all.'

'I might have fudged a few,' she said with a grin, putting her arm through his. 'I hope the other lasses are doing as well.'

Some were, some weren't; he received the daily police reports. But it wasn't his place to say that to her.

The pub was in sight and she was still talking nineteen to the dozen, fizzing over with enthusiasm. He was pleased for her; he knew exactly how hard she'd worked to come this far. The long discussions over whether she should put her name forward as a candidate. It hadn't taken too much effort to obtain the backing of the Suffrage Society. After all, she'd been a speaker for them for a few years. But persuading them and the Women's Co-op Guild to pay the election expenses was another tussle. She had to convince them she had a good chance of winning the Sheepscar ward and ending up on the Board of Poor Law Guardians.

Getting their support was only the start of the work. Sending in her nomination papers. Then she needed volunteers to help with the campaign. There was a manifesto to write, all the ideas and words that taxed her late into the night for weeks. Posters, leaflets. All that before the starting gun for the election. Now it would be non-stop until polling day in November.

76

'You go up,' he told her when they entered the pub. 'I'll be there in a minute.'

She gave him a curious look. But he could see that the energy was starting to leave her face. She'd be asleep as soon as her head touched the pillow.

'Dan,' he said quietly, 'have we had many strangers in during the last few weeks?'

'Always some,' the barman said. 'You know that. People passing through.'

'This one would be well-dressed, in his forties, doesn't sound like he's from Sheepscar.'

Dan frowned. 'Could have been one or two when I was on. I don't really keep track. I just serve 'em and make sure they don't cause any trouble.'

'This one would have probably been quiet.'

He shook his head. 'No one I can think of. Why?'

'Doesn't matter. Just keep your eyes open for someone like that. He might show his face.'

By the end of the week they'd found nothing. But there'd been no trouble at any of the venues, and no more of the women candidates had been threatened.

'It looks like your policy is working, sir,' Ash said. They'd slipped out to the café in the market for their dinner, a hurried plate of warmed-through cottage pie and a cup of tea.

'I'm glad about that,' Harper told him. 'But unless we have something else to go on, we're never going to catch this man.' He snorted. 'Must be the first time I've wanted a crime to happen.'

77

'I don't think he's given up, if that helps.'

'Nor do I.' He pushed a heap of mashed potato on to his fork. 'Did you manage to come up with anything on Terrier John and any missing money?'

'I should be able to finish up this afternoon. But I haven't found so much as a hint. You didn't really think I would, did you, sir?'

'No. But we might have forgotten something or overlooked it. Let me know and I'll drop Billy Reed a line. Looks like Terrier John didn't acquire his cash in Leeds.' He paused. 'By the way, we're going to have a new detective constable from Monday.'

'Dominic Walsh. I know.' Ash gave his enigmatic smile. 'Don't you worry, sir, we'll look after him.'

How the hell did word pass so quickly, Harper wondered? He'd only signed the papers that morning, after Grayson had given his approval to the transfer. But it had always been that way. The police force gossiped more than a bunch of housewives over the Monday morning wash.

He was pleased with the new addition. If Walsh lived up to his promise, he'd have the best squad in the city. No, one of the very best in the country. He'd show them down in Scotland Yard that the provinces could be their equal.

And they'd make a start by solving this case.

'How's Mrs Harper's campaign coming along, sir?'

'Exhausting,' he replied with a sigh. 'I'm no sooner home than we're off out to another meeting. Tomorrow's going to be the test. It's the first

78

hustings. All the candidates on stage together, answering questions. You know how those things go.'

'Boisterous. I worked on one or two when I was in uniform.'

'So did I,' Harper said. He remembered them well. Loud, and often violent. At the Parliamentary elections, the candidates would turn up with their mobs and their bodyguards, and the event was guaranteed to end in a brawl. A wagonful of arrests and bruises that took weeks to fade. This would be much smaller. More genteel, he hoped. But it would probably still be ugly. 'I've arranged extra men at the ones with the women.'

'We'll go to some of them,' Ash said. 'I have to say, sir, so far the meetings have been tame affairs.'

'That's going to change. I can feel it. Our friend is going to want to try again.'

Reed sat at the back of the magistrate's court, watching the man standing in the dock with his arm in a grubby sling. He pleaded not guilty. Never mind that he was caught on an empty beach with a boat full of contraband.

And there was the other one, still in hospital in Scarborough. But it would be a while before his day in front of a judge; the injuries were bad.

As it was an Excise case, there was nothing for the police to do but observe. The prisoner came from Redcar, not too far up the coast, but out of his manor.

Another hearing was set for a week's time, and

the man led away to the cells. Reed made his way outside. Harry Pepper was already there, puffing on his pipe.

'What do you think, now you've had a proper look at him?'

'Like most of the criminals I've seen in my life,' Reed answered with a laugh. 'Did you catch the bigger boat?'

'No. It managed to slip away. They must have had a sharp lookout.'

'What did the smugglers bring ashore?'

'Some good French brandy. They'd taken off two loads before we swooped, so it's a decent haul. Several cases would probably have ended up in your old neck of the woods.'

'Leeds?' Reed asked in astonishment.

'There, Newcastle, Sunderland. It's a network.'

'I never knew that.' He lit a cigarette. 'Did he say anything about Terrier John?'

'From the look on his face when I asked, he's never heard of him. And I've not had a sniff of him at all. Maybe he's just innocent.'

'No,' the inspector said. 'Anything but. I can feel it.'

'Another letter for you, sir.' Sergeant Tollman placed it on his desk. 'Mr Reed again, by the look of it.'

Harper had been planning on writing that morning, after Ash's search had turned up nothing. Billy probably wondered why he hadn't received word yet.

Dear Tom,

The other night I was called out to the arrest of some smugglers not too far away. The Excise people were handling it, but they wanted the police because two men had been shot. After court today, the Excise chap told me that some of the haul of brandy would have been sent to Leeds. Sold to shops and publicans, evidently. Do you know anything about that? I've never heard of it.

It made me wonder if Terrier John might be involved somehow. It's a bit of a leap in the dark, but I'll look into it from this end. I'd be grateful if one of your men could ask a few questions, too.

Sincerely,
Billy

Smuggling? He'd never come across anything like that. And publicans? He'd have to ask Annabelle; she might know something. In the meantime, they could do a little digging.

'Sergeant Fowler,' he called, 'I have a little job for you. It'll keep you out of mischief.'

The hall was already half-full by the time they arrived, people milling around. Chairs and a lectern had been set up on the stage, along with a desk for the chairman. Harper could sense an edge to the mood, one that could quickly turn sour. Not violent, he judged, but angry.

Two of the candidates were standing and talking with their supporters: Mr Moody, a portly older

81

man, the Liberal who'd served on the Poor Law board for years, running on his experience in the job, and Mr Oldroyd, the young fellow put forward by the Labour Party. He worked with the unions, earnest, still fresh-faced, and looking nervous.

'I feel like Daniel walking into the lion's den,' Annabelle whispered.

'You'll be fine. There are some of your people over in the corner. More of them will show up closer to the time.'

Harper circulated, listening, smiling. He knew one or two of the faces, men he'd arrested for this and that over the years. A few more made him for a copper and turned away. Everyone was in their best clothes, as if this was an occasion or a party. Uncomfortable high collars and ties, good wool suits carefully brushed and sponged down, a high shine on the black boots. Sunday frocks on the women. He wondered what they'd all look like by the end of the meeting.

Finally, the chairman banged his gavel for order. The candidates were ready: Moody, Oldroyd, Wilkinson, the Conservative with the long aristocratic nose and condescending manner who didn't have a chance here, and Annabelle.

About two hundred people were jammed into the room, with the close, animal smell of bodies pushed together. Her crowd had arrived just a few minutes before, a mix of women and men, all of them ready to shout for her. A uniformed bobby stood against the back wall, eyes searching the crowd.

'First of all we're going to give each candidate

five minutes to speak,' the chairman bellowed. 'I know you'll give them a fair listen.' He smirked, voice riding over the jibes from the audience. 'Since we're chivalrous here, we'll give the opening turn to the lady. Mrs Annabelle Harper.'

The order didn't matter; whenever she spoke, it was going to be a difficult ride. As she stepped up to the lectern, hat sitting jauntily on her head, hands unfolding a few pages of notes, the catcalls began. She stood, gazing down at the men who were shouting, not saying a word until there was a space in the noise.

'Is that how your mothers brought you up?' Her voice carried easily, trained by four years of public speaking for the Suffragists. 'You.' She singled out a man with a stare, 'Robert Mayhew. Did you used to do that at home when you were a lad? I bet you didn't. I know your mam. If you tried, she'd have given you a clout you'd have felt for a week. My little girl's five and she has better manners than that. Maybe your mothers should all see you now.' It was enough to shame them for a while. Time to start on her ideas.

Her plans were ambitious. Fewer people in the workhouse. More relief at home, especially for the old. Proper training for those children who were in the Guardians' care, seeing that they learned their letters and their numbers and a trade, so they might make something of themselves.

'Aye, but how much is it going to cost us, missus?' someone shouted.

'Not a penny more than you're paying now,'

she answered triumphantly. 'And in a few years, it could even be less. More than that, it treats folk like people. How many of you have known someone on relief? Go on, how many?' A few hands went up at first, then Harper saw more and more, until most of the crowd had their arms raised. 'You've heard all the stories, then. You've seen the way it makes them less than human. All that talk we hear about the deserving poor? Every one of them is deserving. The system we have now makes them crawl in order to get a little help. What I'm proposing lets them keep their dignity.' She folded the papers and stood defiantly.

Harper wasn't sure what to expect. An outburst of barracking? The quiet grew like a bubble over the space of a heartbeat, then came the burst of applause. He felt the relief and pride welling up inside and glanced at Annabelle's face. Surprise and gratitude. She'd given the others a hard act to follow.

She'd almost reached her seat when something arced out of the crowd. A cabbage. It missed her, landing against the back wall. By then Harper was pushing through the crowd, eyes on the man who'd thrown it. He was determined to nip any trouble in the bud. But the bobby was there before him, grinning and giving a small salute as he led the culprit away by the arm.

The chairman was banging on his gavel. A man appeared on stage and whispered in his ear.

'If there's a Superintendent Harper here—' He stole a questioning glance at Annabelle. '—There's someone outside who needs to speak to him urgently. And now we're going to hear from Mr Oldroyd.'

He caught his breath in the open air and looked around. A young constable, red-faced from running.

'What is it?'

'A message from Meanwood, sir. The soldier from the Engineers found a bomb and defused it. Nothing else that he could see. Inspector Ash is on his way there. He said we should tell you.'

'Very good. Who did the soldier inform?'

'Just us, sir. The hustings are going ahead as planned.'

Let's pray the Engineer hadn't missed anything, Harper thought as he sat in the back of the hackney heading to Meanwood. The hall was the spit and image of the one he'd just left, packed inside, the crowd loud and boisterous.

Around the corner of the building he spotted Ash. The soldier stood next to him, his uniform grubby, cradling a package in both hands.

'This is Private White, sir. He found the bomb hidden in a room behind the stage.'

'Call me Chalky if you like, sir,' the soldier said with a wide grin. 'Everyone does.' He held out the parcel. 'This was tucked away at the back of a cupboard. Could have done some real damage if it had gone off.'

'Are you certain it's safe now?' Harper eyed it warily.

'Safe as my Granny's house on a Sunday night, sir.'

'How much harm could it have done? Deaths?'

White thought for a few seconds. 'If someone was standing close enough, yes. Most likely it

85

would have brought down part of the building.'
His eyes flickered over to the window. 'If this
lot had been in there . . .'

'How expertly is it put together?'

'Nothing special, sir. It's much like the anar-
chists used to make a few years ago. I trained
on those things down in London. Doesn't take a
whole lot of brains. Clockwork fuse. It was timed
to go off about half an hour before the hustings.
I didn't tell the candidates. Once I'd disarmed it,
they weren't in any danger.'

'You're sure it won't go off now?'

The soldier grinned again. 'Positive. I've
made it harmless.' He tossed it up in the air
and caught it with one hand. 'God's honest
truth.'

'Right.' Harper took hold of it, surprised by the
weight. He pulled sixpence from his pocket. 'Have
yourself a drink, Chalky. You've earned it.'

'Never say no to a drink, sir, you learn that in
the army. Thank you.' He saluted and walked
away.

'We were lucky,' the superintendent said quietly
as he stared at the bomb.

'Not quite, sir,' Ash said. 'We were prepared.
Chummy's probably wondering why he never
heard an explosion.'

'True.' Could he still be lurking in the neighbourhood? For a moment he wondered if it was
worth searching. Then he thought of the miles
of streets and ginnels all around, the yards and
privies. Too many places to hide. 'We need to
see if he left us another clue.'

'I'll search back there, sir.'

'Be glad the soldier didn't sound the alarm. Can you imagine what it would be like if word got out that we'd found another bomb? We were lucky enough not to see panic after that first one. This would put an end to all the political meetings in this city.'

'Maybe that's what he wants. But it's a nasty way to achieve it.'

A wave of shouting came from inside the hall, two groups of voices in a confusion of sound.

'See what you can find.' He passed over the bomb. 'Leave that at the station when you're done.'

Ash raised an eyebrow. 'Thank you, sir.'

Annabelle was pacing around the parlour, still in the dress she'd worn for the hustings, her hat on the hook behind the door.

'How—' he began, but she cut him off.

'What was it? Why did they need you?'

All the way home he'd been wondering what to tell her. That it was a false alarm? A disturbance that was quelled before he arrived? She'd look into his face and see the lie. It had to be truth. But he'd need to trust her to keep it to herself.

'There was a bomb at the Meanwood hustings.'

'My God.' She covered her mouth with a hand.

'The soldier found it and disarmed it. No harm done. Everything went ahead.'

'What?' she asked in disbelief. 'After that?'

'We didn't tell anyone. And I need you to keep it to yourself. Please. It's vital that it stays quiet.'

Annabelle turned away in a rustle of silk. He could see her breathing, making up her mind.

'All right,' she agreed finally. 'I don't like it, though, Tom. It's not honest. It's not fair to people.'

'It's reality. Even the candidates don't know, and we're keeping it that way. It has to stay under your hat.'

'I just said I wouldn't tell anyone,' she snapped. 'But what's going to happen if you don't discover a bomb and it goes off? Tell me that.'

'You know the answer as well as I do,' he said calmly. 'But I trust the troops. You've met them; they're good at their job.' He needed to start her thinking about something else. 'You really won them over tonight.'

'Apart from cabbage man.'

'He was out of there before you could say Jack Robinson.'

'He won't be playing for Yorkshire any time soon with an arm like that. Missed by a mile.' She smiled wanly. 'You're sure no one was hurt?'

'Cross my heart.'

'It did go well tonight,' she admitted. 'Oldroyd mumbled so often they kept asking him to repeat things, poor lamb. And they wouldn't even give Wilkinson the time of day. What do you expect, a Tory round here? All Moody could come up with was how long he'd been a Guardian. When I asked him about his ideas and plans, he hummed and hawed and said just carry on.'

'Sounds like you came out of it the winner.'

'I'm not going to gloat. And I'm not going to

get my hopes up. I'm not. There's still a long way to go.'

'I know.' Weeks of it ahead of them, trying to keep everyone safe. 'I know.'

Ten

He thought he'd reached Millgarth early, but Ash and Fowler were already in the detectives' office, hard at work. The inspector was completing a report, while the sergeant pored over a pile of folders, pausing often to push the glasses back up his nose.

'No other incidents last night, I hope?'

'All went smoothly, sir,' Ash said.

'We need to be particularly careful from now on. I want those Engineers going over the halls with a nit comb. And every bobby at a meeting needs to be alert for anyone resembling our friend.'

'Yes, sir.' He gave a small cough. 'I gave that room where he'd hidden the bomb a proper going-over. I came up with this. It was far enough away that it wouldn't have been destroyed.' He picked a piece of paper from his desk. Torn from a notebook, just like the others. The handwriting was the same.

Then let me this my life wear out,
And turn my harmless wheel about

'Do you know it?' Harper asked.

'I do.' Fowler raised his head and spoke. 'It's from a song called *The Spinning Wheel*. My mother used to sing me to sleep with it when I

89

was little.' He gave a quick, embarrassed smile and returned to work.

Ash raised an eyebrow. 'Odds-on it's in Mr Kidson's book,' he said.

'I'm not enough of a fool to take that bet. He's offered to help us, if he can.'

'What have you learned about smuggling, Sergeant?' Harper asked.

'Not that much, sir.' Fowler frowned, and the lines on his face transformed him into the old man he'd become in a few decades. 'I've still got a long way to go, but there doesn't seem to be a great deal to know, at least as far as Leeds is concerned.'

'That might be why I've never heard about it.'

'It happens, right enough. The Excise people haven't caught anyone here selling smuggled goods in a bit over three years, though. And there was a gap of four years before that. Of course,' he said with a grin, 'they might just spend their days sitting in the office and playing pontoon.'

'Three years?' Suddenly Harper felt very alert. 'What happened then?'

'A few people rounded up. Cases of French brandy, no duty paid on them.' He dug through the files on his desk. 'Here we are. Nothing very important. A publican, two shopkeepers. They caught the chap who'd sold it to them, but not his contact.'

He'd never asked Annabelle about smuggling. She'd been too wound up, too full of politics and pain, all touched with anger. The time hadn't been right. Tonight, he thought.

'Who were they?'

But when Fowler read the list of the guilty, it contained no names he recognized. Terrier John Millgate wasn't among them.

'You know, when I was going through Terrier's past, a name cropped up, sir,' Ash said from across the room. 'John Rutherford.'

'Who's he?' Harper had never heard the name.

'A wholesaler of spirits. That's what the sign on his warehouse door says, anyway. He and the Terrier grew up together, been friends all their lives, evidently.' He shrugged. 'Might not mean anything at all.'

But perhaps it might. Rutherford . . .

'Do you know where the Excise office is?' he asked Fowler.

'Me? I haven't a clue, sir. Besides, it's Sunday. There won't be anyone on duty today.'

He'd forgotten that. Just over a week since the first bomb. So much had happened in that time. They'd made progress, but not enough of it. The memory of the blast he'd seen – the roar, seeing the caretaker's head with the rubble strewn all around – would stay with him for the rest of his life.

Who the hell was behind it all?

No answer at Kidson's house. He left a note and strode back towards town. Every spare wall was plastered with election posters. For council seats, for the school board, for the Poor Law Guardians. Heavy black type on white paper that was rapidly losing its colour from all the soot and the chemicals in the air.

With no machinery running, the city was cleaner today. Quieter, too. A rest for his ears. Each day all the noise of Leeds grew more wearying. By evening, all he craved was silence. But with a small, talkative child and a wife like Annabelle, Harper knew he had no chance. Sometimes he believed a solitary walking holiday up in the Dales was exactly what he needed. No traffic, hardly any people. Nothing more than nature and his own footsteps.

He'd never do it. He belonged in a place like that as much as the Queen belonged on Noble Street. After a day he'd be itching to come back. A nice idea, but . . . Billy was the one who'd put his dreams into practice.

He'd been shocked when he heard that Reed was moving to Whitby. How could he, after so long in Leeds? The man had kept his application quiet. He hardly said a word about it, even after the news of his appointment was out. He'd heard more through Annabelle nattering with Elizabeth than he had from Billy himself.

Even the official leaving do had been quite muted, over early so Reed could pack his trunk and catch the early train the next morning.

In the weeks after, Elizabeth had been a regular visitor to the rooms above the Victoria, sitting and talking with Annabelle, going over sets of figures as she sold the bakeries. Those had been Annabelle's once. She'd founded them. Elizabeth Reed had built on that, making them even more successful.

They went down to the station to see her off, the children with her looking so tall now. A new life. Starting over.

Perhaps a visit to Whitby was a good idea. Once the election was over, win or lose. Maybe even over Christmas, while there was no school. He had time due, and plenty of it. Walsh would be broken in by then and Ash was quite capable of handling things without a worry.

In winter, Whitby would be quiet. He could wander a little. That might be the ideal answer. Harper smiled to himself as he walked on.

'Smuggling?' she asked as if she hadn't heard him properly. 'I thought that was all in story-books. Like pirate treasure.'

Mary lifted her head, suddenly interested. 'Treasure?'

'Not really,' Harper told her. 'It's just a tale.'

With a pout, she returned to her drawing.

'It's big business in some places,' he said. 'Turns out some people were convicted of selling stolen brandy here a few years ago.'

'I don't remember it.' She raised her feet from the bowl of warm water and towelled them dry. 'That's better. They felt like they were on fire after delivering leaflets all afternoon.' She paused. 'I suppose some of it must go on, but no one's ever mentioned it to me. They never tried to sell me anything that wasn't right. Just as well, too, I'd give them what for. Why do you want to know, anyway? What's going on?'

'Nothing much. It might tie into that letter Billy sent, that's all.'

'No luck on . . .' She glanced down at their daughter, not wanting to say the words.

'Not yet.'

93

'I don't have a meeting until Wednesday. None of us does. That gives a breathing space, doesn't it?'

'Yes.' He ate a slice of buttered malt loaf and a mouthful of cheese. A break also offered a few evenings when he could simply sit at home with his family. Annabelle should be exhausted by the relentless pace of the campaign, but her face was full of life, eyes twinkling. For all her complaints and aching feet, she seemed to thrive on it. The crackle and the excitement of the election blazed all around her. 'What do you have tomorrow?'

'Knocking on doors,' she replied. 'There are plenty of streets I haven't been near yet. It's hard to believe; I feel like I've tramped over every inch of Sheepscar in the last week and a half. I'll be swimming in tea by the time I'm done.'

'How can you swim in tea, Mam?' Mary asked. 'You drink tea, you swim in water. Everybody knows that.'

'A right clever clogs, aren't you?' She smiled. 'It's a saying, that's all. It means you've drunk so much that you think you're full of it.'

'Just make sure you have someone with you,' Harper said. 'Two would be even better.'

'Tom . . .' she began, then stopped. They rarely had words, and never in front of their daughter. 'You should be getting ready for bed, young lady.'

'Mam,' Mary complained, but in a moment she was in her room.

'I'll make sure I'm safe,' Annabelle said softly. 'Now, you go and tell her a story. Maybe the one about the policeman who caught the bad, bad criminal.'

'I thought you didn't believe in fairytales.'

'This is Detective Constable Walsh,' Harper said. 'That's Sergeant Fowler and Inspector Ash. The man on the front desk is Sergeant Tollman. Be nice to him, he's the most important man at Millgarth; he's forgotten more than the rest of us will ever know. If you're stumped on something, ask him.'

'Yes, sir. Thank you.'

Walsh was wearing a black working man's suit of thick, serviceable wool, a collar and a dark tie. He kept turning an old bowler hat in his hands as he stared around.

'Fowler, you show him the ropes. Are you still delving into smuggling?'

'Just a few more files to read, sir.'

'Let me know if Terrier John's name comes up. John Millgate's his real name. Ash, in my office, please.'

'Have you found anything on our bomber?'

'Other than to confirm what we already knew, no, sir,' the inspector answered, twitching his heavy moustache in annoyance. 'Whatever he's doing, he's working alone. No one knows anything about it. If they did, I think they'd dob him in. Even crooks don't like innocent people being hurt.'

That was true enough. They might slash and maim and kill each other, but there was an odd code to violence among criminals.

95

'We're stuck, then. We can't announce that he's trying to wreck the election or we'll cause a crisis in town. But that just makes him so much harder to find.'

'We did put out a description after the attack on Mrs Pease. But none of the tips panned out.'

'He's probably someone that nobody would suspect. Very mild and polite.'

'And completely barmy inside,' Ash said. 'As long as he hides it well, we're going to have a difficult job.' He paused. 'You were asking about Terrier John and smuggling, sir?'

'Yes. Do you know something?'

'I remember that case. I knew someone who used to work for the Excise people. He told me back then that they believed there was someone who'd done well out of it. And the crooks genuinely didn't seem to know who he was.'

'John was never that smart.'

'People learn, sir. A little luck never hurts, either. He was due some of that.'

'It's possible,' Harper agreed thoughtfully. 'Takes his profit and gets out of the way? I'll pass it on to Billy. And if you're thinking about luck, why not say a prayer and hope ours holds so no one else is killed during this election.'

The Excise office was small, only three men, with Captain Burt in charge. No uniforms; the whole place felt curiously informal and careless.

'We cover all the West Riding,' Burt explained. 'Truth is, though, not much finds its way here. That's probably why you've never heard of us. We're almost like the forgotten men.' He gave a

96

laugh with an edge of bitterness, the sound of someone who craved some action and praise.

He went through the case from three years earlier. Everything had hinged on a tip-off. The Excise men watched long enough to allow the goods to be distributed, then swooped. Not a grand haul, prison for those guilty, all done and dusted.

'Does the name John Millgate mean anything?' Harper asked. 'He's known as Terrier John.'

'I'm sorry, Superintendent, it doesn't. Should it?'

'No. I thought I'd try on the off-chance. What about John Rutherford?'

'We know him, of course,' Burt replied. 'In this line of work, you're bound to come across every spirit wholesaler. We perform spot checks of his warehouse but we've never found anything amiss. He seems as honest as the day is long. Why? Do you know something?'

'No. It's just a name I heard. Thank you for your time.'

So much for that. The office seemed very lax to him. And there was something in the way the man had described Rutherford. Too glib, perhaps. Nothing to say Burt was lying, though. But he had some word to pass to Billy, certainly a little more than they'd had before. He could pick up the traces from there. Finding this bloody bomber was far more important.

He'd almost finished the letter to Whitby when Tollman knocked on the door.

'A gentleman and a lady to see you, sir. Name of Kidson.'

'Thank you. Show them in, please.'

They sat side by side, Kidson with his hat in his lap, Ethel carefully taking in every detail of her surroundings.

'You left a note at my house, Superintendent,' Kidson said.

'I did, sir. About a song.' He'd checked the night before; *The Spinning Wheel* was in *Traditional Tunes*.

'Another piece of paper with some of the words?' Ethel Kidson asked.

'Yes. Here.'

'*The Spinning Wheel*.' Kidson glanced at his niece. 'Another woman dying. I wish I understood what it meant.'

'You said you'd like to help us, sir. I'll be honest, we can use every bit of help we can get to find the man who's writing these. He's dangerous.'

'Certainly. But if he's copying them from my book, I don't see how that will help.'

'We do know someone was going around the pubs in Leeds asking about old songs. Not you,' he added with a smile.

'I see. Then the chances are that he doesn't know very much, Mr Harper. Leeds isn't fertile ground for song collecting. Most of the traditions died out a generation or more ago. People don't sit around and sing any more.'

Ethel chimed in. 'What my uncle means is we've had more luck in rural communities where the old ways still exist. We do have one or two sources in Leeds, but they're few and far between. And not usually in the public houses. They're older gentlemen.'

'I can think of some people to ask, if you like,' Kidson offered.

'I'd be grateful, sir.'

'Very good.'

'I'll try to have an answer for you in the morning.'

'Thank you. One more thing, sir: you were going to check whether there are any more references to women dying in your book.'

'Yes,' Kidson replied. 'I'm sorry, I haven't had chance yet. I should tell you, though, there are plenty of songs that mention death, especially women. I only printed a very few in there. I've dealt with more in my columns for the *Leeds Mercury*, if that helps.'

Harper nodded.

Ethel Kidson lingered in the doorway for a moment.

'Harper,' she said, running the name over her tongue, 'is it your wife who's running for Poor Law Guardian in Sheepscar?'

'It is,' he told her with a smile.

'I hope she wins, Superintendent. I'd like to see that.'

'How was your first day, Mr Walsh?'

The detective constable had put on his mackintosh, ready to leave, when Harper caught up with him. The day had dulled and they stood in the doorway at Millgarth studying the sky for rain.

'Different, sir. Definite change from walking a beat.'

'You'll develop a feel for it. The hours can be long sometimes.'

'I've never minded hard work, sir.'

'You'll get your share in this job, I can promise you that. I'll see you in the morning.'

'Da?' She'd been full of questions all evening. He'd hoped to have time to read the paper, but Mary wasn't giving him any peace. 'If two and two makes four, and three and three is six, what's a million and a million?'

'Two million.'

She considered his answer. 'So it's like starting at one and one again?'

'Yes.'

That seemed to satisfy her for the moment, and she returned to her book. Annabelle was down in the bar, talking to a pair of her volunteers and making plans for the next fortnight. When he arrived home she'd handed him the *Evening Post*, folded over to show an editorial about the grace of women and their standing in the home, how they should be above the dirty rough and tumble of politics. He glanced at the writer's name: Gerald Hotchkiss. The same man who'd penned the piece when the election race began.

'If he was any more sentimental he'd be bringing out the hearts and flowers,' she said in disgust.

'I see he managed to evoke the beauty of motherhood.'

'Twice.' She shook her head. 'Honestly, it's pathetic. No one believes this tosh, do they?'

'Of course not,' he assured her. But plenty were easily swayed. Too many.

She was planning, and he needed a scheme of

100

his own, some way to catch the bomber. So far the chief was standing back and letting him handle things. But Harper had no illusions. If he succeeded, the chief constable could take credit for giving him free rein. If he didn't, Crossley wasn't tainted by the failure. He had his chance, but like everything in life, it came with a price.

Maybe Kidson would have some luck, or some glittering insight that opened everything up. There was certainly no predicting what the bomber's next move would be; that was the problem. He seemed to like explosives, but that wasn't the only trick up his sleeve. It was impossible to edge ahead of him.

'Da?' Mary said again, and he was happy to be shaken out of his thoughts.

Eleven

'Mr Kidson, Miss Kidson. Please, sit down.'

Like the day before, the man settled nervously on the chair, while the young woman appeared far more composed.

'Have you found something?'

'I talked to a couple of people I know last night,' Frank Kidson said. 'It turns out there has indeed been someone asking about old songs, as you said.'

'Do the people you know have a name for him? Or a description?' Harper held his breath.

'Both, Superintendent,' Kidson said triumphantly.

'He's apparently in his late forties or early fifties, balding. Oh, and quite well-dressed.'

It didn't sound like their man. He was greying, not bald, and he was younger than that.

'You said you had a name?'

'Hardisty. Dr Hardisty.'

They should be able to track down a doctor very easily.

'Excuse me a minute.'

Ash was still in the office. He passed on the information, seeing doubt flood into the inspector's face.

'I know,' Harper said. 'I'm not sure it's him, either. He wouldn't be stupid enough to give his real name anywhere. But follow up on it. Maybe this Hardisty will have heard about someone else.'

'Yes, sir.'

Back in the office, he nodded at Kidson. 'That could be very useful, Thank you.'

'We promised you more information, Superintendent,' Ethel Kidson said. 'The other songs in the book that mention death.'

He hadn't forgotten.

'Yes.' Nothing else, and maybe the man wouldn't strike again. Then it would be almost impossible to catch him. One more and they'd have a chance. But people might die.

'There are a few more,' she said. '*Lord Thomas and Fair Eleanor*, *Mary of the Moor*, and *The Drowned Sailor*. They all specifically mention dead or dying women. That was what you wanted, wasn't it?'

Three, he thought. Three. Too many.

'It was. You said "specifically". What do you mean?'

'Others imply death, and beyond the songs in the book there are many that touch on the subject. Too many to count. Folk music can be quite violent, I'm afraid.'

'I see.' Dammit. Too much opportunity. The real test would be if some words came from a song that wasn't in Kidson's book. He glanced at the pair of figures across the desk. 'I appreciate what you're doing.'

'I hope you catch him,' Kidson said earnestly. 'He's giving our brotherhood a terrible name.' He realized what he'd said and blushed. 'Of course, what he's doing is awful, but . . .'

'Don't worry,' Harper told him with a smile. 'I know what you mean. If you can keep asking around and pass on anything you learn, that would be helpful.'

'I intend to,' the man promised. 'We feel involved. We'd both like to see him caught, wouldn't we, Ethel?'

'Yes,' she said firmly. 'We would.' She stood and extended a hand. 'Good day, Superintendent.'

It was Kidson's turn to stay behind.

'You said your wife knows some old Irish songs?'

'Yes, but I've no idea how rare they are.'

'Perhaps I might call and see her? Both of us, of course.'

'You probably want to wait a few weeks. She's fighting an election.' When Kidson raised his eyebrows in surprise, Harper added: 'Ask your niece, sir. She knows about it.'

* * *

103

He heard the soft fall of the letter on to the tiled floor in the hall and padded through to collect it. From Leeds.

Billy Reed ripped open the envelope and read the words quickly. Elizabeth came through from the kitchen, wiping her hands on a towel.

'Anything important?'

'It's from Tom Harper. I'd asked him about that chap I recognized. Turns out there was a prosecution for smuggling a bit over three years ago in Leeds. It was the Excise people handling things. The police weren't involved, that's why he didn't know. They never got a sniff of the man behind it, not even a name. But it turns out that the chap I'm looking into is an old friend of a spirit wholesaler in Leeds.'

'Do you think this man you've seen here might be the one pulling the strings?'

'I don't know.' He frowned. It was hard to think of Terrier John as a successful criminal. 'But it's worth trying to find out a bit more.' He looked through the rest of the letter. 'Annabelle's election campaign is going well, but the force has had problems with a man who doesn't like women candidates—'

'Typical,' she muttered.

'Mary's blooming. He sends you all their best. Oh.' He paused in surprise. 'He says they might come to Whitby for Christmas. Wants to know if there's a good guest house that would be open.'

Elizabeth was grinning with pleasure. 'It would be wonderful to see them again, wouldn't it, Billy love?'

He wasn't so certain. At one time he and Tom

Harper had been close friends; Reed had been his sergeant when Tom was still an inspector. But they'd had their differences and Billy had moved to the fire brigade; it seemed like the easiest resolution. Time had healed some of the problems. They were civil enough. But they both knew it had all changed, that there could never be the easy intimacy between them again. Elizabeth and Annabelle, though . . . they'd been almost like sisters from the start.

'Yes,' he agreed. 'It would be good.'

'I'll start asking about decent places to stay. I'm not going to recommend a hovel. I'd have them here if we had more room.'

Thank God they didn't, Reed thought. He liked his privacy, and his home to be his home. He didn't want guests underfoot. At arm's length was much better; he could plead duty and slip away.

The weather promised squalls as he walked down to the police station bundled into his mackintosh. Down below, he could see the River Esk winding out to the sea, and hear the raucous gulls on Pier Road. The air smelled fresh, the brine sharp in his nostrils. On top of East Cliff, the ruins of the abbey stood stark against the sky. Would he ever grow tired of it all?

He hoped not. He was in his middle forties now, finally feeling settled and content. He had a wife he loved, who loved him, and he enjoyed the responsibility for the children from her first marriage. The years of heavy drinking were all behind him, along with the flashes of temper that could spark into violence. These days he could enjoy a glass of beer then walk away without needing another. Life was calm.

He tapped his chest, making sure the letter was still there. A little over three years since the smuggling case, a little over three years since Terrier John had shown up in Whitby with money. They had to be linked. Proving it, though, was going to be difficult. The Terrier had dug himself in well. He looked as if he had friends. And if smuggling was involved, then he was going to be tangling with some dangerous people.

At the bottom of Brunswick Street he changed course, walking down Baxtergate and across the bridge to the Custom House. Harry Pepper was already in his office, puffing on his pipe.

'Good morning. You're out and about early today.' He picked up a mug of tea and drank. 'What can I do for you, Inspector?'

'Who's the best person to talk to about John Millgate and smuggling?'

'I could have brought him in, sir, but it would have been a waste of everybody's time.' Ash sat in the superintendent's office. Outside, the rain was belting down, runnels sliding along the glass. 'Dr Hardisty used to be a surgeon at the Infirmary. He had to retire because he started with tremors in his hands. Not what you'd want if you were making bombs.'

'No,' Harper agreed.

'On top of that, he's a small man and closer to sixty than fifty. I don't see how he could have moved Mrs Pease around.'

'Never mind. It was worth investigating.'

'He did give me one thing, though, sir.'

'Go on.'

'He said there was someone else asking in the pubs around about old songs. Much like I found, if you recall, sir. It quite surprised him; he imagined he was the only one with an interest, apart from Mr Kidson.'

'Does this man have a name?'

Ash shook his head. 'He's going to see if he can find one. But since what we had before was false, anything else probably would be, too.'

Harper glanced at Fowler. He had the other chair, Walsh standing with his back against the wall.

'Do you two have anything?'

'We went to the public library and looked through Kidson's book. There's nothing in these songs, other than the fact he collected them in Yorkshire. Nothing in the words link to the crimes at all, other than they mention dead women.' He shrugged.

'Right.' Dead women; that was a connection enough. Too much of one, a taunt and a threat. 'We're back to meetings for the candidates tomorrow night, gentlemen. What else can we do to keep everyone safe without scaring them?'

An hour of talking and they'd only come up with a single idea. Fowler would spend the evenings at Millgarth, while Ash and Walsh would move from one meeting to another on a set schedule. With Harper at Annabelle's events, if reports of trouble came in, Fowler would be able to locate everyone else very quickly.

By then it would be too late, of course, Harper

reflected as he waited for the tram. The damage would have been done, and their man would be far away. But it was what they had, and they needed to make the best of it.

'Da! Da!' He was barely through the door when Mary was running up to him with an exercise book in her hand. 'Look, Da!'

'Let him hang his coat up first,' Annabelle shouted from the parlour. 'It'll still be there when he's done that.'

He picked his daughter up, groaning in exaggeration at her weight, and carried her through. 'Right. What is it?'

All the letters of the alphabet neatly written out in pencil. Underneath, in pen, a star from the teacher.

'It's for my penmanship.' Mary spoke the word slowly, making sure she had it right.

'That's excellent,' he told her. Sitting by the table, Annabelle was beaming proudly. 'Keep on doing this well and you'll be able to earn enough to support your mam and da when we're too old to work.' He felt in his pocket and pulled out a halfpenny. 'That deserves a special prize.'

Mary studied the coin, then bunched it in her pudgy little fist and smiled.

'Thank you,' she said, and turned hopefully to her mother.

'No. We're eating soon. If you buy sweets from the shop now, you'll ruin your appetite. You can spend it on the way home from school tomorrow.'

'Yes, Mam.' Mary didn't try to hide her disappointment.

'She can be such a little madam sometimes,' Annabelle said quietly after the girl had gone into her bedroom.

'Give her a minute and it'll all be forgotten. Had a good day in the election race?'

Suddenly she was smiling again. 'Listen to this: Hope Foundries have given ten pounds to the campaign and are backing me. And the chemical works at the bottom of Meanwood Road have put in a fiver.'

Very handsome contributions. Those would pay for quite a few more posters and leaflets and hall rentals. More importantly, it meant that they believed in her. They felt that she could take the race, and both of them were big companies in Sheepscar. They bet on winners.

'That's as good as Mary's star.'

'I know. But you'd better not try to fob me off with a ha'penny to spend on sweets, Tom Harper. I'm going to expect something more in the way of congratulations.'

'You might have to wait until later.'

'Patience is my middle name. Didn't you know that?'

He'd had enough of reading and signing reports. Didn't they ever end? Half past three in the afternoon and he'd been at it since morning. Didn't they ever end? He felt almost grateful when the telephone rang.

'This is Superintendent Harper.' The instrument crackled and buzzed against his ear, a woman's voice he didn't recognize.

'This is Dr Gordon's surgery calling.' Just up

109

Roundhay Road from the Victoria, by Enfield Street, right next to Mary's school. 'Your wife is here with your daughter, sir. She asked me to ring. Can you get here as soon as possible?'

'What?' He could feel his heart thudding hard in his chest. 'What's wrong? Are they all right?'

'Everyone's fine, sir.' The woman sounded calm and cool. 'But if you could come, sir.'

'Of course. Yes. As quickly as I can.'

He grabbed his mackintosh and dashed out of the office. As he passed the front desk, Tollman said, 'Sir!'

'What is it? I have an emergency.'

'Just had a report come in. Someone tried to snatch a child on Roundhay Road. Didn't manage it, but he got away.'

Now he understood.

'I'm on my way there. Tell Ash to join me. I want uniforms out taking statements. You know the drill.' He thought quickly. 'If I'm not there, I'll be at the Victoria.'

Twelve

The doctor's surgery stank of carbolic soap. There was an atmosphere of fearful hush in the waiting room; faces jerked up as he dashed in, out of breath and panicking.

'I'm Superintendent Harper.'

The woman behind the desk nodded at a closed door. 'They're in there.'

110

It was a sparse room, no more than a couple of chairs and a barred window that looked out on to a small flagstone yard. Annabelle sat, cradling Mary on her lap. The girl looked very small, pale and defenceless, legs like little white twigs, grazes on her knees where she'd fallen.

'She's . . .?' he began, scared to say more.

'She's fine, Tom. Not hurt.' He stared at her. As his wife looked up he could see the lines where tears had run down her cheeks, and all the colour was gone from her face. 'Honest. She's just shaken up and very, very scared.'

He stroked Mary's hair, but she didn't raise her head. Harper could feel anger so tight in his chest it might crush him. He'd find whoever did this and he'd make sure they suffered.

'What happened?'

'Ellen started to worry when Mary was half an hour later than usual coming home. We went out looking. She wasn't in the playground. Mr Barber said she'd been in the shop with Maisie and Anna. I was on my way over to their houses when I found her. Some of the women on Armenia Place were looking after her. They'd come out when they heard a girl screaming. A man was trying to drag her toward that land by the dye works. They chased him off.' She managed a faded smile. 'Mary had been fighting him.'

'You're very brave,' he told her.

'I'm cancelling tonight's meeting. I can't . . . not with this.'

'Yes.' He agreed without hesitation. He squatted and looked into Mary's face. 'You're safe now.

111

And your mam or Ellen will go to school with you from now on and see you get home with no problem. All right?'

The girl nodded dumbly. He'd seen this reaction so often before, the numbness of shock. But it was plain torture to see it in his own daughter's eyes. He had questions he wanted to ask her, but they could wait. Forever, if need be.

'Do you want me to come home with you?'

'We'll be fine,' Annabelle said. 'I think we'll just sit here a little while longer. You go and find him, Tom. If it's . . .'

She didn't try to finish the sentence. They both knew the answer already.

The bobbies were already out in the Armenias and the Renfields that ran off Manor Street. It was the normal procedure for any attempted child snatching. Flood the area and find as much information as possible. It was about the only time that people were eager to help the police. The uniformed sergeant directing the men saluted as Harper approached.

'Sir. We're starting to piece it all together. As best we can tell, he must have been lurking outside the school and followed the girl.'

'Go on.'

'The lass stopped at the shop over there with a couple of her friends.' He nodded towards the corner of Enfield Street. 'After they left, the others went off home together, and this little one started down Manor Street. Her name is . . .' He looked in his notebook.

'Her name's Mary Harper. She's my daughter.'

112

The sergeant reddened. 'I'm sorry, sir. I hadn't realized.'

'Continue.'

'He must have tried to grab her as she crossed by the top of Armenia Place. Looked like he was going to drag her along. But she fought him and started screaming. Made enough of a racket to bring the women out from their houses. As soon as they saw what was going on, they were on him. He scarpered down there, through the stables and over Gipton Beck into the rhubarb fields. Could have gone anywhere from there. People were more concerned with the girl. No harm, I understand?'

'No,' Harper answered. 'Do you have a description of the man?'

'Average height, in his forties, short hair, going grey. Well-dressed, some of the women said, like he could have been a rent collector. He's probably sporting a few cuts and bruises now. Those women battered him with whatever they could find. One of them said he had blood on his hand. Did your little girl bite him, sir?'

'I don't know,' he answered distractedly. It fitted. The same man. This didn't happen out of the blue. It wasn't opportunism. He'd planned it. He knew about Mary, he knew where she went to school. He must have watched the pub. More than that, he felt very sure of himself to attempt something like this in the middle of the afternoon. 'Let me see the women who got Mary away from him,' Harper said. 'I'd like to thank them.'

He'd just finished talking to them when Ash arrived, a look of dark concern on his face.

113

'I saw the sergeant, sir. He told me all about it. How is she?'

'No damage. None to see, anyway,' he corrected himself.

'Same man?'

'The description is right. I don't need to tell you what I want, do I?'

'No, sir. We always look hard for kiddie snatchers, you know that. But your lass? Everyone on the force is going to be hunting. There are probably reporters on their way here right now. He's going to end up with all of Leeds on his trail.'

No one liked men who went after children. No one would help them. It was one more reason to believe that the man was acting on his own.

'One thing.' He hated himself for saying it, for even thinking that anything could be more important than his daughter. 'We can't afford for this to be tied to the election. When anyone asks, it just happened, and we don't know why yet. Understood?'

Ash eyed him curiously, then slowly nodded. 'Understood, sir.'

At the stables, Harper found one of the grooms brushing down a horse. He'd seen the man as he ran through the yard.

'You didn't try to stop him?'

'He were through here like a flash. Kept glancing over his shoulder like he had the hounds of hell behind him.' The man turned and spat into the straw. 'By the time they told me what he'd done, he were off the far side of the rhubarb fields. I couldn't have caught him if I'd tried.'

Harper would catch him, though. He'd make absolutely bloody certain of it.

Ash had everything in hand, directing all the uniforms. There was nothing more for Harper to do here. He clenched his fists and opened them again, then rolled his neck, trying to work out the kinks and the tension.

'Go home, sir,' the inspector told him quietly. 'Spend some time with them. That's where you're needed.'

He nodded. They weren't going to catch the man tonight. 'You're right.'

'If there's anything, I'll send a message. Let me finish up here and I'll go to those meetings.'

'Thank you.'

He started down Manor Street, the outline of the pub stark on the corner, then retraced his steps to the shop. Mr Barber stood behind the counter in his crisp brown overall, his face suddenly full of concern.

'How is she?'

'Not harmed, thank God.'

'She was in here wanting to spend her money like it was burning a hole in her pocket. If I'd known . . .'

'No one could,' Harper assured him. 'What did she get?'

'This and this.' He pointed at the jars.

'Give me the same, please.'

Barber weighed them out in a paper bag. When the superintendent tried to pay, the shopkeeper held up his hand.

'Your money's no good, Mr Harper. It's the least I can do for her.'

115

The pub was starting to fill with men coming off the day shift. He made his way through, shutting the door on the noise and climbing the stairs. Mary was on her mother's lap, the way she'd been at the surgery.

Annabelle put a finger to her lips and mouthed the word 'sleeping'.

'Do you want me to put her to bed?' he whispered.

'Leave her here. She'll want us around when she wakes.'

In the kitchen he made a pot of tea, going back into the parlour as it brewed.

'It was him, wasn't it?' Her voice was quiet, revealing nothing.

'Yes.' He could feel the fury burning in his belly. 'It was.'

'I don't know what to think, Tom.' She looked down at Mary, brushing a strand of hair off the girl's forehead. 'I never imagined he'd try something like this.'

'Neither did I,' Harper said emptily. 'Who could . . .?'

'Ask him when you arrest him.'

'Believe me, I intend to.'

He poured the tea, placing her cup on the chair arm.

'Sleep's the best thing for her right now, poor lamb.'

'What about you?'

'Tough as old boots, you know me.' But her smile was too quick, too false, fading as quickly as it arrived. 'What do you think he'd have done if he'd been able to snatch her?'

'I don't know.' He'd tried not to think about it, to push it away from his mind. But the question kept creeping back. 'I really don't.'

'Attacking me is one thing. I'm up there, I'm fair game,' Annabelle said. 'But a little girl?'

'He's desperate. Three attempts so far and no one's dropped out of the race.'

'This makes number four, and two of those have been against me.'

'You must terrify him.'

She snorted. 'Me? He's the one who's got me petrified.'

'We'll catch him.' He took hold of her hand, squeezing it gently.

'I know you will.' Her voice was grave. 'But I wonder what he'll do first.'

Impossible to guess. There was simply no knowing.

'How about you?' Harper asked. 'What are you going to do?'

Annabelle let out a long breath. 'I've been going back and forth ever since I found her.' She cuddled Mary a little closer; the girl didn't stir. 'Part of me says I can't stop, because it'll mean he's won. But another bit says I can't risk anything like this happening again. Who knows what it'll be next time? And I'll feel like it's all my fault for being selfish and wanting to be in politics.'

'Don't blame yourself,' he insisted. 'You can't do that.'

'I know.' She sniffled, and reached into her sleeve for a handkerchief. 'I know it up here.' She tapped her head. 'But inside . . .'

'Sleep on it.'

'I will. I think we'd better have this one in with us tonight, in case she has bad dreams.'

But Mary had no nightmares. She barely seemed to stir until morning. Then she was eager for school, acting as if nothing had happened. Not even a mention of the afternoon before. For some people, it was a way of coping. If it worked, fine. But walling it off couldn't last forever.

As he was about to leave for work, he brought something from the pocket of his coat.

'Well,' he said, 'look what I found. Close your eyes,' he told Mary, 'and hold out your hand.'

For the promise of a treat, she was obedient.

'You can open them again now.'

As soon as she looked inside the bag, she stared at him in surprise.

'Daddies have magic powers. Don't you know that?' He rubbed her hair. 'You go and enjoy your learning.'

'Well?' He knew he sounded brusque. But after a sleepless night brooding about the man, he didn't care.

'You more or less know everything already, sir,' Ash told him. 'I sent men around to ask at the far side of those rhubarb fields. A couple of women think they saw him, but they don't know exactly where he went. Dolly Lane, probably. From there, who knows?'

'Any problems last night?' he asked Fowler.

'All went like clockwork, sir.' The sergeant paused, glanced at Ash and Walsh, then said, 'How's your daughter, sir?'

'No damage done. You know that already.'

'We're going to find him, sir. Although he might not look his best by the time he reaches court.'

Harper gave a dark smile. He saw the same determination in them that he felt.

'I'll be at the front of that queue, Sergeant. How do we track this bastard down? That's what I need to know. I want to see his face.'

The squalls had blown out to sea and the evening was clear, millions of stars like pinpricks glowing in the sky. Reed felt the autumn chill in the air as he entered the Scoresby Arms. It was out of the way, stuck on a quiet little dead-end street, the kind of pub that drew its custom from the houses around.

The man he wanted was in the corner, a glass of beer and a box of dominoes on the table in front of him. Reed ordered a pint of bitter, and took a seat opposite.

The man had his cap pulled down, eyes in the shadows. A grizzled face, as weatherbeaten as half the men in Whitby from all the hours out on the water. Thick fingers, dirt rimed into his skin.

'Harry Pepper says you know a thing or two.'

'I might.'

How often had he played this scene in Leeds, the meetings in out-of-the-way public houses with men who wanted to stay anonymous? Reed imagined he'd left all that far behind. It went to show: you could never completely let go of the past.

'There could be a little money for good information. Honest information.'

119

The man took out the tiles, deftly turning them face-down and shuffling them around.

'What are you after?' he asked. 'Draw your eight.'

'John Millgate.'

The man stayed silent for a long time, eyeing the dominoes he'd chosen.

'Double six?' the man asked, and Reed shook his head. With a grin, the man put down a double five.

'I know who you mean. He's a gent with a big interest in night-time catches.' He cocked his head to be sure Reed understood.

'How big an interest?' He laid a tile on the table, five and three.

'More than passing, let's put it like that.' Three and two.

Reed knocked, knuckles rapping lightly on the table. 'How deep?'

'Don't know.' He added another tile to the row.

'Can you find out?' He could make a move now.

'I suppose.' He pondered his hand, then slapped down a double two. 'It'll cost you, mind. Don't know how long it'll take.'

Reed took a sip of the beer, then knocked again. 'How will I get in touch with you?'

'You don't.' The man's fingers went for one tile, then chose another instead. 'I know how to reach you.'

They finished the game in silence. The inspector took a florin from his pocket and slapped it down on the wood. He'd lost, but it was years since he'd played dominoes. Any game, for that matter,

120

including dealing with informants. With a nod, he stood.

'I look forward to the rematch.'

'I daresay.' The man grinned; he had hardly any teeth left in his mouth. 'But I wouldn't place a bet on winning if I were you.'

He'd told no one at the station what he was doing. Sergeant Brown and the others were all Whitby men, born and bred, with too many deep, wide associations in the town. They seemed honest, but he didn't know them well enough yet. He was the outsider and he didn't trust them. All it took was one loose word. Much simpler to keep it all to himself.

The next day he headed south in the pony and trap, going to Hawsker, Fylingthorpe and Robin Hood's Bay. Even with low clouds, he enjoyed the trip, leaving the cart at the top of the hill and walking down the steep slope to the Bay.

He liked the place, always surprised by something he saw; it was unlike anywhere else he'd been. Tiny streets ran off the winding hill of the main road, barely wide enough for one person, never mind two, with shops in the houses. The place was a maze that he doubted he'd ever master. The fishing fleet was in, catch unloaded for the day, the boats safely beached and anchored.

'Used to bring in more fish here than they did in Whitby,' a man told him as he stared out at the sea. 'That's a few years back now.' He was old, his hair white and thick, skin grizzled. 'But it were in my lifetime.'

It hardly seemed possible in a place as small as this. A village. A hamlet, really. Still, he listened, letting the old man reminisce. It wasn't as if Reed needed to be anywhere urgently. The only crime at home was a pair of drunks arrested on the bridge the night before, and that hardly needed an inspector's time. The main thing he had to do was pursue his suspicion of Terrier John.

They ended up talking for an hour, until it was time for Reed to take the long road home.

'Was there a lot of smuggling here?'

'Was?' The man raised an eyebrow and chuckled. 'Born yesterday, were you? When the fishing goes, they have to make a living somehow. There's so many holes in them cliffs you could hide an army. Tunnels up from the pub cellars to the top of the hill, too, they say.'

'Aren't they ever caught?' If it was that blatant, how could they evade the Excise men?

'They're canny lads.' The old man tapped the side of his nose. 'Very canny. And folk round here know to keep their mouths shut.'

Interesting, he thought as he trudged back up the hill, a long, slow pull to the top. Maybe he was looking in the wrong place for Terrier John's activities.

Thirteen

Would she continue or would she give up? Sitting on the tram to Sheepscar, Harper wasn't sure. In his heart he believed he felt Annabelle would carry on, but after yesterday, who could blame her for saying she'd had enough? Whatever she decided, he'd be proud of her.

And he'd find the man who tried to snatch their daughter. Every time he thought about it, his hands curled into tight, hard fists. When Harper found him, he'd make sure the payment was brutal.

All around him the coughs and sneezes of autumn bloomed. The air was thick with the smell of industry and factories. He could tell exactly where he was from the different perfumes: the malt and hops of the brewery slowly shifting to the harsh, sharp stink of the dye works as he came closer to Sheepscar. As soon as he could smell that, his stop was close.

Annabelle was in the parlour, studying her face in the mirror, pulling down the skin under her eyes.

'Mary's having her tea with Ellen,' she said. 'I think they have some sort of secret between them, I keep hearing giggling from upstairs.' She turned to face him. 'Do you think I look older, Tom?'

'Older?' He didn't understand. What did that have to do with anything? 'No, of course you don't. Why?'

'I was out knocking on doors this morning and a woman said that politics made you look hard and old before your time.'

He laughed. She'd answered one question, anyway.

'You look as lovely as the first day I saw you.'

'No soft soap,' she warned.

'I mean it.' The words seemed to satisfy her. 'How's Mary?'

She shook her head in quiet wonder. 'You wouldn't know anything had ever happened. I walked her to school this morning and talked to the headmaster. They're going to keep an eye out. If they see any strange men they'll go after them right away. And she knows to only come home with me or Ellen. At least until the election is over.'

'Meeting tonight?'

Annabelle nodded and gave a tight-lipped smile. 'I have to. We're making sure nothing else can happen to Mary. I thought it through again this morning. He's just another man who wants to scare women. If any of us wins a seat, we show him that his way can't work.'

'Good.' He hugged her close, smelling the scent on her neck.

'I don't suppose you've . . .?'

'Nothing yet. The *Post* and the *Mercury* both had stories this morning, with his description. Someone has to know who he is.'

'I saw the articles. No mention of the election.'

'No,' he agreed slowly. 'It seemed best.'

'Maybe.' After a moment she nodded once more. 'Right, we'd better get down to the hall and make sure your soldier boy has checked it out.'

Standing up there, the audience rapt, she talked very briefly about the incident. Around here word would have already passed; it would have been strange to ignore it completely. People would have wondered what she was trying to hide. Instead, she made it into a passing reference, close to the start of her speech, before going on to attack the way the poor were treated now, and lay out her plans for the way relief should be given.

Annabelle always managed to capture a crowd. She had the gift for it. But tonight there was more fire in her, Harper thought as he stood in the back corner, eyes scanning the room very carefully. Every word seemed to blaze and burn, and the people responded, reflecting her heat.

When she finished, half of them were straight on their feet, applauding and cheering. Others sat and clapped. Only a very few, dotted around the room, stayed stony-faced and silent.

On the platform she was smiling, looking a little surprised. Her face was shiny with sweat, her eyes glistening happily.

It was another half-hour before they left the hall. Harper waited with a grumbling caretaker as Annabelle talked to everyone lining up to meet her. He watched them, tense and ready to move at the slightest problem, but there was nothing.

By the time they walked home the excitement was draining from her. She clung tight to his arm, walking mechanically, dead on her feet. She didn't speak, and he was content in the silence. The booming echo of voices in the halls always taxed his hearing, forcing him to concentrate to make out words and conversations.

No other footsteps on the road. Most of the houses were already dark, families trying to get their sleep before the call for morning shift. No one had come to drag him out of the meeting; it looked as if trouble had stayed away for another night. When that was a victory, it said little for their success, Harper thought sadly.

Annabelle had a dreamy smile on her lips, as if she was floating back to the Victoria. It felt as if something had changed, that out of yesterday's horror she'd tapped into a seam deep inside herself and folk had responded.

He'd only seen that once before, when the union organizer Tom Maguire addressed a crowd of striking building workers down on Vicar's Croft. Maguire was dead now and mouldering in his grave, but he'd grown up near Annabelle on the Bank. He'd watched her progress with the Suffragists and encouraged her. He'd be proud of what she was doing now.

She never mentioned Maguire these days, but he knew she thought about him from time to time. Harper did, too; the occasions they'd sit over a cup of tea in the market café, and he'd enjoy the man's sense of humour. But Maguire had gone too early, coughing out his life with pneumonia all alone in his empty room. A sad, terrible end.

A few stragglers remained in the bar at the Victoria. Dan was already wiping down the table, most of the glasses washed and stacked. A quick goodnight and they were up the stairs. Annabelle was asleep as soon as she lay down.

'It looks like we had another quiet night,' the superintendent said, then saw Fowler glance awkwardly at Ash. 'What is it?'

'Not completely quiet, sir,' the sergeant told him reluctantly.

'Mrs Morgan, one of the candidates in Holbeck, was robbed on her way home.' Ash took over. 'She was one who hadn't wanted a copper with her all the time. Even refused an escort from the one on duty at her meeting.'

'Was it our man?'

'Her description's a bit confused, but it sounds like him. He told her she'd better stay at home where she belongs from now on. Made off with her reticule. No violence, though, no threats of more.'

'Why wasn't I told?' Harper kept his voice cold and hard. 'You had your orders: any trouble and I was to be informed. You know how badly I want this man.'

'Yes, sir,' Ash agreed. 'But there was nothing you could have done. He was long gone. At first we weren't even sure it was him. I'm still not completely convinced. It seemed like an ordinary robbery. I told Sergeant Fowler not to disturb you.'

'An order is an order, Inspector. As far as I'm aware, it's not optional.'

'Yes, sir. I'm sorry, sir. I take full responsibility.' At least he had the grace to look abashed.

'In future you let me know about the smallest things. Anything that might involve him. Dismissed.'

Alone, Harper had to laugh to himself. How many times had Kendall given him a similar dressing-down? All those occasions when he realized the super's presence would add nothing, and the news could wait until the morning. Now the boot was on the other foot and it didn't feel comfortable,

Ash was right. There was nothing he could have done. He'd have ended up standing around in the dark and feeling like a spare part.

He waved the inspector back into his office. 'What was in Mrs Morgan's reticule?'

'Not much, sir. A comb, some pennies, that's about it. Rubbish, really. Like in Shakespeare.'

'What?' Harper stared at him, confused.

'There's a quotation, sir – "Who steals my purse steals trash." It's from Shakespeare. *Othello*.'

Shakespeare. Ash was full of surprises. 'I see. Did he leave a little bit of paper, by chance?'

'Nothing we've found so far. But it was windy.' Ash shrugged.

A thought struck Harper. 'Did he run away after the robbery?'

'He must have.' The inspector stood and tried to remember. 'Took off, she said. Yes, I'm sure of it.'

'How was she?'

'Very shaken, upset. What you'd expect, sir.'

'Go back and see her this morning. Find out if he ran off. And how? Loping? Sprinting? Somehow I haven't pictured our man as an athlete. How many men in their forties can run fast?'

'He did it the other day, sir, after he . . .'

Yes, after he'd tried to snatch Mary. Like the hounds of hell were after him, the stable hand had said.

'Have you gone round the neighbourhood? Maybe someone saw something.'

'The uniforms over there are doing that, sir.'

Harper nodded. 'And thank you for reminding me of the way I used to be.' He raised an eyebrow. 'Just don't make a habit of it.'

'No, sir,' Ash said with the barest of grins.

Meetings, meetings. The bane of his life. They served no purpose beyond generating enough hot air to warm Leeds all winter. Without them he'd have been able to keep on top of his work *and* have enough time to go out and do some real policing. This one, though, offered something worthwhile: sitting with the superintendents from the other divisions, working out ways to keep the women candidates and the public safe.

Harper was wearing a dark blue suit Moses Cohen had made up for him. After his promotion Annabelle had insisted he bought one appropriate for his rank. Two years on, he only dragged it out for occasions like these. Most of the time he was stuck at Millgarth, where appearance hardly mattered.

In the end they hammered out one or two small ideas. But the simple fact was that much of it would be down to luck. Old Pemberton from E Division had suggested a plain-clothes officer following the women who refused protection. The chief looked at him, aghast.

'Good God, man, you can't do that. They'll be screaming for a bobby and your copper will end up arrested.'

By the time he left the Town Hall, Harper had a headache. He stood on the steps, by the lions, and buttoned his overcoat. The balmy weather had lingered so late in the year they'd all hoped it would last longer. But now the season was changing with a vengeance. There was a bitter edge to the breeze. Soon enough all the children would be out chumping, gathering wood for the bonfires, then stuffing old clothes with straw and asking for money for the Guy. One of those rituals that never changed.

The air felt thick as he walked. He could taste soot in his mouth and see some of the smudges on his clothes. Years of it had left all the buildings dark as the devil. Even the Town Hall looked as if it had always been black, although he could remember the pale glow of the stone when he was young and it was still new. Industry brought money along with all its dirt. And jobs. Muck was the price they paid for brass, but there weren't many here who'd refuse the bargain.

'What have you found?' he asked as he stood in the detectives' room at Millgarth.

'Our man definitely ran, sir,' Ash told him. 'Like he'd been entered in the mile, according to Mrs Morgan. She's calmer today. And this isn't going to put her off being a candidate, she says.' Under his moustache, the inspector's mouth flickered into a smile.

'But I don't suppose she's willing to have one of our lot with her all the time now?'

'Actually, she is. Walsh persuaded her.'

'Really?' He turned to look at the detective constable. 'Well done.'

'Bit of the blarney, that's all.' He grinned. 'My Irish charm and good looks, sir.'

'Maybe I'll send you to talk to the other

holdouts, see if you can work your magic on them. It would make our lives a lot easier.'

'Any time you like, sir. My pleasure.'

'There's been time to search the area. Any pieces of paper?'

'Not yet, sir,' Ash said. 'But like I said, it was windy. Blew all night, too.'

There could have been something and it vanished. And, he reflected, he'd probably have learned nothing new from it.

'What do we have tonight?'

'I'm manning the fort here, sir,' Ash told him. 'Fowler and Walsh will be out and about.'

'I want a special eye on Mrs Pease. After he grabbed her and threatened rape, he might see her as a weak link. And after last night, Mrs Morgan.'

'Yes, sir.' The inspector gave a small cough. 'What about your wife, sir? How's she?'

'Staying strong. She's not going to let him win.'

'And your little girl, sir?' Fowler asked.

'Acting as if nothing had happened.' He walked towards the door; he didn't want to discuss that. 'And remember . . .'

'Anything at all and we'll let you know, sir.'

Fourteen

The days crept past. The man tried nothing new. The candidates made their speeches and delivered their leaflets. Harper was out every

131

evening with Annabelle at her meetings. A few hecklers, someone who tried to start a fight, but nothing important. By political standards, mild stuff: he'd seen too many broken heads and pools of blood when he'd worked at these events, with bruises as badges of honour. This was polite by comparison.

Autumn was here to stay. The day before had brought another heavy wind that whipped through the branches and threw showers of leaves to the ground. Today, drizzle persisted, leaving him grateful for once that he was stuck in the office.

He was putting the finishing, frustrating touches to the station budget when Sergeant Tollman knocked on the door.

'Mr and Miss Kidson to see you, sir.'

'Show them in, please.' He glanced out of the window. 'And do you think you could find three cups of tea, please?'

'I'm sure I can manage that, sir, don't you worry.'

The superintendent kept the conversation inconsequential until the tea arrived. The door closing behind Tollman was the signal to become serious.

'Have you found something for us?'

'I might have,' Kidson said warily. 'Whenever I've seen people I know, I've kept asking if others have been looking for songs. There are only a few of us, up and down the country. And certainly not many around here. I've tried to make it sound very casual.'

'That's good,' Harper told him with a smile.

'This week, two different men said they'd been

132

approached by someone. It was three months or so ago.'

'Go on.'

'He seemed like an educated gentleman, from what they told me. But definitely not a scholar. He didn't seem to know what pieces had started out as broadside ballads. Those are—'

'I'm sure Superintendent Harper doesn't need to know the history of broadsides, Uncle,' Ethel interrupted him gently.

'Yes, yes. Of course.' Kidson composed himself. 'He was interested in songs about death. As I told you before, there are a fair few.'

'Did he give his name?' Harper felt his body tense, praying for some good news.

'Yes,' Kidson began, then paused. 'That is, he gave each of them a different name.'

'What were they?' Harper picked up his pen.

'Mr Carter and Mr Worthington. But I'm certain it's the same man. How many can there be with those specific interests? Two of them appearing at the same time?' he said. 'That would be too much of a coincidence.'

'It would,' the superintendent agreed. 'What did he look like, sir? Did you ask your friends?'

'I did, and he sounds just the way you described your . . .'

'Bomber.' Ethel Kidson supplied the word.

'Yes, your bomber.'

'Did he give an address at all?' Harper's chest was tight. It was him, beyond a shadow of a doubt. All they needed was something, one fact, one solid lead to start prying things open.

133

'No,' Kidson said. 'There was no need, was there?'

'Why was he interested in these particular types of songs, sir? Did he say?'

'No one asked. Why would they? People all have their own fascinations, Superintendent. I'm sure you understand that.'

'Yes. Of course.' He felt disappointment rise as hope ebbed away. 'Have your friends seen anything of him since he approached them for songs?'

Kidson shook his head. 'No. A single session each, that was all. But he did ask if they knew others familiar with old songs. That's how we work, you see. Passed from person to person like a parcel. They told him about two other men. I'm going to see them.'

'Thank you. Be careful, though.'

'Oh, I will, of course. But he'll have been and gone by now, I imagine.'

'I can't make head nor tail of this song angle, sir,' Fowler said. 'Why leave these little bits at the scene for us?' He smoked a cigarette, waving his hand in the air.

'Taunts? Clues? A signature?' Harper said, and looked at the others. 'Any other suggestions?'

Both Walsh and Ash shook their heads.

'After that first letter I thought he was a bit barmy,' the inspector said. 'So far I've seen nothing to change that theory. Quite the opposite.'

'I agree. Something's broken inside him,' Harper said. He held up the fragments of paper the man had left at his crimes. 'These aren't normal.'

'I think it's his way of letting us know who did it, like you said, sir,' Walsh suggested. He leaned against the door jamb, arms folded, frowning with thought. 'Like someone signing his work. He has the notebook in his jacket, and leaves a sheet. He can do it quickly, then go. It identifies him, that's all.'

It made as much sense as anything he was likely to hear, more than some of the thoughts that had wandered through his head.

'He's done nothing since he robbed Mrs Morgan. If that was him.'

'I'm positive it was, sir,' Ash said. 'I'd put good money on it.'

'Then we'll include that. He hasn't given up, people like that never do. They become more obsessed. We need to keep a very careful watch. None of the women have withdrawn from the race. He's not receiving the results he wants.'

'Where should we be tonight, sir?' Fowler asked.

'I've arranged to have a uniform monitoring messages so we can all be out. We all know where I'll be,' Harper said with a grin. 'One of you with Mrs Pease, so that leaves two to float around. Any questions?' He looked at a row of shaking heads. 'And anything at all, you let me know. You know I have a very personal interest in finding this bastard. Don't forget it.'

'At least I don't have any meetings tomorrow,' Annabelle sighed as she sat back in the hackney. The coach bumped over the tram tracks, bouncing them up and down.

135

'Still have to be out and about, though.'

'I think my feet must have grown a layer of steel, with all those miles I've walked.' She closed her eyes and let out a long, slow breath. 'I feel like I could sleep for a week.'

He glanced out of the window. 'We're almost home. You can have eight hours' rest, anyway.'

'Good.' She put her head on his shoulder and yawned, hand covering her mouth. 'I hope I win after all this.'

She was the likely victor. Even if she didn't see it herself yet, it was clear to him from the way audiences reacted. They believed her, as if they knew that everything she said was more than just another politician paying lip service to ideals. People had come up to him on the street to tell him with pride that they intended to vote for her.

It was a small election, really. Whoever paid much attention to the Poor Law Guardians? He couldn't name a single one of them, he'd never given them a moment's thought. But having women involved had made it into an important issue in Leeds. The newspapers still carried their editorials, urging voters to support the male candidates. But in Sheepscar, at least, not many people appeared to be listening.

The cab drew up outside the Victoria and he shook her gently awake, paying the driver as she unlocked the front door. It was late, but a light still burned in the bar. A policeman sat at one of the tables, his hat in front of him.

Annabelle glanced worriedly at Harper.

136

'You go on up,' he told her. 'I've a feeling I'm going to be a while.'

He was quick enough to flag down the hackney before it turned around. The constable had said little, only that the Superintendent was needed, and he didn't know what had happened.

At the station, Harper paid the cabby and dashed in, leaving the uniform behind. Ash and Fowler were in the detectives' room. The sergeant's jacket hung over the back of a chair, his sleeves rolled up to show thick, dark hair on his forearms.

'What is it?'

'As bad as it gets, sir,' Ash told him. 'Murder.'

'Who?' The question came out in a parched croak. He had the image of one of the female candidates lying dead in the street.

'Mr Cain, sir. His wife is running to be a Guardian.'

'But . . .' It took him completely by surprise. She'd been one of those who'd accepted police protection, happy to feel safer. Ash told the tale: her husband worked the late shift at a boot factory in Meanwood. The constable had escorted her home. She'd barely been inside the house for five seconds when she started to scream. Moments later the bobby was back outside, blowing furiously on his whistle.

'How did it happen?'

'Knife, sir, at the kitchen table. Pot of tea there and two cups.' He picked up a scrap of paper from his desk. 'And there's this.'

They cry out that poor Mary died,

137

With the wind that blew o'er the wild moor.

The same ink, the same writing. Another dead woman in the words. No doubt about the killer.

Could he have guessed it might happen? No. Nobody could have predicted this. Nobody could have prevented it; that was more to the point.

'Where's Walsh?' he asked.

'With Mrs Cain, sir. He has a touch with women, I thought he could calm her down. She was in a bad way when I was there.'

Christ, anyone would be. Coming home to find that someone had murdered your husband in his own kitchen?

'House-to-house?' Harper asked.

'Already going on, sir. When I left, nobody had mentioned anything strange. No noises.'

Cain must have invited the man in. Made him tea, asked him to sit down. Was it someone he knew? The Superintendent tried to think, to work out the possibilities.

'Check with the constables who've been guarding Mrs Cain. Was anyone hanging around? Men passing by too often, things like that.'

'They're already under orders to report anything like that,' Ash told him. 'I asked, and there's nothing.'

'Whoever he is, he did his homework. He knew where she lived, he knew her husband would be home and there'd be no copper there.'

'The address could be easy to find,' Fowler pointed out. 'They'd be in the street directory.'

Harper shook his head. 'Too general.' He considered for a moment. 'Her election papers. They'd have her address.'

'Town Hall,' Ash said. 'As soon as they open, I'll go and see if anyone's asked to see them.'

'Good. Now, how did he know the husband would be at home and on his own? What time did his shift finish?'

'Nine,' Fowler answered. 'The factory's only five minutes' walk away. Looks like he'd been home long enough to give himself a thorough wash. His hands and face are clean.'

'Look at the people who work for the bootmaker. Clerks, management, people like that. It might be one of them. He invited the man inside . . .'

'It could have been someone who said he admired Mrs Cain's campaign and wanted to meet her.'

All too easily.

'Yes,' he admitted. They simply didn't know. 'Where's the body?'

'I sent him over to Dr King, sir,' Ash said. 'Post-mortem tomorrow, although the cause of death is obvious. Knife to the heart.'

'One wound?'

'Yes, sir.'

'So he knew where to aim,' Harper said thoughtfully. 'Could be worth looking at that doctor again, the one interested in folk songs.'

'He doesn't match the description in any of the other incidents, sir,' Ash said.

'Find out where he was tonight, anyway.' He was going to cover everything.

The duty sergeant arrived with tea. The superintendent perched on one of the desks.

'Even after he tried to snatch Mary, I never imagined he'd go this far. I even thought the death from the bomb might be an accident. But now I don't believe he has a conscience. Just a goal.' He shook his head. 'Who in God's name would kill to stop a woman running for office?'

'Someone who's very seriously disturbed,' Fowler suggested. 'But who probably hides it quite well.'

'That doesn't help us at all.'

'The newspapers will be all over this,' Ash said. 'Plenty of juicy scandal there for them – "Candidate's Husband Knifed To Death".'

Harper grimaced. He hadn't even thought about that. His eyes strayed to the clock. Not even twelve. It was going to be a very long night.

Harper took advantage of a lull in the investigation to slip home for breakfast. At least he could deliver the news to Annabelle himself. It was becoming a habit.

All the colour drained from her face in an instant, and he thought she might faint where she stood. But she tightened her grip on the chair back until her knuckles were white.

'Poor Alexandra,' she said. 'You know, she was one of the first I met after I joined the Suffragists. She'd do anything to help people. That's why she wanted to be elected. I talked to Harry Cain a few times, too. He was always cheery. Pipe stuck in the corner of his mouth every time I saw him.' A smile of memory came and vanished in a moment. 'What can I do to help her?'

'Go and see her. She can probably use plenty of comfort right now.'

'I will.' She nodded.

Mary wandered into the kitchen, still in her nightdress, bare feet padding across the wooden boards, a book tucked under her arm. She looked at their faces.

'Is something wrong, Mam?'

'No, sweetheart.' Annabelle composed herself and swung her daughter up into her arms. 'Your da just had some news that surprised us and came home to tell me. Now, you want me to hear you read from that book before school, don't you?'

'The elections office remembers a man coming in and asking to see the papers of all the women running to be Poor Law Guardians,' Ash said.

'Was it him?'

'The clerk didn't pay too much attention. But from what he remembers, I'd say it probably was.'

'Did he have to leave a name and address?' He seemed to recall that was needed to see the documents.

'It was in the ledger. Mr William Smith.' He raised an eyebrow. 'And where he lives doesn't exist. No such street.'

Harper ran a hand through his hair. The man knew where all the candidates lived. He could have watched every single one of them. That explained how he knew about Mary.

'I know some of the women didn't want police protection. But like it or not, they're going to get it.'

'That might not go over too well, sir.'

'I don't care. It's a damned sight better than

141

him killing them. And I want their families warned to watch out, too.'

'I've already done that part, sir. First thing this morning.'

The superintendent nodded. He was lucky to have a man like Ash, someone who could think and plan and act. A polite cough drew his attention.

'What about Mrs Harper, sir? Are you going to have a man on her?'

She'd hate it. It would spark a furious argument. But he had to do it. It was impossible to assign constables to the other women and not her.

'Yes,' he said reluctantly. 'But you'd better be prepared to bury me with full honours once she knows.'

'Inspector . . .' Dr King began, then smiled and shook his head. 'I mean Superintendent. I'm not sure I'll ever become used to calling you that.'

'I don't know that I'll ever be used to hearing it,' Harper admitted.

The police surgeon had to be in his mid-eighties, round, most of his hair long gone apart from a set of long, wispy grey side-whiskers. But there was still an air of vitality about him. He enjoyed his job down in King's Kingdom, the mortuary under the police station on Hunslet Lane. He was completely at home among the corpses and the heavy, biting smell of carbolic.

'You must be here about last night's body,' King said. 'It's the only one I've had recently. You police must be doing your job well, it's been a quiet year for murders.'

142

'Be grateful for small mercies. Have you taken a look at him yet?'

'Yes. It was cut and dried, if you'll forgive the rather awkward pun. A single blow, pierced the heart. The assailant wasn't more than two feet away. A thin blade, very sharp.'

'Skilled?'

'Yes,' King replied after a moment. 'He knew where to strike.' The doctor took a cigar from his waistcoat pocket, chopped off the tip with a scalpel, lit a match and began to puff. 'Why? Do you have someone in mind?'

'Is it knowledge a doctor would have?'

'I'd sincerely hope so. Although I'd trust no physician would ever do something like that. The Hippocratic Oath.'

'You know people as well as I do,' Harper began, but King shook his head vigorously and held up a hand.

'I hope I never know humanity as intimately as you do, Superintendent. I see the results of what they do, and that's bad enough. I don't want to know the reasons for it.'

'The dead man, what was he like?'

'Fifty-two, and he looked every day of it. Balding, the little hair he had left was mostly grey. A manual labourer from the look of him. His knuckles were gnarled with the start of arthritis. Palms heavily callused. Clean, but there was a smell of leather on his skin.'

'He was a bootmaker,' Harper said, and King nodded.

'What else would you like to know? Death would have been immediate.'

143

'Any sign of a struggle on the body?'

'Nothing. I'd say he was taken completely by surprise.'

Fifteen

The wind was fierce. Even from the top of the hill he could hear the waves crashing over the pier, loud as cannon fire. Billy Reed turned up the collar of his mackintosh and tapped his hat down on his head.

'I hope you don't have to go anywhere today,' he told Elizabeth.

'The café,' she told him. 'I'm expecting a load of dishes to be delivered.' She peered over his shoulder at the rain bouncing off the pavement. 'If they can make up it up here from Scarborough.'

'Stay as dry as you can,' he said as he kissed her.

By the time he reached the police station on Spring Hill, his trouser legs were sodden. None of the boats would be out today, surely. Not in weather like this. Sergeant Brown greeted him with a smile as he took off the coat and shook himself like a dog.

'First big blow of the season, sir. Plenty more of these to come before the herring fleet heads out again in the spring.'

'Is there much crime here in the winter?'

'A bit more drunkenness and fighting, maybe,'

Brown answered after a little consideration. 'But not *crime* crime, if you understand, sir.'

'I think I do.' It made sense if you were a copper.

'I lit the fire in your office. Should be cosy by now. And tea's brewing.'

'Thank you, Sergeant,' Reed said, his gratitude genuine.

An hour later he felt warm and dry. The wind might have eased a little, he thought hopefully as he looked out of the window. Maybe there'd be a lull. He had an appointment with Harry Pepper at Custom House at eleven and he didn't fancy another soaking.

No such luck. He saw the boats bobbing in the heavy swell along St Ann's Staith, glad the towering waves couldn't penetrate into the harbour, then ducked through the door and up the stairs.

Pepper was on his own in the office, the air thick with pipe smoke.

'Makes me glad I don't work the boats any longer,' he said as he stared out towards the North Sea. 'Still two of them out there, did you know that?'

'Will they be all right?'

'Let's hope. Experienced skippers. They probably put in somewhere to wait it out. Still, there'll be plenty of people praying today.' He sighed. 'How was your meeting?'

'Hard to tell. He didn't have much to say.'

'That's his way,' Pepper said with a grin. 'He spends words like they were money. But if he tells you something, you can take it to the bank.

And if we can arrest some more smugglers, I'll be happy. Especially if there's a ring operating out of here. The Coast Guard will be pleased, too. It'll give them something to do instead of sitting around and pretending they're Jolly Jack Tars.'

'Terrier John is mine, though,' Reed told him.

Pepper shrugged. 'You're welcome to the collar. Tell me, did our friend make you play dominoes?'

'Yes.'

'A word of warning: don't ever beat him. He likes to think he's the best.'

'I'll make sure I remember that.'

He dashed along Church Street, as if he might be able to dodge between the raindrops, then into Elizabeth's café.

She was sorting through a crate of crockery, checking every plate and cup for breakages or cracks, while the delivery man waited impatiently. Finally she was satisfied; she signed his invoice and let him leave, muttering under his breath.

'I thought I'd take you out for something to eat,' Reed said.

Her eyes brightened. 'Billy, love, you know just what to say to a girl. Let me get my coat.'

The showers had passed and the clouds had lightened by the time Harper stood in the doorway of Millgarth police station, buttoning his overcoat. The hackney drew up and he climbed in, giving an address in Meanwood.

Officially Harry Cain's murder was Ash's case,

146

but the superintendent wanted to see the widow. He'd met her twice with Annabelle, and he needed to assure her that the police would do everything they could. For whatever worth words might have when she was bereft.

Alexandra Cain was dressed in black. A neighbour sat with her in the parlour. The door to the kitchen stayed firmly closed, the room where the killing happened. Harper balanced a saucer on his lap, holding a teacup in his fingers.

'Your Annabelle came by this morning,' Mrs Cain said. 'Not long after that detective constable left.'

'She said she would.'

'Wanted to offer her sympathies. I told her what I'm saying to you now: I'm not going to go on and run for office. I can't. Not after this.' She pulled out a handkerchief and dabbed at her eyes.

'I understand.' It was what he'd expected as soon as he saw her face, as if all the hope had been ripped from it. She'd been married to Harry for thirty-one years, she said. Knew from the moment she saw him that he was the one, and never stopped loving him. They hadn't been blessed with children, but half of the kiddies in the neighbourhood had ended up at their house one time or another.

'Your missus is a right 'un,' she said with approval. 'Couldn't have been kinder.'

'I'm glad. And we will find him, Mrs Cain.'

'I know you will, love.' She sighed, the weight of time heavy on her. 'I know you will. But a lot of good it'll do me, unless finding him brings my Harry back.'

And they both knew the answer to that. He made his farewell, looking up and down the street as the door to the terraced house closed behind him. Everything was so ordinary. Most of the houses were neatly kept, windows sparkling, steps donkeystoned. Completely unremarkable. But now, for years to come, it would be known as the place where the murder happened at number fifteen.

Two dead. The killer had finally achieved something; he'd made one of the women drop out of the race. But there were still six left. For most, something like this would terrify them. For some, it would only stiffen their resolve. He'd need to wait and see on that.

Meanwhile, the police had enough on their plate trying to find the man who'd knifed Harry Cain and contain the fright he seemed determined to spread.

It wasn't far to Roundhay Road. He ducked into the Victoria. Might as well face the ructions with Annabelle. Instead there was only Dan, shaking his head.

'She's out with that politics stuff again, Tom. And we need to make a beer order. Tell her, will you?'

Even with his hearing, Harper made out the sound of the children at the primary school from a hundred yards away. Playtime, he thought, then pulled out his pocket watch. Dinner time, he corrected himself; where had the morning vanished? He stood by the railings until he picked out Mary. She was running around, playing tig with some of the other girls.

She'd said nothing more about being grabbed. No nightmares that woke her, she hadn't seemed anxious. For all the effect it had, it might never have happened. But it would be pushed down somewhere, simmering away. He'd seen that happen with coppers. Sometime later, a few days, months, years. It would boil up to the surface. He didn't want that with his daughter. Yet he didn't know what he could do about it.

A tram was coming and he ran to the stop, arm out. On board, he gazed at the streets as they passed, knowing them all so well. Home, Harper thought. Home.

'Give me some good news,' he said to Ash when the inspector returned to the office, Walsh trailing behind him.

'Wish I could, sir. We've got nothing. All the houses along the street had their curtains drawn. No one heard a thing. It's easy enough to get anywhere from there, too. No one's going to remember a man who looks respectable.'

'That's his shield,' Walsh said. 'Respectability. He's the type no one notices. He's mad as a bloody hatter, but he looks completely normal, so no one pays attention. He can hide behind it. And he's well-spoken, so no one would think of questioning him.'

'Good,' Harper nodded. It was a succinct analysis. But it still didn't help them catch him. 'Mrs Cain is dropping out of the race.'

'She told me last night, sir. I didn't know if she'd change her mind. Can't blame her, can

149

you?' The constable gave a small, tight smile and sighed. 'Poor soul.'

'No, I don't blame her at all.'

'What has Mrs Harper said about the police protection, sir?' Ash asked.

'I haven't seen her yet. What about the other women?'

'They've accepted it. Reluctantly, but in the light of what's happened . . .'

Better to be safe. But none of them could really be safe until this man was caught. He had an agile mind, he looked beyond the obvious, and he went for things that would hurt the most.

'If you were him, where would you strike next?'

Before anyone could answer, Sergeant Tollman appeared at the door with a newspaper folded under his arm.

'Begging your pardon, sir, but I thought you'd like to see the *Evening Post*.' He placed it on the desk and left.

The murder was the headline, of course. But the reporter had done his homework. He noted that it was the culmination of a series of attacks against the women candidates. He'd joined the dots and concluded that someone was trying to force them to abandon the race.

There should have been outrage on the page. But instead of fury at the intimidation, the writer felt that the female candidates should put the welfare of their fellow Leodiensians first and cede the ground to the men, to let them battle it out at the polls.

'Christ,' he said and tossed it down again. 'Just what we need. He'd better hope no one decides

150

to imitate the killer in order to scare off the women candidates. I'll tear him apart if that happens.'

'Maybe it'll bring in a few tips,' Walsh suggested.

'Don't hold your breath. There's not even a description in there. Where's Fowler?'

'He said he might have a lead, sir.' Ash shrugged. The sergeant had quickly developed his network of informants, and they'd given him solid information in the past.

'Right. Back to where we were before this rubbish turned up. If you were the killer, where would you strike next?'

'I'd lie low for a few days,' Walsh said as he lit a cigarette. 'He has every copper in Leeds looking for him. A little while and they won't be paying quite as much attention.'

'Or he could change his appearance a little,' Ash said thoughtfully. 'I don't know. I'm just guessing.'

'That doesn't answer my question,' Harper told them. 'What's he likely to do next?'

The silence grew around them. It had been a hopeful question, he decided. If they really knew, they'd have stopped this bastard already.

'What?' Annabelle exploded, exactly the way he knew she would. 'No, Tom, I'm not having it. Simple as that.'

She stood, glaring daggers at him, fists bunched on her hips. Mary was upstairs with Ellen. At least she wouldn't see this. But she'd probably be able to hear it through the ceiling.

'The other women have accepted it. I'm just trying to keep everyone safe. And alive,' he added pointedly.

'They can take it if they want. I'm not going to. We've been through this once. How's it going to look if I traipse around Sheepscar with a tame bobby at my heels? How can I look people in the eye and say I'm one of them if that's going on? It's bad enough with that rubbish in the paper today. I don't expect anything better from them. But now to have you saying this . . .'

'Look—' he started, but she was blazing.

'I know you have your job to do. But I have mine, too. I put my name on those papers to run for office. Fine, you want to keep us all safe. But how about all those women who end up beaten and raped every single day of the year? What are you going to do about them, Tom? Are you going to give them all a personal copper?'

'It's not the same,' he told her quietly. 'You know that full well.'

'Maybe it's not,' she acknowledged sullenly. It was an olive branch of sorts, before things went too far. But he knew it wasn't over yet.

'I can't have the others guarded and not you.'

Annabelle shook her head. 'No. I've told you, Tom. I'm not going to have people say I'm mollycoddled.'

She could insist all she wanted. This time he was going to have his way.

'I'd rather they said whatever they like and have you alive. I don't give a monkey's what people think. If they've got an ounce of sense, they'll know why we're doing it. Any order I can give that helps stop this man, I'm going to give it. Think about it, for God's sake. He's killed two people. He tried to snatch our daughter. You know what he's done to some of the women.'

'He won't do that to me,' she said.

'No,' Harper agreed, staring at her. 'Because he won't have the chance.'

He'd said his piece. She'd either give in with good grace and accept it reluctantly, or this would rumble along between them for a long time.

'All right,' she said after a long while. 'I'm not happy about it. But if the other women have said yes, then I will, too. But,' Annabelle warned. 'I don't want him breathing down my neck the whole time. When I'm knocking on doors, he keeps a little distance.'

'Close enough to act if there's a problem,' Harper told her, and she nodded.

'And his protection ends at the front door of this pub. You're here, Dan's here, the customers.'

'Yes.'

'Then you can tell him to start tomorrow.' Her mouth turned into a smile. 'But you'd better have picked me a good-looking one, Tom Harper. I don't want to be walking round with a bobby who has a face like a wet Whit Sunday.'

'I'll select him myself.' He opened his arms and hugged her.

'I know you, you'll pick the ugliest one you can find.' She sighed. 'I'm not happy about it, but I know you mean well.'

Ash raised his eyebrows when he saw Harper was already in his office.

153

'I wasn't sure if you'd be in today, sir.'

'Why on earth not?'

'Well, since you were telling Mrs Harper about her protection last night, we had a bet on whether we'd find you here or at Dr King's mortuary. How did she take it?'

'You know her. How do you imagine?'

'Any broken plates or windows?'

'No. We came close, though.'

'Who have you put on her, sir?'

'Martinson.'

'The ugliest man in Millgarth?' Ash chuckled. 'I'm sure she'll appreciate that.'

Harper grinned. 'No problems at the meetings last night?'

'Not a sausage.'

Fowler arrived, shrugging off his overcoat.

'How did your lead pan out yesterday?' Harper asked.

'I'm not sure yet, sir. I was thinking about bombs and what you need to make them. Turns out it's not much in the way of explosives to damage a hut, but you still have to buy it from somewhere.'

Dammit, Harper thought. They should have considered that right away.

'Go on.'

'I'm sure you'll be glad to hear that there aren't too many places where you can buy explosives, sir.'

'Does that mean . . .?'

He shook his head. 'Unfortunately, it's not that hard to make your own, with a little knowledge and care. All you have to do is mix sulphur,

154

charcoal, and saltpetre, and those are easy enough to pick up without arousing suspicion. I asked around, and it's safe to say that our man didn't try to buy gunpowder already mixed. So he must have made his own.'

'That tells us he's clever,' Harper said. 'We already knew that.'

'And careful. I know, sir, we were aware of that, too. Anyway, I started wondering where you'd learn how to make gunpowder.'

'Books,' Ash said.

'The library.' Fowler nodded. 'They were very helpful. One of the books with the information was taken out two months ago. Returned on time.'

'I hope after all this you're going to tell me who borrowed them,' Harper said.

'The librarian thinks she might know, sir. I'm going back this morning to talk to her again.'

'That's excellent work.' A very good piece of deduction. But, Harper berated himself, if he'd had his wits about him properly, they could have done this after the first bomb. Should have done it.

'No guarantees, but I'm hopeful, sir.'

'If you come up with a name, I want to know immediately.' The superintendent turned as the door opened. 'Mr Walsh. Bearing good tidings, I hope?'

'Sorry, sir. Hold-up on the tram. A cart shed its load and stopped traffic.'

The eternal problem. Between the carts, the carriages, the cabs, the omnibuses and the trams, there were just too many vehicles in Leeds. The roads were clogged; close to the market there

155

was barely room for anything to pass when they were parked. He'd brought it up at divisional meetings, but no one had a solution.

'Any problems last night?'

'A chap who thought he was being clever by heckling.' He grinned. 'The constable on duty and I took him outside and persuaded him of the error of his ways.'

'We've been lucky. I thought some men might have been encouraged by that piece in the *Evening Post*. Be alert.'

'Well?' Harper asked as he stopped at Fowler's desk. 'Did you get a name?'

'I did, sir.' He should have been looking triumphant. Instead, he appeared doubtful. 'But she's not at all positive it's the right man. It was two months ago and plenty of people borrow books.'

'Who is he?'

'His name's Surtees. He lives on Chapeltown Road, sir.'

'Let's go and talk to him. Ash, Walsh, grab your coats.'

Sixteen

It was a respectable address, no more than a stone's throw from the house where Harper had lodged before he was married. It was close enough to have witnessed the explosion at the church hall.

'What do we know about him?' They stood at the corner of the street, an odd grouping of men with their heads together.

'No police record.' Fowler looked at his notebook. 'Going back in the city directory, he's been in the house for at least five years. That's all.'

'I'll go to the front door with Walsh. You two cover the back. The usual drill. If he's our man, he probably won't be expecting us to find him.'

'If he puts up a fight, sir?' Ash asked, and Harper gave him a withering look.

'Let's hope the librarian was right and we can put a stop to things now.' He straightened his back and began to walk.

Number eight was one of a series of three-storey villas. A cellar where the maid-of-all-work did her job. A pocket-handkerchief garden at the front, the small patch of grass trimmed close and square. The houses were no more than ten years old but they already had that dark Leeds patina, the drift of smoke and soot up from the factories in Sheepscar and Meanwood, with the faint tang from the gasometer scenting the air. He took hold of the polished door knocker.

'Ready?'

'Ready, sir,' Walsh replied.

The man who answered resembled the description they had. Tall enough, greying hair, in his forties, neatly dressed. But when Harper announced himself, he looked confused.

'Police?' he asked. 'What have I done?'

157

'Might we come in, sir?'

'Yes, yes, I suppose so. The girl's gone to the shops or I'd offer you some tea.'

Once they were seated in the parlour, Surtees asked again: 'What have I done, Superintendent?'

If he was acting, he was very good. Harper felt the urgency starting to trickle away. Five minutes later he was certain that Surtees wasn't a criminal.

'I do go to the library quite regularly,' the man admitted. 'But I've never taken out a book on explosives.' He sounded faintly amused by the idea. 'And I'm not sure I'd know a folk song if you stood there and sang one for me.'

'Would you mind if Detective Constable Walsh took a look through the house, sir?'

'If you think it's necessary, feel free,' Surtees agreed. 'But there's nothing remarkable to find, besides my collection of butterflies.' He looked at Walsh beseechingly. 'Please be careful with them; it's a lifetime's work.'

When the detective constable returned with a sad shake of his head, Harper stood and made his apologies.

'I quite understand, Superintendent. I hope you find him soon. I heard that bomb go off, it was terrible. From what you've told me, someone like that needs to be behind bars.'

'It was still a good idea,' Harper said once they were back at Millgarth. 'You were on the right track.'

'Can't blame the librarian, either,' Fowler agreed. 'She did say she wasn't certain.'

'It might be worth having another word with her. You know, get in touch if something springs into her head, that sort of thing.'

'I will, sir.' He sat back and chewed his bottom lip. 'This man we're after, he's a right little tin god, isn't he? Wanting to show how powerful he is, and in everyday life he's probably nobody at all.'

'He's going to be somebody when we find him. We'll have him on the gallows.' Harper gave a dark smile. 'They can make up a song about him.'

'I could cheerfully kill you,' Annabelle said as they walked to the evening's meeting.

'This might be a good time,' Harper answered. 'There's no copper behind us.'

'That's what I'm talking about. Did you have to assign that one to me?'

'Amos Martinson? He's a very good constable.'

'I daresay he is. But he's got a face to scare small children and the dourest manner I've ever come across.'

'You wanted someone who wouldn't be bothering you,' he reminded her.

'I know. I also asked for handsome, remember?'

'He'll do a good job and still give you elbow room. Do you think I'd stick my own wife with a waster?'

She arched an eyebrow. 'You'd better not, Tom Harper.'

'No problems today?'

'None. I went over to visit Alexandra Cain again this morning.'

'We thought we had the killer earlier today.'

159

He felt her arm tense against his. 'Mistaken identity.'

Tonight it was Cross Stamford Street, in the large upstairs room of the Jewish Tailors Union building. The soldier from the Engineers was outside waiting for them.

'Is there a problem?' Harper asked.

'Yes and no, sir.' The man presented himself at attention, well over six feet tall in his cap, eyes staring straight ahead.

'Stand easy. Tell me about it.'

'I've been through the building, except for one room. All the rest of it is clear, but that's locked.'

'Doesn't the caretaker have a key?'

'He sloped off earlier, sir. They've sent someone for him, but he's not back yet. It means I can't say the place is safe, sir. If you want my advice, you won't go in until I've had time to check that room.'

Harper pulled out his pocket watch. Half an hour until the meeting was due to begin. The caretaker should return very soon. It was a chilly evening, but dry, not too bad for standing outside.

The superintendent looked at the soldier. Harper was the one who'd wanted every place checked before a meeting. What was the point in using an expert if you didn't heed his advice?

'Very good,' he agreed. 'We'll wait.'

Five minutes became ten, and there was still no sign of the caretaker. More than twenty people had gathered on the pavement, ready for tonight. Annabelle moved among them, talking, shaking hands, keeping them at ease and apologizing for the delay.

Finally, after a quarter of an hour, Harper turned to the soldier.

'What's your recommendation? I can't keep them here all night.'

The Engineer bit his lip. 'You'll hate me for saying it, sir, but I think you should abandon the meeting. The chances are there's no problem at all, but you brought us in to make sure everything's safe. As it stands, I can't guarantee that.'

The crowd had risen to nearly thirty, growing restless and muttering. Harper whispered in Annabelle's ear. She shook her head.

'Of course we're not going to take a risk.' Her voice bristled. She looked around, then up at the clouds. 'There's some waste ground, over where they're starting to build that bonfire. I can use that. It doesn't look like rain.'

She'd do it, he knew that. Harper was torn between going with them and standing guard or staying with the soldier.

'You go on, sir,' the Engineer told him. 'I'll give this caretaker a few minutes more. If he doesn't show his face, with your permission I'll go on back to the barracks.'

'Yes, that's fine.'

'If your wife keeps them that far away, they should be safe if this does go up.' He slapped a hand against the brickwork of the building. 'Not that I expect it.'

'Let me know what happens.'

She'd been talking for ten minutes, standing on an old fruit box she'd found, when Harper heard the sound of footsteps. He turned, body tense, but it was only the soldier. He was wiping

161

sweat from his face with a handkerchief, looking worried.

'I think you'd better come and take a look at this, sir.'

'Why? What is it?'

'Nothing to worry about.' He grinned, suddenly looking more like a boy than a man. 'Not now, anyway. But it's just as well you didn't go ahead with the meeting, after all.'

'Where's the caretaker?'

'Ran off as soon as I spotted the bomb. It's small, not a lot of charge, it wouldn't have done much damage.'

It looked exactly like the one they'd found in Meanwood, a package.

'Safe now?' he asked warily.

'Completely.'

'That's very good work. Thank you.'

'Part of the job, sir. It's crudely made, but effective enough. Or it was. Simple to defuse.'

'Was it hidden behind anything?'

'Out in the open, once we had the door unlocked. By my reckoning, it was set to go off somewhere around now. Nothing like working against the clock to keep you alert.'

'I'm very grateful. My wife is, too, I'm sure of that.'

'All part of the service, sir.'

'Was there a piece of paper there with some writing on it?'

'I've no idea. I was only looking for a bomb. Why, sir?'

'It doesn't matter. I can check.'

'It's all locked up again now.'

Never mind; it could wait for the morning. It wasn't as if he had any doubt who was responsible. Harper brought out a shilling and handed it to the soldier.

'Buy yourself a drink on the way back to the barracks. If your sergeant asks, say it was an order from me.'

'Don't mind if I do, sir. Thank you.' He paused. 'Would you have any objection if I took the bomb? Only I'd like to show the boys.'

He laughed. 'Be my guest.'

By the time he returned the crowd had thinned a little, a few discouraged by the thin wind that cut along Roseville Road. Annabelle was still talking, but from the tone of her voice she was close to the end.

He hung back, leaning against a street lamp, waiting until she was done and the audience dispersed.

'I saw you go over to the building.'

'There was a bomb. It's defused. Gone now.'

She took a slow breath and closed her eyes for a moment. 'Nobody hurt?'

'Everything safe.' His voice was grim. 'We were lucky.'

'Harry Cain wasn't lucky, Tom. Mr Harkness at St Clement's wasn't lucky. Mrs Pease wasn't lucky when she was attacked.' She let out a long, frustrated sigh. 'It's like he's at war with women.'

'I think you've about summed it up.'

They cut through the back streets, beyond the dark, open space of the rhubarb fields where the man had escaped after trying to snatch Mary, and past rows of back-to-back houses. They'd just

163

reached Roundhay Road when he saw the constable waiting outside the Victoria.

'It's not good news.' Harper looked at Annabelle.

'You're needed at Millgarth, sir,' the bobby said. 'Soon as possible.'

Seventeen

The message had come during the afternoon. Reed was walking home, head down against the wind, holding on to his hat, when someone bumped against him. As he looked up to apologize, a voice said, 'Eight tonight, same place,' before moving on.

Now he was sitting in the Scoresby Arms, a glass of bitter in front of him and a domino tile in his hand, ready to play.

'Be plenty of people thankful round here tonight,' the man across from him said.

'Why's that?' Reed asked.

'You haven't heard? Them boats as didn't make it back all found safe harbour. Telegram arrived this afternoon.'

'That's good news.'

'Aye.' Without hesitation, he laid down a double two and smiled with satisfaction. 'Weather like this will keep the smugglers indoors.'

'Including the man I asked about?'

'He's a strange 'un. Seems to know everybody, but don't none of them ken too much about him. A foreigner.'

'From Leeds.' He rapped his knuckles on the table: no move he could make.

'What I said. Folk listen to him, and some of them are people who'd rather talk than hear someone else.'

'What do you mean?'

'They respect him.'

'Is he involved in smuggling?'

'Don't know that yet. Can't just come out and ask, can I?' With a flourish, he slapped his last tile on the table and grinned. 'Don't have a chance of beating me at this, do you?'

'No,' Reed agreed. He didn't care about dominoes. Only about Terrier John. There was something going on. He could feel it. All he needed was some proof. He counted out a florin in change and pushed it across to the man.

'I'll let you know when I have something.'

'You look worn out,' Elizabeth said when she saw him.

'Long day. And I'm off to Ruswarp and Sleights tomorrow. I hope the rain holds off.'

'Maybe you'll be all right. Someone told me this afternoon that this will blow itself out tonight. I'm blessed if I know how they can tell.'

'Fisherman's knowledge.' He felt the teapot; it was still warm.

'That's been mashing for ages. I'll brew some fresh if you want.'

'This will do. Where are the children?'

'Upstairs, writing to their friends in Leeds.'

A pen and a sheet of paper lay on the table. A

list, some items crossed out. He looked question-
ingly at her.

'Plans for the tea room?' Reed asked.

'All the things I still need to do before I open.
I no sooner think of one and write it down than
two more pop into my head.'

'No rush, is there?' he asked, looking through
what she'd written. It seemed thorough enough.

'No,' Elizabeth agreed. 'I want it all to be just
right. Oh,' she said, 'I found a place where
Annabelle and Tom can stay, Billy love. It's over
on Crescent Avenue. Very nice. I took a look at
it this afternoon. So you'd better write your own
letter to Leeds and let Tom know. I asked: they
have vacancies over Christmas, and they'll do a
full dinner.'

Well, he thought, she'd given him his orders.
But he needed to let Harper know what he'd
learned about Terrier John. For whatever it was
worth.

'Two other bombs?' Harper said in disbelief.

'The soldiers found and defused them both,'
Ash said. He looked haggard, all his heartiness
gone, his skin pale and almost yellow in the light
from the gas mantles. 'No damage done. They
were easy to spot, too. It's as if he wanted them
to be found.'

'Three in one evening. What the hell is he
doing?' He ran a hand through his hair.

'If he's trying to run us ragged,' Fowler
suggested, 'he's doing a fine job of it.'

One bomb in Woodhouse, another in Cross
Green, and the third Harper had seen for himself.

166

Their man had been busy. He must have spent the afternoon wandering blithely around the city. Probably smirking at his own invisibility.

'They were small bombs, if that really matters. They couldn't have done much damage,' Ash told him.

'It was the same where I was.'

'Sounds as if it's more for show than anything else,' Walsh said. 'To let us know he can do it and keep us on our toes.'

'Taunting us,' Fowler agreed, pushing his spectacles up his nose.

'Bits of paper,' Harper said. 'Did he leave any?'

'On your desk, sir.'

'Go home,' he ordered. 'There's nothing more we can do tonight. Let's come at it with fresh eyes tomorrow.'

The same handwriting. By now it felt almost as familiar as his own.

I broke a stake out of the fence
And beat this fair maid down

That was one. The other seemed to continue from it:

Oh, Willie dear, don't murder me here
I'm not prepared to die

He took the copy of Kidson's *Traditional Tunes* from his drawer and started leafing through the pages. But he couldn't find a song like this. He wondered what he'd discover at the Union building. Harper ran his palms down his face.

167

He felt too tired to think clearly. It was time to follow his own advice and go back to the Victoria.

Annabelle stirred as he climbed into bed. Harper had spent a minute standing in the doorway of Mary's room, staring down at his daughter as she slept. Only the top of her head showed above the blankets, a thick, wild tangle of dark hair. For a moment he almost believed he could hear her soft breathing. But it was a trick of the night; it was a long time since his ears had been that sharp.

'What was it?' Annabelle asked sleepily.

'Nothing,' he told her softly. 'No one hurt, no damage done. Go back to sleep, everything's fine.' She grunted as rest took hold of her again.

He was late, dashing through his washing and shaving, gulping a cup of tea for breakfast as she quizzed him on what had happened. At least the answers seemed to satisfy her, Harper thought.

Martinson was waiting outside the Victoria, offering a hasty salute as the superintendent hurried past.

The caretaker was unlocking the union building as Harper arrived.

'That politics is nobbut trouble,' he complained as he searched out the right key. 'There. It was in the middle of the floor. Don't know what this world is coming to. Bombs.'

'I just need to search in here,' Harper told him, staring until the man shuffled away.

It sat in plain view.

168

But he beat her all the more
Till all the ground for yards around

Was it the same song?

The Wexford Girl. Kidson had recognized it immediately. Not from his book, but he'd written about it in his column for the *Mercury*. A deep, dark murder ballad. But at least the killer died at the end.

'Let's hope the outcome is the same here,' the Superintendent said as he left the Kidsons' parlour.

'I'm sure you'll catch him,' the man said.

'They all happened on the same night, so he used quotes from the same song,' Fowler said and shrugged. 'It seems quite obvious to me.'

'It's like we said, he's leaving his calling card,' Ash agreed. 'So we know it's him.'

'As if there could be any doubt about it.' Harper sipped his tea. It was almost cold, but he barely noticed. 'I'd rather he left us his name and address. How's he getting into all the places? Are they unlocked?'

'Probably,' Walsh said. 'But there's not much point asking the caretakers. They'll just swear they turn the key every time they leave a room.'

'Where are the meetings tonight?'

Ash checked through a file. 'There's one in Holbeck, round the corner from Marshall's Mill, and another in a church hall on South Accommodation Road. There should have been a third in Meanwood, but Mrs Cain has withdrawn.'

169

The mention of the name was enough to make them all pause for a second and think of the murder.

'Walsh, I want you on that church hall. Fowler, you can go to Holbeck. Spend the day watching in case he shows up to plant a bomb. Keep your eyes peeled around you, too. The way this character operates, he could be watching *you* and waiting for his chance.'

'Where do you want me, sir?' Ash asked after they'd left.

'I don't know. I do owe you an apology, though. All this should have been your case and I took it away from you.'

'I don't mind, sir.' He smiled. The colour had returned to his face after a good night's sleep. 'After all, you want to look after Mrs Harper.'

'I do. But it makes me wonder if I'm too close to see it all properly. If you want to do something, review what we have so far. See if we missed anything. Maybe I've made some mistakes.'

The thought had come to him as he sat on the tram into town. Maybe he'd missed something. Maybe the answer was right there, staring him in the face if he cared to look.

'We can get someone in if you like, sir,' Ash answered. 'But honestly, I don't think they could do it better. I trust you. We all do. Seems to me that this one's leading us quite a dance.'

'Then what's going to happen when the music stops?'

The papers on his desk had grown from a molehill to a mountain. He couldn't put it off any longer.

By dinnertime he'd made a dent in it all, but little enough to feel discouraged.

'Come on,' he told the inspector. 'I'll buy you something to eat.'

'I won't say no, sir, but I'm going to wonder what price I'll be paying for it.'

White's Chop House on Boar Lane. He was hungry, the food was decent, and on a superintendent's pay he could afford to splash out every once in a while.

'What do you make of Walsh?' Harper asked as they ate.

Ash cut the last piece of lamb from the bone and considered the question.

'It's early days yet, but so far he seems very good. Bright, and he fits in well with us. I can probably tell you more once he's found his feet. I think he'll work out well, though.'

'What's Fowler's opinion?'

'He's impressed, too. I think we have a keeper, sir.'

'Good. I thought he had the look about him.'

'Reminded you of yourself, sir?'

Harper chuckled. 'Maybe a little. But I wasn't ever as cocky as that.'

'If you say so, sir.' Ash wiped up the gravy with a slice of bread and chewed slowly. 'This investigation,' he began when he was done.

'Is turning up nothing,' the superintendent said. 'I know.'

'It's not that. We're doing everything right. There are just limits on what we can do. We don't have enough men to look after everything.'

171

'And we haven't had any luck second-guessing him,' Harper pointed out. 'Go on.'

'Last night he proved he could go anywhere and do what he wanted.'

'Agreed.'

'He was playing with us. Small bombs. A bit of a taunt, if you like. The next time is going to be far more serious.'

'Please tell me you know what he's going to do next.'

'I wish I did, sir.' Ash frowned. 'No crystal ball. But I think he'll go after Mrs Harper.'

The superintendent looked up quickly. 'Why?'

Ash settled his large hands on the tablecloth and stared at them before answering.

'She was his first target. He's gone for her twice now, three times if you include last night's little exercise. With all the others it's only been once.'

Harper nodded. He hadn't looked at it that way; he was too close to everything to see it clearly. Why Annabelle, though? Could the man be someone she knew, someone who'd taken against her in particular?

'Do you know when I'd do it, if I were him?' Ash continued. 'The night before Guy Fawkes. Mischief Night. It's always bedlam then.'

'No.' The superintendent shook his head. 'That's too close to the election. They vote the day after. The ballot papers would already be printed. He wants to make sure no women are on there at all. It needs to be sooner.'

When, though? And how?

* * *

172

Annabelle didn't have a meeting that night, a small lull before a full week of them. Harper was looking forward to a quiet evening at home as he sat on the tram. He wriggled his fingers; they still ached from signing and initialling all the reports on his desk. Still, everything was clear, at least until morning. More would be waiting for his attention then, appearing overnight as if the fairies had magicked them there.

But when he climbed the stairs from the Victoria and opened the door to the parlour, she was dressed to the nines. A new lilac frock with broad, leg-of-mutton sleeves and a purple bodice. A tiny bustle at the back, and brilliant white lace at the cuffs.

'I thought you had a free night,' he said, confused.

'I do.' She was looking into the mirror, adjusting the hat on her head before securing it in place with a pin. 'The hackney's picking us up at half-past, so you've just time for a wash and to change into your best suit.'

'Why? Has something happened?'

'I thought we deserved to go out. All three of us. Mary's putting on her sailor outfit. Now all we need is for you to get a move on.'

As he buttoned on a fresh collar and fastened his tie, he could hear Mary chattering away merrily. He really wanted to be at home, to stretch out and do nothing. But she deserved this. So did their daughter. Since the election campaign began, she'd spent most of her time with Ellen. And her behaviour since the attempted snatch had been almost too normal.

Yes, he decided, Annabelle was right. A meal out together might do them all some good.

Mary slept between them as the cab bounced and jolted its way back to Sheepscar. Her eyes had closed almost as soon as the horse began to move.

The meal had been tasty, Beef Wellington in a heavy gravy. They'd talked about the little things, everything remotely connected with the election carefully ignored for a night. He'd relished seeing his wife and daughter laugh together. Like a family.

He loosened his tie and collar stud and turned to look at Annabelle. She wore a dreamy look, hands clasped lightly in her lap.

'What are you thinking?' he asked quietly.

'What it'll be like after November the fifth?'

'You'll be a Poor Law Guardian. You'll be busy with meetings and God knows what.'

'I might not. Everything could be back to the way it was.' She gave a small laugh. 'Mind you, I'm not even sure I can remember how they were before this madness started.'

'You had more time to yourself. Apart from looking after the pub, the Suffragist meetings and all the other things.'

She laughed softly. 'You've made your point, Tom Harper. You know I can't just sit at home with my feet up.'

'I do, and I'm glad.'

The hackney pulled up in front of the Victoria. Lights blazed through the window. Someone was playing the piano, banging out the chords to *The Cat Came Back* as a few voices joined in.

174

Annabelle listened for a moment, then said, 'I wouldn't give this up for the world. Never.' Mary was still deep asleep, her body limp. 'Can you carry her? She's too heavy for me these days.'

He'd wanted an evening at home, Harper reflected as he drifted off to sleep. But as nights out went, this had been wonderful.

Eighteen

'Progress, gentleman?' Harper asked as he looked around the faces. Walsh stared at the ground. Fowler's mouth tightened. Ash sighed. 'Come on, there must be something.'

'Nothing more than we had yesterday, sir.'

'We're policemen,' the superintendent said. 'We should be able to come up with clues.'

'Some of the campaigns are faltering, I can tell you that,' Fowler said. 'Mrs Bolland only drew twenty to hers last night. And I heard Mrs Pease could only manage ten.'

'Almost fifty at the last one for Mrs Morgan, though,' Walsh added.

'They're not all going to win,' Harper said. 'No one ever believed they would. But they'll give the men a run for their money. That was the point. And our job is to make sure they have the proper chance. As long as the killer's still out there, that can't happen.'

'Where do you want us today, sir?' Fowler asked.

175

Six of the women were holding meetings tonight. Assigning the men anywhere was going to be a lucky dip. And no guarantee that anything would happen at all.

'I'll let Inspector Ash give out the assignments.' If nothing else, he could pass along the responsibility. He glanced at his pocket watch. 'That's all.'

Paper and dead leaves, sweet wrappers and cigarette ends caught in the wind and swirled along the gutter on the Headrow. But Leeds needed a good breeze to clean it up. Not that anything could leave it looking like a new penny. That chance was long gone. The Town Hall clock boomed quarter to the hour. He was in plenty of time for his meeting with the chief constable.

After the discovery of three bombs in one evening, he'd known he'd receive a summons. At least the chief was a fair man. Very fair, he hoped, since he had no suspects to offer.

'I'm going to get straight to the point, Tom,' Crossley said. 'Where are you on this case?'

There was nothing to be gained by lying or exaggerating. Not when lives were at stake.

'We've made some progress,' Harper said. 'But not enough. We don't have the faintest idea who's behind it.'

'We already have two people dead,' the chief constable reminded him.

'I'm very aware of that, sir. Believe me, I am.'

'That's not to mention the other incidents, sending uniforms out with the female candidates every day, and soldiers checking venues for bombs before a meeting.'

Stated baldly, it sounded like a long list. A damning one, too, as if every one of them was his failing.

'I know.' He nodded and accepted it.

'We're looking worse with every new thing that happens. Three bombs in one day? For God's sake, is he mad?'

'I think he probably is. Certainly when it comes to women in politics.'

'Be honest. Do you think you're too close to it all, since your wife's running for office?'

The big question. Exactly the one he'd asked Ash the day before. He thought about the inspector's answer before he replied.

'I don't believe so, sir. I think I can still do a fair job. And I have very good men working for me.'

'I'm not doubting any of that, Tom.' The chief leaned back in his chair. 'I know you and your people are some of the very best. But we need to close this case long before the election. I'm sure you can see that.'

'Of course.'

'I'll be honest. I'm wondering about bringing in someone from one of the other divisions to head up the investigation.' He held up his hand to stop any interruption. 'Not yet, no need to worry about that. And don't imagine I'm saying you've done a bad job. Quite the opposite. You've achieved wonders so far. Just that a fresh set of eyes might help.' He paused. 'Someone who's not quite so involved in things.'

Harper swallowed hard. 'Yes, sir.'

Funny, he thought. Yesterday he'd suggested the same thing himself, offering to stand aside. Now, faced with that as a real possibility, it felt like a slap in the face.

'I had a case taken from me once.' Crossley's mouth twisted into an awkward smile. 'It still rankles a little, I'll admit that. But looking back, it was the best thing to do. They solved it in three days. We can't afford to have too much pride. We need to catch the criminals, you know that.'

'Yes, sir. We do.'

'That has to be my concern in this. I need you to understand, Tom. I just wanted to let you know in advance that I might want someone else to handle things. For now, though, you're still in charge. You have a remarkable record.'

And one that would look tarnished if this case was handed to someone else.

'Thank you, sir.'

'And if I do need to bring anyone in, that won't change it in any way.'

'Yes, sir,' he replied, although he knew the words were a lie. It would stand there, a black mark in his career. A failure.

'I know you're doing everything you can. You've made some excellent progress. Finding that folk song connection was good. But what does it mean?'

'I haven't worked that out yet, sir. It seems to be his signature, or something.'

'We can ask when we catch him.' The chief picked up a pen and turned it end over end. 'I have faith you can do that.'

'Let's hope you're right, sir.'

'We both know the clock's ticking, Tom. But I can't let it tick forever.'

He was in no hurry to go back to Millgarth. He needed to think. He felt as if his skin was burning, that everyone would see the shame on his face. Bloody hell. His hands made fists in his overcoat pockets.

The real problem was that the chief was right. They needed the killer, and Harper was so deep among the trees that he couldn't make out the forest. Maybe it did need someone who could look at it all from the outside. But he wanted to arrest this man himself. He wanted to see his eyes as the cuffs went on, then have a few minutes alone with him in the cells. For Annabelle. And especially for Mary.

At least he had a little time yet. Crossley had given him that. He needed to make sure they used it well.

He found himself on Leeds Bridge, leaning on the iron parapet and staring over the water. Boats thronged the moorings by the warehouses, loading and unloading their cargos, three deep in places. The city was thriving. The pall of smoke from hundreds of chimneys was a testament to prosperity.

He wanted that man. And he was damned well going to have him.

The detectives' room was empty. They were all out, watching meeting halls. Harper gathered up the file and took it into his office to go through the pages and try to absorb it all. Every little

179

detail. By six o'clock he felt as if his head was bursting, and he was only halfway through. But Annabelle had a meeting tonight and he needed to be there.

'What's wrong?' she asked as they turned from one street to the next, exchanging one long terrace of back-to-back houses for the next. 'You were quiet all the way through supper and if your face was any longer you'd be tripping over it.'

He told her about the meeting with Crossley. She cocked her head and glanced at him as they walked.

'Would it be for the best?' Annabelle asked. 'If someone else took over.'

'I really don't know.' He let out a frustrated sigh. 'But I'm certain that I want to find this man more than I've ever wanted anything in the job.'

'Maybe you care too much.'

'That's more or less what the chief said,' Harper admitted. 'But it's important to me. Because of you and Mary.'

'He hasn't kicked you off it just yet, has he?'

'No.' He smiled wanly. 'He's giving me more time to finish it.'

'Then don't complain,' she told him. 'You still have your chance. You can do it, I know you can. Come on, there's the soldier boy outside the hall.'

'None of us spotted anyone suspicious around the halls yesterday, sir,' Ash said. 'I think we're wasting time we could use better than spending all day watching and hoping.'

'What do you suggest?' the superintendent asked.

'Something that involves hunting, not waiting,' Fowler said. 'He's out there. We're hanging about for him to make the next move.'

'Then how do we flush him out?' He looked at their faces. They didn't know the answer any more than he did. Harper was all too aware of the hours moving by. 'How? Until he acts again, we're helpless.'

'We know what he looks like, sir,' Walsh began. 'We know he speaks well, and his interests—'

'And that's all we know,' Harper said. 'That description is very general, and he might have set up that interest in folk songs to send us off in the wrong direction. Did you ever think of that?'

He'd only just considered it himself. But it was a possibility.

'If that really is the case, he's even more devious than we thought,' Ash said.

'Maybe he is.' He'd confounded them so far. The man had planned his campaign carefully. He would already have his next moves worked out. 'We need to disrupt what he wants to do.'

'Don't we need to know what he intends first?' Fowler asked.

'That's simple. He wants the women to drop out of the election. Nothing less will be enough. Only one has so far, and polling day is drawing closer. He might be starting to feel a little anxious.'

'He hasn't show any sign of it yet,' Ash said. 'What did you have in mind, sir?'

181

Harper shook his head. 'I haven't a clue. But let's do something quickly, gentlemen. Very quickly.'

The inspector lingered after the others had gone.

'I heard you had a session with the chief yesterday.'

He should have guessed that Ash would hear. It seemed no one on the force took a breath without him knowing about it.

'That's right.'

'I gather he's keeping you in charge of this.'

'For now. If we don't make an arrest, then yes, then he might appoint someone else to run the case.'

'The rumour is that it would be Superintendent Davidson. So we'd better see it doesn't come to that, sir. I haven't mentioned it to the others. They'd do their best, anyway. We all would.'

'Thank you.'

Ash straightened his jacket. It was tight on his big frame, the waistcoat stretched over his chest.

'I just wanted to let you know, sir. That's all. And I'll see if I can work out how to put a spoke in our friend's wheel.'

'I appreciate it.'

Loyalty, he thought as the door closed. Something that couldn't be bought. And he was grateful for it.

Exactly as predicted, the gale had blown itself out, leaving cloudy skies and temperatures that carried the first signs of winter. But everything

182

was so still, Reed thought as he walked to the police station on Spring Hill.

The last of the leaves had tumbled down, mounded in damp piles. A few branches lay in the gardens, torn off the trees. But all the violence of the storm had passed. He'd never realized nature could be so brutal in England.

'Bit calmer today, isn't it, sir?' Sergeant Brown said cheerily as he entered. 'The first blow of the season always cleans things out. And that was a fair wind.'

'Does it get worse than that?'

'Sometimes. That's when you stay inside and make sure everything's shut tight.' He pushed a folded piece of paper across the desk. 'This came for you first thing, sir. From Mr Pepper. He'd like you to call on him as soon as you can.'

Reed pursed his lips. 'Did he say why?'

'No, sir, that's all there is. Did you hear about the body washed up last night?'

'Body? What happened?'

'Old Ken Jones was walking his dog and spotted something just past the spa ladder out to the east pier. The Coast Guard pulled out the corpse.'

'Who was it? Do they know?'

'His face was battered, but they reckon it was Tom Barker.'

'I don't know him.'

'You would if you'd ever met him. Loved to play dominoes, always said he could beat anybody.' Brown sighed. 'He'll have his chance in heaven now, eh?'

* * *

183

'I heard about Tom Barker.'

'Yes,' Pepper said. He smoked his cigar and stared out of the window at the harbour. 'You worked out who he was, then?'

'Yes.' Reed lit a cigarette.

'I went to see the body first thing. He had a fair few injuries.'

'From the rocks, do you think?'

Pepper shrugged. 'Possibly. Or someone beat him to death then dropped him in the water.'

Reed let out a low, slow breath. 'How likely is that?'

'He was informing on smugglers. If someone discovered that . . .'

'We were very careful.'

Pepper turned. 'It doesn't matter. This is a small town. A *very* small town. You'd be amazed how many people see things. And how whispers get around.'

'What do we do now?'

Something caught his attention. 'We look. Come here. You might want that spyglass.' Pepper pointed at the pier. 'Tell me what you see.'

Reed focused the lens, until he could pick out the scene clearly, everything so close that they might have been just a few yards away. Two men whose faces he didn't know were preparing to push off in a boat. But he knew the third figure. Terrier John was talking to them urgently, waving his hands and giving orders.

'Interesting. But what does it mean?'

'I've heard a rumour that same boat went out yesterday straight after the storm had passed, too. Not for long. Funny, though, no one will confirm

184

it,' Pepper said. 'Do you fancy a walk on the cliff tops, Inspector? Maybe we can keep an eye on where they go.'

Reed smiled. 'That sounds like a very good idea to me.'

Nineteen

By four o'clock Harper could feel the frustration pounding in his head. He'd finished re-reading the file, and the killer remained as elusive as ever. Sometimes he imagined he had a glimpse of him, then it would fade to nothing like a will-o'-the-wisp, always just out of reach.

He hadn't managed to come up with a plan. How could you pursue someone who could switch from letters to bombs to threats to murder in the blink of an eye? How could you guess what he'd try next?

There were two meetings tonight. Annabelle had the evening off; she was probably already soaking her feet in Epsom salts. But he wouldn't have a chance to spend time with her. Not when he had the possibility of another copper taking the case hanging like an axe over his head.

He jerked up at the tap on the door. Sergeant Tollman, holding a letter.

'This came for you, sir, and that Mr Kidson and his niece would like a word.'

'Thank you. Show them in, please.'

The man was in his usual dark suit, his hair

brushed and tamed today. Ethel Kidson was the one with poise, he decided. She had a look of anticipation on her face, a faint smile, while her uncle appeared as earnest as ever.

'I think we might have found something for you, Superintendent,' she said.

'What is it?'

Kidson took a folded sheet of paper from his jacket.

'Some names. I've asked around everyone I know, trying to discover who's been looking for songs in recent months. It turns out there have been three more of them. That's all, I'm afraid.' For a moment he looked abashed. 'I told you it was a small field.'

'Quite honestly, we were surprised to find that many,' Miss Kidson added.

Harper looked at the list. All men. All three in Leeds. Names *and* addresses. He realized he was gripping the paper tightly.

'This is very, very helpful,' he told them gratefully. 'Do you know anything about these men?'

'I met Mercer once,' Kidson said.

'What does he look like?'

'He walks with a stoop,' the man replied after a moment. 'Has a beard. I'd say he's about sixty.'

'That's fine, thank you, sir.' No resemblance. One to cross off immediately. 'And the other two?'

'We don't know them at all,' Ethel Kidson said. She stood and smoothed down the front of her gown. 'We won't take up more of your time, Superintendent. I'm sure you have plenty to do. I hope this can help you.' She took her uncle by the elbow and led him out of the office.

186

'Ash, Fowler, Walsh,' Harper called. 'We have a couple of visits to make.'

Two men to each address. It would save time. He felt the hope pushing as the cab moved out to Headingley.

Across from him, Walsh was quiet, staring at nothing. Readying himself. It was the way Harper had been himself when he was younger and all this was still new. Back when there was the thrill of danger about everything in plain clothes. Now . . . there was still the joy of the hunt, but he'd learned not to grow too excited about every possibility. Too many of them turned out to be nothing.

The house lay in the streets behind St Michael's Church. Solid places, not rich, not poor. When he found the one they wanted, Harper sent the constable around to the ginnel to cover the back door. The usual procedure. The curtains were closed, but a light showed in the front room.

He took a breath, climbed the three steps to the front door, offered a quick prayer that this would be the man, and knocked.

And if it was him, it might end up being a while before the superintendent let Walsh in. There was payment due for trying to snatch Mary, for threatening Annabelle, and he intended to exact every last ounce of it. Resisting arrest, he'd call it, and who would say it was a lie?

He was smiling at the dream of it when the door opened to show a man of thirty, with dark hair and a thin moustache. He blinked quizzically.

'Can I help you?'

187

'Mr Reynolds?'

'That's right. Might I ask who you are?'

'I'm Superintendent Harper with Leeds City Police, sir. Are you the John Reynolds who's interested in folk songs?'

'I am,' he replied suspiciously. 'Why? What's this about?'

'Then I'll offer you my apologies, sir. I believe we have a case of mistaken identity.' He raised his hat and left. Dammit. A whistle brought Walsh from his hiding place. Harper glanced up at the church clock. A little after seven and dark now.

'Go on to Mrs Morgan's meeting,' he ordered. 'I'll be back at the office.'

Perhaps Ash and Fowler had enjoyed better luck, he thought as they rode the tram back into town. If they had him . . . but deep inside he knew it would be another dead end. This man they were after was clever. Too clever. He covered his tracks, and laid plenty of false ones.

Harper was right. A scrawled note on his desk simply read *Not him. Gone to meeting*. There was nothing else he could do here tonight. He might as well make his way home.

Harper walked. He'd just missed a tram. By the time the next one arrived he could almost be home. North Street was quiet, many of the businesses closed for the night, only the Hope Inn, the White Stag, and the Eagle spilling noise and light out into the darkness.

He stood on the other side of Sheepscar Street, looking at the Victoria with pride. Home. More comfortable and more welcoming than anywhere he'd ever lived. Home is where the heart is, that was what they said, and his was in those rooms above the bar, with Annabelle and Mary. Harper sighed with satisfaction. He was about to cross the road when he caught a movement at the corner of his eye and froze. Someone climbing over the wall, out of the yard behind the pub and into the ginnel.

He began to run.

There couldn't be more than fifty yards between them. The man turned his head as he heard the sound of feet, then began to sprint.

But Harper had a good start. He'd found his pace and he had a heart full of urgency and anger to spur him along. By the time they reached the end of the street he'd narrowed the gap to twenty yards. He was breathing hard, eyes ahead, ready to take this man.

A missing cobble. A gap instead of stone. His foot landed in the space and he started to fall, desperately flailing at the air for balance. Harper landed on his shoulder and rolled. He started to rise, pushing himself up with his hands.

By the time he was standing, the man had gone. Somewhere on the edge of his hearing he could make out someone running. Too far. Too late. He'd never catch him now.

Then the thought hit him. The pub. Christ.

He fumbled with his keys at the gate, darted through the back door, fingers awkward as he put a match to a lantern and the flame soared. Outside, in the yard, and there it was, right up against the building. A package. Exactly the same as the bombs the soldiers had defused

'Dan.' He took the barman aside, speaking

189

quietly. 'Get the customers out of here. All of them, as soon as you can.'

'Why? What's happened?'

'Tell them there's a gas leak, anything, but get them out.'

'Tom . . .'

'Now.'

Harper dashed up the stairs. Annabelle turned as he entered the room, her face bright with expectation until she saw his expression.

'What?'

'Fetch Mary and Ellen and get out. There's a bomb in the yard.'

For a second she couldn't speak. 'But—'

'Please, get out of here. Can you stay with Ettie Parsons?'

'I suppose so—'

'Go. As soon as you can.' He kissed her and ran back down the stairs. He needed a telephone.

'All taken care of, sir.' Sergeant Buckley stood under the gas lamp and brushed some dirt from his uniform.

'Everything's safe? You're certain of it?' Harper asked.

'Absolutely.'

They were standing on the other side of the road, staring at the Victoria. The exact spot he'd occupied when he'd seen the man. The soldier and Harper, Annabelle with them. She'd left Mary and Ellen with the Parsons and returned. At first he'd wanted to send her away again, to keep her safe, but this was her pub. Her livelihood. Her life, in so many ways.

190

'I have to say, sir, he gave me a couple of hairy moments,' Buckley said. 'Our friend has changed the wiring a little, and I had to work it out. But I'll pass that on to the boys for the future.'

Let's hope there weren't any more bombs, Harper thought.

'How close was it to going off?' Annabelle asked in a dry, cracked voice.

Buckley pushed his lips together, then said: 'It was set for the middle of the night.'

'And how much damage would it have done?' She stared at him. She wanted the truth.

'Enough,' Buckley answered finally.

'Come on in and have a drink,' Annabelle told him. 'I think you've earned it.' She reached out and took Harper's hand. 'I think we all need one.'

'I wouldn't say no to a drop of brandy, ma'am.'

While Annabelle and the soldier sat and talked inside, Harper trimmed a lamp and went out into the yard. He stared at the place where the bomb had been, breathing slowly and feeling the cold clamminess on his skin. If there was a bomb, there would be a piece of paper.

He finally found it folded and wedged into a window frame. The same writing, of course.

There was blood all in the parlour
Where my lady she did fall

Harper leaned his back against the brick wall. Luck, he thought. Sheer bloody luck. That was what had saved them. If he hadn't come home at just that time. If he hadn't caught a glimpse of the man leaving the yard. If . . .

They would all have been blown to Kingdom Come.

Harper had come so close to catching him. As it was, he hadn't even managed a decent sight of the man's face. No more than a hint of a feature.

'What are you thinking?' Annabelle put her arms around his waist.

'How we'd been lucky. Where's Buckley?'

'Gone back to the barracks. Where was it?'

'Over there.' He pointed.

'If it had gone off . . .' He held her as she began to shake, out in the darkness. Already he was working out how to make sure it didn't happen again, to stop anyone getting into the yard. A layer on concrete on the top of the wall with broken glass embedded in it. It would look more like a prison than a damn pub. It was extreme. But these had become extreme times.

Annabelle began to sob quietly. He kept his arms tight around her, not saying a word, letting her tears come. Sometimes even the strongest person needed a rock to crash against. He waited until it all subsided, until each jerk of her body became no more than a gentle hiccough. Slowly, he wiped the tears from her cheeks with his finger, and kissed her skin.

'For God's sake, Tom. I'm running for Poor Law Guardian, not Prime Minister. It's important to me, but it's just a tinpot election. Why is he doing this?'

'Fear?' he said and sighed. 'Maybe he thinks if women can stand now, soon you'll all be MPs. I don't know. I wish I did.'

192

So close, he thought again. So bloody close. Perhaps almost being caught would scare the man away. But he knew he was just hoping.

'Come on,' he whispered. 'Let's go to bed.'

Ash's frown deepened as the superintendent told him about the night.

'He's after your wife more than all the others. I said so the other day, sir.'

'I know.' He'd been worrying at the thought all night, try to come up with a reason he'd target her in particular. 'But he's hardly limiting himself to Annabelle, is he?'

'How is Mrs Harper, sir?' Walsh asked.

'Scared out of her wits but determined not to let anyone see it. She'd no sooner dropped off last night than she was awake again.'

'When you chased him, sir, were you able to see his face at all?' Fowler said.

'Not enough to register. He looked over his shoulder a couple of times, but it was there and gone. Middle height, quite agile. That's about it.' He shook his head and smiled wryly. 'Goes to show. They say coppers make the worst eye witnesses.'

'I think you were more concerned with bringing him down.'

'Did he leave words from another song, sir?' Walsh said.

Harper produced the paper from his waistcoat. 'Right here. I looked in Kidson's book, but I didn't see it. I'll go out there and ask him.' He looked at the men. 'I'm sure Inspector Ash has told you: if we don't catch him soon, the chief might bring in another officer to head up the chase. I don't want that. I don't think you do, either. So let's find him before any of that can happen. Understood?'

'I'm sorry, Superintendent, but my uncle's not here.' Miss Kidson sat primly on the edge of her chair, balancing a saucer in one hand, holding a cup with the other. 'He's out researching some pottery.'

'Pottery?' He wondered what that had to do with folk songs.

'It's a passion of his. He and my father wrote a book about the old pottery in Hunslet. Anyway,' she said as she replaced the cup, 'what can I do for you? Did the information we gave you help at all?'

'Unfortunately, none of those men was the one we were after. But I have another note. Like the last set of words, they don't seem to be from your uncle's book.'

'I'm sure I know this,' Ethel Kidson said as she read them. 'Give me a moment.'

She moved to one of the bookcases and took down a volume, going through the index, replacing it and selecting another.

'Here it is. The song's called *Lamkin or Long Lankin*.' She looked at him. 'It's in Professor Child's book.' Miss Kidson thought for a moment. 'I'm certain my uncle wrote about it in his column a year or two ago.'

Confirmation that their man read all Kidson's work, and saved it. But how did someone who loved old songs square with a man who could kill quite blithely, without conscience, who didn't baulk at destruction, who feared and hated women?

'You're very quiet, Superintendent,' Ethel Kidson said.

'I'm sorry. Too many questions in my mind.'

'If you have words from another song, does that mean he's struck again?' she asked. 'I didn't see anything in the newspaper.'

'He tried. Luckily no damage was done, no one hurt.'

'Good. As my uncle said, we feel that in some sense it's our fault, the way he's using these songs.'

'Don't,' he told her. 'You can't be responsible for a madman.'

'I've had men out searching the ginnels around the pub, sir. More doing a house-to-house, in case anyone happened to spot our friend.'

'Any luck?'

Ash smiled, the grin vanishing into his heavy moustache.

'As a matter of fact, I think we might have something.' He opened the drawer of his desk and pulled out a handkerchief. 'That's the very best lawn, sir, quite expensive. I think you'll agree it's not something most people in Sheepscar are going to own.'

'No.' If any of them possessed something of this quality, it would be in the pawnshop every Monday to put food on the table. It was a luxury, an extravagance. The material was plain, no initial embroidered on the fabric: any help like

195

that would be too much to hope for. But it brought them one step closer to him.

'There can't many places in Leeds selling anything this good,' the inspector continued. 'Fowler and Walsh are out checking. If we're lucky . . .'

If. A tiny word, but very big. If. He wasn't going to hold his breath and hope. It was too slim, no more than a thread. And threads had a habit of breaking.

'Let me know as soon as they find anything.'

Before he went upstairs at the pub, he checked the yard. Pointless, he knew; the man wouldn't be stupid enough to try the same thing again. But he needed to assure himself, to stop his heart racing.

In the parlour, Mary was curled up on the rug, fast asleep in front of the warm fire. Annabelle was sitting at the table, writing. She put a finger to her lips and tilted her head towards the kitchen.

'What's wrong?' he whispered. The only time Mary did that was when she was poorly.

'The headmaster brought her home during the morning.' Annabelle took a breath. 'She started crying in the middle of the class and couldn't stop. Didn't matter what they tried. I gave her some warm milk and cuddled her until she was done. We did a jigsaw puzzle, then she settled down there. She's been like that for the last two hours.'

'It's all coming out,' he said quietly. 'Last night, the snatching. Everything.'

She nodded. 'What am I doing to her, Tom?

196

For God's sake, I never dreamed it would be anything like this. It all seemed so simple. Straightforward. I've been sitting there trying to put together a letter withdrawing from the election.'

'Are you going to send it?' It had to be her decision. But he could only imagine the guilt and the fear that was surging through her.

'I'm not sure. Maybe.' She stopped talking, staring down at the ground. 'You know what Mary's like. Most of the time she's so sharp, so full of questions that I forget she's still a little girl. I don't want her hurt any more by all this.'

'I know.' He squeezed her hand.

'Then I think, if *I* don't fight for all this, how can I expect anyone else to do it? I want to win the battles now so Mary doesn't have to do it when she's older. I don't think I've been more petrified by anything in my life. But I'm a grown-up. I can see what he's trying to do. I can grit my teeth and keep going. Mary can't. Right now she's suffering for what I want to do, and she's not old enough to understand. How can I do this to her? The same as Mr Harkness, the caretaker at St Clement's. What did he have to do with any of this?'

'You're not the cause,' Harper told her. 'Don't go telling yourself that you are. That's what he wants you to think. It's him. No one else. Just him.'

'Oh, I know. I know it in my head. And you can repeat it till you're blue in the face. But I'm still trying to convince myself here.' She put a hand over her heart.

He could see the strain on her face and hear it in her voice. It had been building since the campaign began. Last night had come close to sweeping her over the edge. And now this, with Mary . . . but he understood his wife too well. Down at the core of her there was iron. She would never break. Yet she was the only one who could decide how much this was worth fighting for.

'You have to do what you feel is right.' He stroked her cheek.

'That's the trouble,' Annabelle said bleakly. 'I don't know. I can't think straight.'

Harper looked through the doorway at the little girl lying on the hearth rug. 'What are we going to do about her?'

'Whatever we can. Make sure she knows we love her and that we'll do everything to look after her. How much can anyone do?'

Nobody lived without their scars and pain. There were no guarantees of anything, they all knew that. In this world, it was impossible to become an adult without a litany of the dead trailing behind. Many of those he'd grown up with were already gone, and in twenty years it would be the same for Mary. That was reality. But that didn't stop him wanting to protect her, to keep her safe. But yes, how much could anyone do? Annabelle was right.

Mary woke quiet and a little dazed. After tea they listened to her read, and drew with her on a sheet of brown paper Annabelle had begged from the butcher. Harper told her a story once she was in bed, carrying on until her eyes were firmly closed and her breathing even.

She was different, he thought, muted, as if she'd put a little distance between herself and the world. But everyone coped in different ways. Everyone.

In the parlour, Annabelle sat and gazed into the flames.

'Thought any more about it?' he asked, and she nodded. 'Decided what you're going to do?'

Twenty

For a portly man, Harry Pepper could walk quickly. As they followed the rough path along the cliffs towards Sandsend, Reed was hard pressed to keep pace.

'Watch yourself near the edge,' Pepper warned. 'This stuff can crumble right under your feet. And it's not a pleasant drop on to the rocks.'

They kept an eye on the boat. Its sail was raised, and it stood a good quarter of a mile out to sea.

'Do you notice where we are?' Pepper asked.

'Isn't this close to where you arrested those smugglers?' Reed asked.

'The same spot, as near dammit.' His voice was thoughtful.

'What do you think they're doing?'

'Well, I doubt it's a pleasure cruise. No other craft close by.' He raised the spyglass to his eyes and looked over the water. 'They're moving out. Going where it's deeper.'

'What do we do now?'

'Wait,' Pepper said. 'And hope they don't decide to go round that point to the north or we'll lose them.'

'It looks like they've stopped again.'

'Yes.' He took up the glass once more and remained silent for a long time. 'I think they're hauling something on board. Maybe the Coast Guard missed something. Most of them aren't worth the cost of their uniforms.' He stood for a minute longer. 'Come on, let's get back to Whitby. I want to search that boat when it docks.'

He hurried off, arms pumping, and Reed followed.

'Contraband?' Reed asked.

'I wouldn't be at all surprised.'

'In broad daylight?'

'Why not? That's a fishing boat, out there, pulling something out of the water. Most people aren't going to give it a second glance. It's like hiding a tree in a forest. Come along, I need to get my men out, and alert the Coast Guard. See if they can do something right this time.'

They were waiting fifty yards away, hidden in the shadows, as the boat shipped oars and moored a few yards from the harbour office. Reed had spent the last five minutes watching Terrier anxiously pace up and down, watching the entrance to the harbour. As the fishing boat approached, he stood by a capstan, hands on his hips.

Pepper led the way, his men fanning out behind him. He placed a hand on Terrier John's shoulder and spoke a warning into his ear. Then he hurried down the wooden steps, another Excise officer right behind him. The Coast Guard drifted alongside in a small vessel.

Reed hung back. This wasn't his business; the police had no role here. He kept well away, smoking a cigarette. The two men from the boat were escorted on to dry land to stand with Terrier as Pepper searched the vessel. Finally he clambered back up, carrying a case of brandy.

'You haven't been too clever,' he told the captain. 'There's another one on board, too.'

The man said nothing, simply shrugged and spat. With a sigh, Pepper put the liquor on the ground and straightened his back. Then, in a swift, hard movement, he grabbed the captain by his jacket, lifting him until his feet barely touched the ground.

'Thought no one would notice another boat on the water, eh? You were wrong, Charlie Dennison, and you'll have some jail time to think about it. I'll have to see about impounding that boat of yours, too.'

'You can't do that.' That threat made the man explode with anger, pulling free and glaring, his hands curling into fists. 'That's my bloody livelihood.'

'You'll have a chance to think about it when you're behind bars, Charlie. There's always a price to pay.' He pushed the man away and nodded to other Excise men. 'Take him.' Pepper glanced at the others from the boat. 'Sam Carpenter, too. But maybe we'll hold Mr Millgate back for a quiet word.' To the Coast Guard he yelled: 'Tow the boat up to Whitehall Dockyard.' With a malicious grin, he looked at Dennison.

'Tell them it's government property for the moment. Evidence in a crime.'

'Why have you brought me here?' Terrier John asked once they were in the Excise office. He looked at the faces around him, all of them except Reed.

Harry Pepper took his time, filling his pipe from a pouch then tamping down the tobacco, before striking a match and puffing until his head was wreathed in smoke.

'You were there when a crime was committed, Mr Millgate. You seemed eager for their return and you were talking to them right before they left. That makes you as guilty as they are in my book. But you're an outsider here. You're certainly not a fisherman. I have to wonder about your involvement.'

'And you have a past,' Reed said.

The words made Millgate turn his head sharply.

'Sergeant Reed?' Terrier asked, as if he'd never noticed him before.

'Inspector Reed now,' Pepper corrected him. 'And you're a bloody awful actor, so don't even try. Now, Mr Millgate, why don't you tell us your story.' He puffed on the pipe again. 'I'll warn you, though, we already know a few parts, so we'll be able to tell when you're lying.'

'Well, what did you think of that?' Terrier John had been taken off to jail by one of the Excise men. Tomorrow morning he'd be up in court.

Reed lit a cigarette. 'I didn't believe a word. Just having a friendly chat and he'd promised to buy them a drink when they returned? He has too long a history for that.'

'What matters is if he can convince the magistrate,' Pepper said with a sigh. 'The trouble is, he probably can. He's an upstanding citizen here, remember, not a blot on his character in Whitby.' He puffed thoughtfully on his pipe. 'There's something else about this that worries me: why go out in the middle of the day to collect two cases of brandy? Especially right after Tom Barker's death. Seems to me that someone's trying to send us haring off in the wrong direction, and also portray your friend Millgate as quite the innocent.' He stared at Reed. 'Why, though? That's the question.'

'Tom?'

She stirred as he rose. Her voice was half-smothered by sleep.

'It's still early,' he told her. 'You can rest for a while yet.'

'I can't give up, can I?'

'No,' he assured her. 'You can't.' But whatever her decision, he'd back her completely. And between them, they'd take care of Mary.

'What have you found out about that handkerchief?' Harper asked.

'There are eight shops selling linen of that quality in Leeds, sir,' Walsh answered. 'Evidently it's about as good as you can buy. Definitely not cheap.'

'You know what to do this morning. Visit them all. I doubt if they can identify it, but try to get a list of all customers who've bought handker-chiefs like that in the last . . .' He tried to think.

'Let's say a year, sir,' Ash suggested.

'A year,' the superintendent agreed.

'If they even keep records like that,' Fowler said. 'Bought by men, or anyone?'

'A man.' He didn't hesitate in his reply. It seemed impossible to imagine their killer receiving gifts.

'The Irish Linen shop on Commercial Street,' Fowler said. It was late afternoon, still dry out no matter how the clouds seemed to threaten. The sergeant looked weary, but there was a smile on his face. 'They're certain it's one of theirs, although I've no idea how they could tell.'

'And do they know who bought handkerchiefs like that from them?' Harper asked.

Fowler shook his head and pushed the spectacles up his nose.

'Eight people have bought them in the last year. They can tell me when, how many, even the time of day they were sold. But no names. They don't write them down and the shop assistants don't remember; I asked. I'm sorry, sir.'

'Never mind. It was a good try. Well done.' The sergeant left the office.

What could they do, he wondered? What could they bloody do? He could feel each moment passing, like grains of sand in a timer. He wanted to be the copper to catch this man. He wanted to look into his eyes as he was arrested, to see the defeat and the hatred and the fear. Harper needed this victory.

Sergeant Tollman rapped his knuckles on the door frame.

'Sorry, sir, I meant to bring this through earlier.' He placed a letter on the desk. 'Another one from Whitby. Looks like you and Inspector Reed have a regular correspondence these days.'

'Terrier John.'

'Let's hope Mr Reed finds something good on him. We never nailed him for much in the past.'

He sliced open the envelope and read. The social things first, with the name and address of the hotel that Elizabeth approved. He'd drop them a line very soon, and have them reserve rooms over Christmas.

Then to the heart of the matter, about the smugglers, the arrest, the questioning of Terrier John and the way he protested his innocence. Harper glanced up at the clock on the wall. The man would have been up before the beak by now. Decision already made. He wished Billy well in getting his man for something. But he had more urgent things on his mind.

The parlour was full of women. He stood in the doorway, astonished at the sight. Young, old, in good gowns and cheap cotton dresses, they counted out piles of paper and tied them up with string, chattering merrily.

Annabelle moved from one to another, giving instructions, smiling and looking happy. There was no sign of last night's distress on her face.

'More leaflets arrived from the printer this afternoon,' she told him in the kitchen. 'We need to get them out tomorrow. They all volunteered to help.'

He searched her face, looking into her eyes.

'I'm fine, Tom,' she told him. 'Honestly.'

'And Mary?'

'She woke up this morning as if nothing had happened. No problems at school; I asked her teacher when I picked her up. On the way home she was her usual self, talking about the lessons.' Annabelle looked over his shoulder at the women moving around. 'Why don't you take her out for fish and chips? This lot will be here for a little while yet.'

Mary held his hand as they walked up Roundhay Road, chattering away, pointing out this class-room and that as they passed her school. No sign that yesterday her tears wouldn't stop falling. Had she purged it all from her system, he wondered? Could it really be that easy, that quick?

No, of course not. It would all return. But he couldn't do anything about the future. All he could take care of was the here and now.

The fish shop was small and steamy, with the greasy, welcoming smell of hot dripping. Cod and chips twice, doused in salt and vinegar and wrapped in yesterday's newspapers. He watched grease soak through on to another editorial about the election. At least someone had found a good use for it.

There was no rush to go home; the hurly-burly would go on for a some time yet. Instead he strolled with Mary, talking idly as they ate. Sometimes it seemed miraculous to him that this small person with thoughts and opinions, a girl so quick and bright, could be his. She seemed to remember everything she learned. She considered it, and asked questions when it didn't make sense. How long before she wanted to know things he hadn't a hope of answering?

Mary was precocious. Her teacher had told them so, looking dismayed while she said it, as if an intelligent girl might have some kind of curse on her.

They were lucky. They had to money to help her. When all her classmates vanished into service or the mills and factories once they were nine years old, their daughter could be properly educated. She'd have a chance, as much as the world would allow.

At the corner of Manor Street they leaned against the wall, watching all the carts and trams pass. Suddenly she looked up at him quizzically.

'Da, what do you know about—' she took a breath, concentrating to make sure she pronounced the word correctly '—rhinoceroses?'

God help him, Harper thought as he burst out laughing. There were years of this ahead of him.

'Sir,' Walsh said, 'I think we might have a sniff of him.'

'What?' Harper asked. 'Go on. How?'

'There was a man at the meeting last night who had a resemblance to the bomber. Well-dressed, greying hair. I know, there are plenty of those, but he seemed out of place there.'

'Which meeting?'

'Hunslet, sir. Mrs Morgan.'

'Did you talk to him?'

'He didn't do anything wrong so I had no reason to stop him. Just listened quietly, then left once it was over. I thought I'd wander off behind him and see where he went.'

'Spit it out,' the superintendent told him. 'You must have something.'

'He walked back into Leeds then caught a tram. It was almost empty, so I had to go upstairs. I got off the stop after him and ran back, but he'd gone.'

'Where was this?'

'Hyde Park, sir. Just the far side of Woodhouse Moor. Victoria Road.'

Miles away from Hunslet.

'Good work,' he told Walsh. 'This morning I want you out, talking to the beat coppers who cover that area. See if they recognize him at all. If they're any good at their job they should be able to narrow it down to a few men.'

'Gladly, sir.' He was grinning at the praise as he left.

'I wish he'd brought him in for questioning,' Ash said worriedly.

'So do I,' Harper agreed. 'I'd have done it. You would, too. But he's still new. He's finding his feet here. Sticking to the letter of the law.' He sighed. 'Still, I suppose we can't really go grabbing people off the street. Sometimes I wish we could. It would make our lives a damned sight easier. We're getting closer, though.' His mouth flicked into a grim smile. 'I can feel it in my water.'

Twenty-One

'What happened in court?' Reed asked. He'd dashed over to Custom House from the railway station after seeing the chief constable on to the Scarborough train. Inspection morning, a chance for the top brass to see how the new man was settling in.

It had gone well, he thought. Sergeant Brown and his bobby had cleaned the police station on Spring Hill so well that it seemed to glisten. The smell of beeswax, all the files carefully arranged and aligned, not a single scrap of paper out of place.

Reed was in his dress uniform, medal ribbons on his chest from his army service in Afghanistan, two more for bravery he'd earned when he was still walking the beat, the last pair for his work with Leeds City Fire Brigade. If nothing else, they added a splash of colour to the dark blue. And they impressed the chief, which mattered more.

He could breathe easily, for another six months, at least. But he'd missed Terrier John's court date. Now he hoped that Harry Pepper had some good news for him.

'Three months each for the captain and his man,' the Excise man replied. 'With fishing season over, that's not going to be a big hardship for them.'

209

'How about Millgate?'

'Not guilty, free to go.' He shook his head. 'Even the captain said your friend had nothing to do with it. He was probably paid to say that. I don't believe a word of it, but the magistrate did. Man of unblemished character and all that waffle.'

'No one brought up his record in Leeds?' Reed asked in disbelief.

'They didn't even come near it.' He reached into his pocket and pulled out his watch. 'It's dinnertime, near as dammit. Let's go and get something to eat. It might take this taste out of my mouth.'

'What do you think is going on?' Reed asked as they left the pie shop. One thing he'd noticed about Whitby; they didn't stint on the portions. Meat and potato pie with plenty of mashed potatoes and a hefty pile of carrots.

Pepper paused long enough to get his pipe going, and stared down Flowergate towards the harbour.

'I'm not sure. We took a small haul and put two men away. That makes us look efficient. They chanced their arm, going in the middle of the day like that. Maybe they thought we wouldn't notice. It's strange, though; normally they'd wait until dark to do their business. It makes me think they have something bigger going on. I'm starting to suspect your Terrier John has some power. He looked to be the one sending them out yesterday.'

'Add Tom Barker's death to that.'

'I know,' Pepper said with a nod. 'It *could*

be an accident. But with the timing I don't believe it.'

Reed smoked his cigarette as they cut through the ghaut, the little cut that led down to Pier Road.

'You know this area. What do you think they're going to do? And where?'

Pepper snorted. 'If I had the answers to those, I'd already have the culprits in custody. But I'm convinced Millgate's involved. He was lucky, that's all. I'll be keeping a close watch on him now.'

'If there's anything I can do . . .' Reed offered, and the Excise man smiled.

'I'm sure we'll find a few things. For a start, you can pick up the bill next time.'

'The bobbies have come up with ten possibilities,' Walsh said. It was late in the afternoon, already feeling like night. Rain was falling, and the pavements shone as if they'd been polished, reflecting the lights from the gas lamps.

'How many have you spoken to?' Harper asked.

'Five so far. I never knew how much of a warren it was back there. Miles of streets. But none of them is our man. I'm going back out there later to try and catch the rest.'

'He could be someone the uniforms didn't think about,' Fowler said. The others glared, and he set his jaw. 'Well, it's true. I don't care how good they are, they can't remember everyone. We've already said this man's big asset is his invisibility.'

He was right, the superintendent thought; this

211

whole time had been like chasing a ghost. But this was the best lead they'd had.

'Let's hope he's one of those on your list,' Harper said wearily. 'There probably won't be much of a turnout tonight in this weather.'

The piles of wood that children were accumulating on waste ground for their bonfires would be sodden. Dismal, he thought as he waited for the tram. But there were months of this ahead, an entire winter. Worse, probably, if snow arrived in January.

First, though, they had to find their killer. He wanted it to be one of the men Walsh was going to see. But somehow he couldn't summon up the faith to believe it. It all felt as if it was slipping away from him.

Harper stood at the back of the hall. The air was heavy with the smell of wet wool, the mood one of duty, not excitement. Even Annabelle had little inspiration as she spoke. She was going through the motions, not able to find the spark in herself.

The door opened with a loud squeak and Harper turned. A copper, still in his helmet, gazing around.

'What is it?' he hissed.

'Sorry, sir. Inspector Ash wants you at Millgarth.'

For a second he could hope they'd found the killer, then the uniform said: 'He asked me to tell you that they haven't caught him, but no one's hurt, either. His exact words, sir.'

Very enigmatic, Harper thought. It meant something had happened, but no damage done. He glanced over his shoulder at the stage.

'You stay here, then escort my wife home.'
'Yes, sir.'

'Now we know how he got Harry Cain, anyway,' Ash said. He sat at his desk with a half-drunk mug of tea in front of him, the surface of the liquid turned a thick, scummy brown. He ran a finger on each side of his moustache.

'Go on,' Harper said.

'You're aware that Mrs Lockwood is one of the Poor Law Guardian candidates, of course, sir.'

Harper nodded. He knew the names of all seven women so well he could have recited them in his sleep.

'She had a meeting tonight,' the inspector continued. 'Her husband, his name's Charlie, he's not been well for a while, so he stayed at home. About half an hour after she left there was a knock on the door. When he answered it, a chap was standing on the step. Said he was one of her volunteers. She'd left some notes she needed, and could he come in and pick them up.'

'A fairly plausible story.'

'Possibly, if Charlie Lockwood had ever seen him before. With everything that's happened, he was on his guard. He said no, then this man tried to barge his way in. Didn't manage it, because Charlie's a big lad, then he gave up and went tearing off down the street.'

'That's some good news, at any rate.'

Ash began to smile. 'It gets a little better, sir. Turns out Mr Lockwood is a dab hand at drawing with a pencil.'

213

'We have a sketch?'

With a flourish, the inspector opened his desk drawer and pulled out a sheet of paper, like a magician performing his best trick.

'It was too dark to see the man's face properly, and he had his hat pulled down, but . . . yes, sir, we do.'

Harper picked it up by the edges, handling it as if it was a rare work of art.

Ash was right; Lockwood was a natural artist. There was a sense of the man in the drawing, as if he could almost step off the paper and into the room. He was alive and moving. But there was little detail in the face. The suggestion of shape in the nose and the cheekbones, enough to give a feel – and the rest hidden in shadow.

'It's very good . . .' Harper began.

'I know, sir. It's not going to help us catch him.' He paused and squinted at the page. 'You feel he's right there, though, don't you?'

'If only he were.' The superintendent handed the sketch back. 'One thing – he's failed again.'

'Agreed, sir. Funny, though, even his failures are successes in a way. They all spread that seed of fear and doubt. I don't want to imagine what Mrs Lockwood is feeling right now.'

'I can guess,' Harper told him. 'All too well.' He sighed. 'Have you had the uniforms on a house-to-house?'

'They haven't turned anything up yet. But we're getting closer, sir. Each time we have a little bit more.' He put a heavy finger on the drawing. 'This. The handkerchief. The man Walsh followed on the tram.'

'Who wouldn't have been home tonight because he was out trying to kill Mr Lockwood . . .' Harper picked up the thought.

'That could narrow it down.'

Could, might, should, ought to. Words he'd heard too often. He felt a wave of exhaustion rise in him, all the anticipation and excitement flooding away.

'Let's see what we have in the morning.' At the door, he turned back. 'It's good work. And you're right. We're closer. That hand's coming down on his collar very soon.'

But would it be soon enough?

Annabelle was standing in the doorway of Mary's room, staring at their daughter. He felt a moment's panic when he saw her, thinking that something had happened. But the ghost of a smile crossed her face as she moved towards him.

'Just checking,' she said quietly. 'Sleeping like a lamb. And she was her old self tonight, Ellen said. Questions coming out of her ears. Maybe it was just a blip.'

'Maybe,' he agreed, although they both knew that nothing was ever resolved so easily. Or so quickly.

'And your trouble can't have been much if you're back so soon,' he told her as they undressed and washed. Lying in bed, his arm around Annabelle's shoulders, her head lying on his chest, he could feel her voice as much as hear it.

'Nobody hurt. That's something.'

'I'll take any good news at all,' he said. 'I just want to be there when we catch him.'

215

'So do I. I have a bone to pick with him.'

'The meeting seemed quiet tonight.'

'Yes,' she agreed. 'I couldn't find any oomph.' She snuggled closer. 'It'll come back.'

'How many of those men do you have left to see in Hyde Park?' Harper asked.

'Three, sir,' Walsh answered.

'You know what happened last night. You've seen the drawing.'

It was pinned to the wall, staring down at them like an accusation.

'He's still laughing at us,' the superintendent continued. 'And he's got the luck of the bloody devil. Let's see if we can wipe the smile off his face today.' He turned to Fowler. 'Go back to that Irish linen shop. See if anyone's memory has been jogged.'

'Yes, sir.'

'And, Walsh,' Harper added as the men rose to leave, 'if any of those men bear even the smallest resemblance to that drawing, I want them down here before they can say a word. Understood?'

'Done, sir.' He smiled. 'My pleasure.'

The office was quiet as Harper began to plough through his paperwork. Sometimes bad hearing could be a blessing; it kept the world at bay and let him concentrate. But he'd barely been at it for ten minutes when he was disturbed by a tap on the door.

'Mind if I come in, Tom?'

Superintendent Davidson, the head of C Division, with a tentative look on his face.

216

'I'm not disturbing anything, am I?'

'Just the usual.' He waved a hand at the pile of folders on the desk.

'I won't feel too guilty, then.' He sat down and reached into his jacket for a cigarette.

'Come to take over the bomber case, Peter?'

'No, no. You've heard that rumour, too?'

'The chief said he'd give me a while before he brought someone else in.' Harper shrugged. 'Someone told me it was going to be you.'

'If it is, I've heard nothing official. That's why I stopped in. I wanted to let you know. As far as I'm aware, Crossley hasn't talked to anyone about it yet.'

He felt a surge of relief, as if someone had removed a noose from his neck. It was still no more than a thought in the chief constable's mind.

'I appreciate that.'

'Starting to feel the pressure?'

'Yes. Even more with my wife involved.'

Davidson nodded. 'Can't be easy. I won't say that I think women in politics is a good thing. But the law's the law. And it looks like this killer of yours doesn't care who gets hurt. Is that him?' He nodded at the sketch.

'Done by someone he tried to kill last night.'

He let out a low whistle. 'He drew that straight after? I'm impressed.'

'I came within a few yards of him myself a few evenings ago.'

'I heard about that. A bomb at your pub. Horrible. Cowardly. I just wanted to tell you that all of us are behind you on this, Tom. None of us are looking to supplant you. We'll do every-thing we can to help you.'

'Thank you.'

'If one of us arrests him, we're happy to arrange for him to disappear for a few hours so you can talk in private.'

Harper grinned. 'Thank you.'

'You'd do the same for us.' He stood. 'Anyway, it was just a quick visit to put your mind at rest.' He glanced at the sketch again. 'Nasty looking sod. We don't need characters like him around.'

The *Evening Post* appeared around noon, the paperboys crying out the headlines as they tried to hawk copies on the street. Harper counted out tuppence and glanced at the headlines on his way to dinner. More celebrations in Australia and New Zealand for the Queen's Diamond Jubilee. All the fuss and parties felt like a lifetime ago. Had it really only been four months since they'd been waving flags and cheering?

At the George on Briggate he sat down to cottage pie, feeling the building rattle as trains passed on the viaduct. He leafed through the newspaper, glancing at a paragraph here, a head-line there. Very little to interest him. He didn't care about tittle-tattle of grandees from the empire and he wasn't much bothered by whatever they were debating in Parliament.

He turned to the editorials. An amusing one about a London taxi driver convicted for drink driving. And then one to make him push the paper away before his blood began to boil. More about the fitness of men for elected office and how women were too delicate to become involved in politics, in case they should become nervous and hysterical.

Harper looked at the author's name, expecting Hotchkiss, but it was simply credited to the editorial board. He tried to finish his meal, but suddenly it had become tasteless.

He hoped some of the women would win on polling day, if only to give a black eye to men like this. It would do them the world of good.

And it would show their killer that he didn't have a chance of stopping history.

Twenty-Two

'What do you have for me this morning, Sergeant?' Reed asked as he entered the police station on Spring Hill. The morning had been sharp as he walked down, but not bitter yet. When he first arrived in Whitby, one of the neighbours had said the place seemed to have its own weather. It made no sense at the time, but now he was beginning to understand. He'd been over in Sleights the day before, no more than four miles away, and found the morning frost still white on the ground, most of the plants died back for winter. On the coast the earth was still green and alive.

'Absolutely nothing, sir,' Brown answered with relish. 'Things went well with the chief constable, did they?'

'He seemed happy enough when I saw him on to the train.'

'I heard there were some smugglers in court yesterday. Mr Pepper must have been happy.'

'I daresay he was. Do you know them?'

'Charlie Dennison is my cousin's sister's husband. Good sailor, but none too bright.' The sergeant gave a sour grin. 'That chap from Leeds got off, though.'

'So I heard,' Reed said. He still wasn't sure how far he trusted Brown in all this. The web of family was heavy here. Some things were better kept to himself. Terrier John would certainly be out and gloating today, demonstrating that the law couldn't hold him.

Towards dinnertime he strolled into town. Along Pier Road and past the moorings the smell of fish persisted; it probably never vanished completely. The gulls paraded and flew, hoping for something to scavenge.

Men worked on their vessels, cleaning and starting on their winter repairs, while others stood and talked with them. Reed stood at the end of the pier staring at the waves. The tide was out, sand packed hard; not a single footstep disturbed the surface. On the other side of the river, women searched for limpets in the tide pools, gathering them in wicker baskets, calling to each other and laughing.

Strolling back, he saw the Terrier chatting with a group of fishermen. He looked happy, like the cock-o'-the-walk with his tale to tell. Time to prick that balloon, he decided.

'Good morning, Mr Millgate,' he called, and

the man turned expectantly at the sound of his name. 'A good decision for you in court yesterday.' Reed raised his hat. 'My congratulations.'

'Thank you, Sergeant. Sorry. Inspector.' John's eyes were suspicious. His companions stared at him.

'You must have been pleased to be believed.'

'Of course.'

'Relieved, too, after all those sentences you've served in Leeds in the past.'

If looks could have killed, the gaze would have felled him on the spot. But Terrier composed himself.

'A new life, a new man.'

'A rich one, too.'

'Comfortable,' Millgate replied.

'Exactly,' Reed agreed with a smile. He started to walk away, then said. 'That matter we were discussing the other day . . . I'll find you when you're not so busy so we can continue. Good day.'

He strode off briskly. With luck, that might raise a few suspicions. Drop a stone in the pond and see how far the ripples travelled.

'I'm flummoxed, sir,' Walsh said. 'I saw those other men in Hyde Park, but there's not one of them who's our killer. And none of them were at that meeting in Hunslet. I'm positive about that.'

'Then he must be one the beat bobbies don't know,' Harper said. 'It happens.'

Invisible in his respectability. Damn. And the assistants at the Irish linen shop hadn't been able

221

to help. All they had was the drawing. Good as that was, it remained vague and incomplete.

'I should have brought him in when I saw him.'

Yes, the superintendent thought. But Walsh had stuck to the law, and there was no point in regrets.

'You said he went down Victoria Road?'

'Yes, sir. I'm positive of that.'

'Then be there early tomorrow morning. Keep watching the men on their way to work. He may well be among them. And you know what to do if you see him.'

'No hesitation this time, sir.' Walsh smiled and left.

Ash stretched out his legs and let out a long sigh.

'That sounds a bit desperate, if you don't mind me saying so, sir. Like going fishing and not taking any bait.'

'We *are* desperate.' Harper grimaced. 'Unless you've had any sudden ideas.'

'I wish I did. I was talking to my Nancy about it last night. I thought she might spot something we've missed.'

'Did she?'

He shook his head. 'She doesn't see what else we could do.' He glanced at the sketched pinned on the wall. 'If that was better, we could ask the newspapers to run it. As it is . . .'

As it was, they were still nowhere. They knew plenty about their man, just not enough to identify him.

'Then we'll keep on with what we've been doing. All those failures must be tearing at him. That's when mistakes happen.'

'We'd better be ready to pounce.' Fowler looked up as he spoke. 'Not give him a chance.'

'We will be,' Harper told him. 'Ready and willing.'

'Did you see it?' Annabelle asked as soon as he walked through the door. Her voice bubbled with pleasure.

'See what?'

'In the paper.' She picked it up from the table and held it out. 'Right there.'

The letters page. From the Suffrage Society in support of their six women candidates. Signed by Isabella Ford, it was sensible and compassionate, laying out the values and qualities they represented. The compassion, the fairness.

Eloquent, but would it really sway any minds, Harper wondered? Still, everything helped.

'She writes well,' he said.

'I thought it would make a good poster. We need something new. People don't even notice the old one any more.' She was bustling around the room, not settling at anything for more than a few seconds. 'Mary's having her tea at Maisie's house. I said you'd go over for her at seven.'

'Busy day?'

'The usual. Leaflets and door-knocking.' She shrugged. 'I think the people round here must be sick of the sight of me by now.' She shook her head in wonder. 'I'm certainly sick of hearing my own voice.' She gave him a pointed look. 'And if you're thinking of saying a word about that, don't.'

He laughed. 'My lips are sealed.'

'Good. I need to prepare for the hustings tomorrow.' The second debate between the candidates. With the election looming, it should draw a large crowd. If the bomber was targeting Annabelle more than the other women, maybe he'd show his face there. 'The rumour is that the Tories have given up on Wilkinson. They know he doesn't have a chance here,' she said. 'Oldroyd doesn't seem to be gaining much support, either. People think he's too young.'

There was some truth in that, Harper thought. The man looked like he was barely old enough to shave; how could he expect to be taken seriously as a candidate?

'It's between you and Moody, then.'

'The old system and the new ideas.' She raised an eyebrow. 'That draws the lines clearly, doesn't it?' She flitted from table to sideboard to mantelpiece.

'What's wrong?'

'I'm nervous about it.' Annabelle hesitated. 'And scared by everything.' She sat down for a moment, on the edge of a chair, as if she was immediately ready to rise again. 'There are two women who have a real chance of winning in this election: me and Mrs Pease. I'm not being hopeful or boasting, Tom. That's what people reckon. If this man can stop the two of us, he'll achieve what he wanted. I just have this horrible feeling that someone else is going to end up dead before it's all over.'

'We're going to make certain that doesn't happen.'

'Can you?' She stared at him. 'Honestly? No flannel, can you do that?'

'No,' he admitted. 'But we'll do everything we can.'

The statement seemed to satisfy her. Annabelle's mouth moved into a dark smile.

'Go downstairs. Have a drink or something. Give me a little time to do my work.'

He bypassed the bar and went out to the back yard, checking quickly behind the crates and barrels. Everything safe, nothing worse than a rat that scurried away. He let himself out through the gate. With luck he'd reach the doctor's surgery before it closed.

He had to insist on using their telephone. The doctor had left for the day and the young woman at the desk was reluctant to give permission. Finally, Harper leaned on his rank. Police business. He asked the operator for Millgarth Police Station.

It was strange to hear Ash's voice without seeing his face.

'You caught me right as I was leaving, sir. Off to one of the meetings.'

'I want more men on Mrs Pease.'

He noticed the hesitation.

'I'll arrange it, sir. Do you have a tip?'

'Supposedly she and Annabelle are the two who might win their elections. If you were our man and wanted to stop everything, who would you go after?'

'Point taken, sir. But what about your wife?'

'I'm here, and there's Martinson during the day.'

Ash coughed gently. 'I wonder if it might be worth having someone keep watch on the pub at night, sir. Especially after what happened.'

225

Harper opened his mouth to speak, then closed it again. The idea made sense. He'd promised Annabelle the police would do everything they could.

'Yes,' he said. 'You'd better assign someone.' He chuckled. 'The chief will go through the roof at the budget.'

'He'll do worse if anything happens.'

On the way home he stopped to collect Mary. The Taylors lived at the top end of Manor Street in a terraced house that always smelled of soap, as if everything had been freshly washed. Arthur Taylor had started at the brick works in Burmantofts when he was nine. Twenty years later he was still there, a foreman now, a man who took his delight in sensational novelettes and the racing pigeons he kept in his yard. Every time he visited, the constant cooing of the birds felt like a gentle lullaby at the edge of Harper's hearing.

He wasn't allowed to leave until he'd had a cup of tea, while Mary packed her satchel. Then the walk home, hand in hand. He searched her eyes for any hint of fear or pain, but found nothing. Instead, she told him every detail of her day, all the things she'd learned. Full sentences, not stumbling over words, either. It was hard to believe she'd barely started at school.

The copper was at the end of the ginnel, a heavy cape over his uniform. He rocked from one foot to the other, smiling and saluting as he spotted the superintendent.

'Had the duty all night, Bryant?' Harper asked.

'I have that, sir. Shift over soon as the day man arrives. I've hardly seen a soul, and definitely no troublemakers. We can't have anything happening to your missus, can we?'

'No. We certainly can't have that.'

'My wife reckons we need more like her.'

'Speaking for myself, Constable, I think one Annabelle Harper is quite enough.'

'How's the protection on Mrs Pease?' Harper asked.

'Up to snuff, sir. She's been back in her own house for a little while and I've made sure someone's watching the property while she's out. No trouble last night. And there's one on yours, too.'

'Bryant. I saw him this morning. We have hustings tonight. I don't believe our friend will be able to keep away. Walsh, you think you've seen him, so I want you at Mrs Pease's event. Fowler, you go with him. If there's anyone you suspect at all, haul them out and question them.'

'Yes, sir.'

'Where do you want me?' Ash asked.

'Here, in case there's trouble anywhere else.' He could see how the long, fruitless days were wearing on them all. 'It can't be much longer now. He needs something decisive well before election day. And if there's one small consolation, gentlemen, it appears that Chief Constable Crossley doesn't intend to replace me on the investigation after all. At least not yet. So you're stuck with me.'

'I daresay we'll manage, sir,' Ash told him with a grin. 'Hard as it might be. What do you want us doing before tonight?'

Twenty-Three

'Can you carry these, Tom?' She handed him a bundle of paper tied with string. 'The new leaflets. I had them printed up today, and I thought this would be a perfect time to put them out.'

Annabelle didn't seem nervous. Instead she looked perfectly calm as they walked through the back streets. She wasn't wearing her best dress, he noticed, but one that was two years old. Just enough out of fashion to look past its prime. And not silk, but fine wool, long enough to sweep at the ground, and with a hint of a bustle at the back. The cape that kept her warm was one she'd owned as long as he'd known her, one she still wore every winter. But not for best.

She'd picked her clothes very precisely, Harper decided. Well-dressed, but without overdoing anything. She greeted people, asking after families, talking to wives about their husbands who were customers at the Victoria.

By the time they reached the hall she stood a little taller and appeared more confident. Her supporters were already there, a knot of them clustering around her. The soldier from the Engineers had left after giving the place the all-clear. Harper busied himself by putting a leaflet on every chair, glancing up to watch each new arrival. The constable on duty was attentive and alert.

Moody appeared with a large, boisterous group trailing behind him. Harper assessed their faces, searching for his man, but no sign of him. Oldroyd turned up with a gaggle of Labour supporters. But his face was careworn, as if he already realized he didn't have a chance in this election. Finally, not even five minutes before the start, Wilkinson came through the door, only three others beside him.

This time the moderator didn't call on Annabelle first. He'd learned that lesson. Instead it was Wilkinson, then Oldroyd. That gave the crowd a chance to barrack and shout, to be ready for the main attractions.

Harper circulated, inside the hall and out. The constable kept an eye on the crowds, ready to step in if things grew too rowdy. The streets were quiet, nobody lurking around.

The hustings had pulled in at least two hundred and fifty people. The hall was crammed and hot, women fanning themselves with Annabelle's leaflet; at least it was doing some good, he thought wryly. Plenty were here for the politics, but the crimes surrounding this election had attracted more.

Not the killer, though. He hadn't spotted anyone resembling their man. Not a soul acting suspiciously.

Moody's crew tried to give Annabelle a rough ride as she spoke. They attempted to drown her out, but she wasn't having any of it. The years speaking for the Suffrage Society had taught her well; she could modulate her voice without effort, making sure she was heard, and she had stinging comebacks for all the hecklers. She made people laugh and think at the same time. It was a rare quality, Harper thought. Very rare. And she spoke with passion. She believed.

He found himself caught up in her voice. Not because she was his wife, but because she had things to say. Real things, important things. She listened to the questions that were asked and tried to offer honest, straightforward answers. None of the usual guff that edged around the topic and ended up saying nothing at all.

She had them. He looked at the other candidates' faces. They knew it, too. Even Moody looked worried, his usual, complacent expression scrubbed away. Now he was no more than a portly old man in a frock coat and high collar. No importance about him at all as he stood at the lectern and smoothed out his notes like a man already defeated, someone seeing an era change before his eyes and not understanding why.

His supporters were loud in their cheers. Then a voice cried out, 'Let's make her wish she'd never run!' and the mayhem began.

He couldn't pick out the man who'd yelled, but before he'd even finished, Harper was wading into the group. He'd brought his truncheon and now he used it, hoping the bobby was doing his bit.

Fists hit him, but they didn't do any damage. Bruises, nothing more. But he was trained, and he was ruthless. He had someone worth defending.

By the time it was done, he was covered in sweat and panting as if he'd run five miles. His jacket was ripped, and he could feel a small trickle of blood down his cheek. The men who could still walk had fled. Some lay groaning on the floor. One was out cold, another cradled a broken wrist. More were bleeding and dazed. Harper didn't care; they'd brought it on themselves.

How long had it lasted, he wondered? It felt endless, but it couldn't have been more than two minutes at most. He looked around. The hall had cleared, chairs were knocked over, the doors stood open wide. The candidates had all vanished from the stage. Where was Annabelle?

He took a pace and felt a hand on his arm. The copper, looking the worse for wear but grinning widely and nodding at the group nursing their wounds.

'Do you want me to get a wagon to take them away, sir?'

'Yes,' he said, and hurried off. In his head, the panic was rising.

She was out on the pavement, her supporters gathered around her. Guarding her. Harper closed his eyes and felt relief wash over him.

'Tom,' she said, concern growing on her face as she made out his injuries. 'My God, are you all right?'

'Fine.' He realized he was still gripping the truncheon tightly, and slid it into his jacket, wiping his damp palm. 'Did they hurt you?'

'I came out the back way.' She had a stunned expression. 'What happened? I heard that man, but . . .'

'He came to start a riot,' he told her. 'Moody's people.'

'I thought it was *him*,' Annabelle said. 'It made my hair stand on end.'

'You're safe now.'

She nodded absently, pulled a handkerchief from her sleeve, spat on it, and dabbed at the cut on his temple.

Had it been the killer behind all violence? He hadn't seen the speaker, but he could still hear the voice clearly. And he could have sworn no one resembling their man's description had been in the hall. All it took, though, was to miss one small thing.

Most likely he'd never know the answer. Tempers flared at political meetings. Violence was common enough. He'd waded into far worse before.

'Why?' Annabelle asked as they walked home. 'Why do they need to do it? Why can't they just talk?'

'You already know the answer,' he said.

'Because they're men and it makes them feel like they're someone.'

'Partly.' Nothing was ever quite that cut and dried, he'd learned. They were angry, frustrated at their own lives, and they were powerless to change things. Win or lose, fighting gave a momentary outlet. The physical satisfaction of bone on flesh. And for men who'd never had a chance to learn the words to express how they thought and felt, it was the only way.

By the time they reached the Victoria all the glow of battle had faded; only the aches and pains remained. He ushered Annabelle inside, then wandered round to the ginnel. Bryant was there, standing so still he might have been made of stone.

'Nothing?'

'Not back here, sir. Sounds like they've been having a high old time inside, though.' He caught a glimpse of Harper's appearance. 'Ructions at the hustings, was it?'

'A bit of a scrap.'

'I miss those,' Bryant said wistfully. 'We used to have plenty of 'em in the old days. Do you remember, sir?'

He could recall it well enough, but he didn't miss those times at all. Policing by sheer force. It wasn't that long ago.

'You'd better keep a sharp watch tonight. After that, he might be in the mood to try something.'

'Having an extra man to watch Mrs Pease's house turned out to be a good idea, sir,' Ash said.

'Why? What happened?' He could feel every part of his body this morning. Aches and soreness where he'd forgotten he even had joints and muscles. The bruises had bloomed on his face. His skin had been tender as he shaved.

'The constable on duty spotted someone walking around the neighbourhood just after midnight. A well-dressed man. He didn't look as if he belonged there. But as soon as he approached him, the chap ran off.'

'Did he chase him?' Harper asked. 'Did he catch him?'

But they were pointless questions. The answers were obvious.

233

'It was PC Cannon, sir. He's not quite built for running. And he said his orders were to stay at the property.'

God save him from coppers with no initiative, Harper thought. 'Did he at least get a decent look at him?'

'The man was careful to stay clear of the gas lamps. Cannon says he couldn't see much.'

Cautious, dangerous, going for a vulnerable woman, running off at the first sign of danger . . . it sounded like their man.

'I suppose we should be thankful for small mercies.'

'At least this time we were one move ahead of him,' Fowler added.

That was true, but he couldn't find any satisfaction in it. They hadn't arrested him. Next time he'd have another idea.

'I want the area searched,' he said. 'Maybe he dropped something from one of his songs. The same with the hustings hall from last night. The caretaker should have cleaned it up. Walsh, you can handle that. The new man gets the dirty jobs.'

'Yes, sir.'

'Seems to me we've got him on the run a bit,' Ash said once they were alone. 'Nothing he tries is working any more.'

'He's clever. He'll come up with something different,' Harper told him. 'It's not over yet. Not by a long chalk.'

'Da,' Mary said when she saw him that evening. 'Have you been fighting?'

She stood on tiptoe, peering at his face and

234

frowning. She'd been asleep when they returned the night before, and he was gone before she woke.

'I've been doing my job,' he explained. 'Sometimes it can be rough.'

'Miss Mobley said it's wrong to fight. She told us all when Clem and Arthur started in the playground.'

'She's right,' he agreed. 'But being a policeman means that sometimes you have to stop people fighting, even if they don't want to.'

She considered that. From the corner of his eye, Harper could see Annabelle in the kitchen, listening to the conversation.

'Couldn't you punish them? Keep them in after?'

He tried to hide his smile.

'That's what we do sometimes. Going to jail is a bit like that, but worse.'

'What did you do to the ones who hit you?' For a fraction of a second, her eyes glistened with excitement. 'Did you batter them?'

'That's enough of that, young lady,' Annabelle called out sharply. 'Your da doesn't batter people.'

But that was exactly what he'd done. They'd threatened his wife and he'd relished his revenge. Not that he'd ever say so to Mary. Or to Annabelle.

No meeting tonight, and he wasn't going to be tempted out of the house. All day long he'd been looking forward to a hot bath to soak away all the pains of the night before. A few years earlier, Annabelle had spent money on a boiler. Hot water from the tap instead of heating pan after pan. It

235

had seemed like a luxury, but this evening he'd gladly indulge himself.

He'd barely settled in the water, just starting to feel the heat soak into his joints, when she opened the door.

'Detective Constable Walsh is here,' Annabelle said.

Never a moment's peace, Harper thought. The responsibility of rank.

'What does he want?'

'He says it's important, Tom.'

'Hell.' All he wanted was a little peace and quiet. But he knew the man wouldn't have come if it wasn't urgent. 'Tell him I'll be there in a minute.'

'Leave the water,' she said as he climbed out and began to towel himself dry. 'I'll have a bath myself. It'd be a shame to waste it.'

He remembered growing up. Bath nights when the zinc tub was taken down from the wall in the kitchen. His father first, then all through the family. He was the youngest, and the water was filthy and almost stone cold by the time his turn arrived.

'I saw your eyes when you came out of that hall last night,' Annabelle told him. 'You enjoyed it, didn't you? You did give them a battering.'

'I was trying to keep order. I wanted to look after you, to make sure no one hurt you.'

She had an ocean of sadness in her eyes. 'That's one of the reasons I'm fighting this election. To show that women can do things, that we don't need men taking care of everything. I'll tell Mr Walsh you'll be ready soon.' She turned abruptly and left the room.

He tried to do the right thing, Harper thought. But even then it turned out wrong.

'You'd better have something important.'

His hair was still wet, slicked down on his head, but his clothes were fresh and he felt clean. Walsh looked around with a start as the superintendent spoke. He was standing by the piano, examining the sheet music on display.

'Sorry to disturb you at home, sir. But I thought you'd want to see this.' He held out a wadded piece of paper. Harper didn't even need to ask what it was. Part of a folk song.

'Where was it?'

'In the hall where the hustings were held. I caught the caretaker just before he was going to burn everything. It wasn't too far from here, so . . .'

'Thank you.' Why hadn't he noticed the man in the crowd? How could he have missed him?

'The inspector's given me the evening off since there are no meetings.'

'Then make sure you enjoy it.' He nodded at the piano. 'Do you play?'

'Not really. I had a few lessons when I was young, when we could afford it. I keep thinking I'd like to start again, but we don't have the room for one.'

'You're always welcome to come over and use this,' Annabelle told him as she appeared from the kitchen with a teapot and cups. 'Isn't he, Tom? It's just decoration here, really.'

'Yes,' he agreed, surprised. 'Of course.'

237

'Thank you.' He stood. 'I'll be on my way, sir.'

'I've just made some tea.'

'I'd better not, ma'am. My missus will be happy to see me. Goodnight, sir.'

'What did he want?' she asked after he'd gone.

'To bring me this.' He showed her the paper. 'It was our killer who started that riot last night. He left it at the hall. Probably slipped out as soon as he'd shouted.'

But soon this pretty damsel she lay down by his side

And in a few moments she kissed him and died

A dead woman again. Harper leafed through Kidson's book. There it was. *The Drowned Sailor*. Set on Stowbrow, near Robin Hood's Bay. Billy Reed's territory, he thought idly.

Annabelle stood still, the cup in her hand, breathing slowly.

'I just . . . that he was there, in the same room. So close.'

'I know,' he said. 'I know.'

But why hadn't Harper spotted him?

Twenty-Four

Reed stood on the bridge over the Esk, looking out along the estuary to the sea and breathing in the thick salt air. A cloudy day, but still no real sign of winter cold.

'Hard to get sick of the sight, isn't it?' Harry

Pepper leaned on the railing and puffed at his pipe.

'What do the fishermen do all winter?'

'Hope they've made enough money to survive until spring,' Pepper replied with a shrug. 'Some might try a spot of smuggling if the weather's kind.'

'Have you found out anything more about that?'

'Did you know your friend Millgate's been down to the Bay a couple of times in the last four days?'

The Bay. Robin Hood's Bay.

'No.' He'd heard nothing about Terrier John since their brief encounter on the pier. 'Any idea why?'

'More smuggling there than anywhere along this coast.'

Reed thought back to his last visit to the place and the old man who'd told him that it was still rife, how it helped the town survive.

'Can't you stop it?'

Pepper snorted. 'We had a man down there a few years ago. On his first day he was warned that if he didn't leave, he'd be dead in a week. He was back here before the Sunday. You might as well try and stop breathing as end the smuggling down there.'

'You think Terrier's tied in to that?'

'It makes sense, doesn't it? I hear you talked to him the other day. What did you say?'

'That I'd enjoyed our conversation and we'd continue it soon.'

'Someone must have passed the word. Our Mr Millgate was probably summoned to answer some awkward questions.' He puffed smoke for a few moments. 'Shame, eh?'

'Worried for his life, do you think?'

'That depends if they believed him. Seems to me they've done a lot for him.'

'Maybe I'll have another chat with Terrier John,' Reed said thoughtfully. 'See what that brings.'

'Remind him that he's always welcome to turn Queen's evidence. That might help.'

It took an hour to find him, traipsing all over town, up and down the steep hills of West Cliff. He was sitting quietly at a table in the far corner of the Inglenook Tea Room, a half-eaten piece of cake pushed away.

A worried man, Reed thought. A very worried man who looked like his world might be crumbling. Good.

'Hello, Terrier,' he called out. 'I've been looking all over for you.'

Trapped. Reed saw the man's eyes dart around, searching for a way to escape.

'Inspector.' He tried to smile, but his heart wasn't in it. 'Here's a surprise.'

Reed took a seat across the table and ordered a cup of tea when the waitress approached.

'I hear you've been visiting the Bay,' he said with a smile.

'Maybe he wore a disguise of some kind,' Fowler suggested. 'That's why you didn't spot him at the hustings, sir.'

'We've mentioned that possibility before,' Ash

240

pointed out. 'He must know we have a good description of him.'

'Possibly.' In his mind, Harper tried to search through the faces he'd seen the night before. But there had been too many jammed into the hall to remember every one of them. He'd been there, no more than a breath away. And once again he'd slipped out. Set things in motion then vanished. Probably not a mark on him.

He'd struck again, and in a way none of them had anticipated. Not to kill this time, but to disrupt.

'I hear he left his calling card,' Ash said.

'Another folk song. *The Drowned Sailor* this time.' The superintendent sighed. 'I'm starting to feel like we're the ones going down for the third time.'

Criminals usually had their ways of operating and stuck to them. But this one was too slippery. Just when they hoped they'd blocked his path, he found another.

'We could . . .' Walsh began, then shook his head.

'What?' Harper asked.

'I was going to say we could offer a reward for his arrest, sir. But we'd probably end up with so many tips he might slip through the net.'

'The chief would never go for it. If we do that, we might as well admit defeat.' He looked up. Sergeant Tollman was standing in the doorway.

'Just had a report of a fire, sir. The brigade is on its way.'

'What about it?'

241

'It's in the hall where your wife is supposed to be speaking tonight.'

By the time he arrived, the blaze was out. Half the building was destroyed; the rest looked almost normal, except for the choking smell of charred wood in the air. Harper spotted the arson investigator, Inspector Binns, walking around the perimeter of the wreckage, stopping to peer more closely here and there.

'Deliberate?'

'No question, Tom,' Binns answered. 'Lamp oil. Spilled it around the floor and on the walls back here. At least the alarm went up quickly. Our lads were able to save half the place.' He nodded at the firemen, looking sooty but cheerful as they rolled up their hoses. 'My guess is he got in through the back door somehow. Thirty seconds to throw the liquid around. Toss in a burning rag as he left and bob's your uncle.' He frowned. 'Amateur but effective. Mind you,' he added, 'if he wasn't careful, that first flash of the flames might have given him a burn if he didn't close the door straight behind himself. Some people like to see their handiwork. Make sure it's actually caught.'

'Is the rest of it safe?'

'No,' Binns told him. 'It'll have to come down. But if you want a look it probably won't fall on you.'

Harper left the investigator to his observations and calculations and let his gaze roam around what was left of the floor. Puddles of water pooled like small lakes. Where would the man hide his piece of paper? Nowhere it could be destroyed; there was no sense in that. Outside. It would need to be outside.

It was on the low brick wall that separated the hall from the street, weighted down under a stone to make sure it wasn't blown away. The man wanted it found, to claim responsibility and credit.

The usual writing. Another pair of lines.

That some drops of this lady's heart's blood
Ran trickling down her knee.

Harper didn't recognize the words from Kidson's book. But a trip to Burley Road would give him the answer.

'Superintendent.' Ethel Kidson greeted him with a smile. 'I hope this doesn't mean there's more trouble.'

'I'm afraid it does, Miss.'

'Come in. My uncle's in the parlour. He has a cold, but if we can help you at all . . .'

The man was leaning over the table, head covered with an old towel as he inhaled from a steaming bowl. He sat up and Harper caught the sharp smell of mustard. Good for clearing the chest, his mother had always insisted.

'My apologies.' Kidson fumbled for his glasses and set them on his nose. 'I picked up a chill in the Dales.' He sniffled, pulled out a handkerchief and wiped his nose.

'We've had another pair of incidents. You might be able to help me with these.'

'That one's in my book,' the man replied as he glanced at the paper. 'This one, though . . . it's

243

Little Musgrave and Lady Barnard, isn't it, Ethel?'

'Yes, Uncle.' She glanced up at Harper. 'Another that Professor Child collected. It's very bloodthirsty.'

Kidson tapped the note with a fingernail. 'I've written about this one in the *Mercury*, too. Not in detail, of course, because of consideration for the ladies. I think I have three or four versions. Some go back at least a hundred years. But it's almost certainly older than that.'

'It was at the scene of a fire this morning.'

'I see.' He placed the paper on the table and smoothed it out carefully. 'I'm not sure what else I can tell you, Superintendent. I'm sorry.'

'You published something about it. That helps. All the fragments so far are from your books or columns. Since we've had no luck among the song collectors you mentioned, it's probably safe to assume he's finding these in things you've printed.'

'Plenty of people read the *Mercury*, though.' Kidson sounded apologetic.

And the paper always supported Liberal candidates. The shout at the hustings had come from the knot of Moody's supporters. The Liberal candidate. Was there a connection?

'Do you remember, Uncle, a few months ago Mr Ericson was saying that someone had been asking about you and your work?'

'Was he? I don't recall it.'

Ethel Kidson turned towards the superintendent. 'He's another collector,' she explained. 'He mentioned it in passing. It just sprang into my head.'

244

'Did he say who it was?'

'I don't think so,' she replied hesitantly, then brightened. 'We can go and ask him. You'll be fine without me here for a little while, won't you, Uncle?'

In the hackney she was full of questions about Annabelle and the other women running for office, genuinely curious to know. By the time the cab stopped in one of the silent streets off Headingley Lane, Harper felt as if he'd been well and truly pumped for information.

The house was set well back from the road, standing at the back of a large, untended garden. The building had an air of benign neglect, a slate hanging loose on the roof, a corner of stonework beginning to crumble.

'Mr Ericson is a little bit eccentric,' Ethel Kidson whispered.

The man himself was in his sixties, sitting in a parlour buttoned up in a thick Melton overcoat while a miserly fire flickered in the grate. He had thinning white hair smoothed down with pomade, spectacles with gold rims, and a face that seemed more heavy jowl than bone.

He was genuinely happy to see Ethel, and curious when she introduced the superintendent.

'Are we criminals?' he asked with interest. 'Have we broken the law?'

'You told my uncle that a man asked you about him.' She'd raised her voice, the way people often did around the elderly and the deaf. How long before people started that with him, Harper wondered?

245

'Yes, yes,' Ericson nodded. 'It was back in the early summer. He said he admired Mr Kidson's book and his columns.'

Harper could feel his hopes beginning to rise. But how often had they been dashed before on this case?

'The superintendent would like to know about him.'

'Would you?' He turned a pair of very clear, alert blue eyes on Harper. 'Why?'

'Police business, sir. Probably best if I leave it at that.'

For a second, Ericson's face reddened, as if he was angry. Then he shrugged. 'Really, eh? Well, no matter, no matter. I didn't know the chap, someone must have pointed me out to him.'

'Did he give you his name?' Harper asked.

'I suppose he must have,' Ericson answered. 'But for the life of me, I didn't pay any attention. He wanted to talk about music, and what Mr Kidson had done.' With a smile, he nodded towards Ethel.

Of course. To have a name would be too easy.

'What did he look like, sir? What did he sound like?'

The description matched. He'd felt certain it would.

'Very pleasant man,' Ericson said. 'Genuinely interested in folk songs and collecting. Not an expert, but he seemed to know a little.'

'And you've no recollection of his name? Or who pointed you out to him?'

'No. The only reason it stayed in my head was that it seemed so odd.'

246

'Odd, sir?'

'It's the first time anyone's asked me about it.' He gave a knowing smile. 'Most people just think it's strange. Especially at the club.'

'The club? Which club?'

But there could only be one. The Leeds Club on Albion Place. Members only. Wealthy men and their guests.

'You're certain it happened there, sir?'

'Positive,' Ericson told him coldly. 'Now, was there anything else?'

'Yes,' Harper replied. 'Was he a member, do you know, or someone's guest?'

The question surprised the man. He pinched his lips together as he thought.

'I'd never seen him before. But that doesn't mean much; I don't often go there. If I had to guess, I'd say he was a guest. He didn't seem quite at home, if that makes sense.'

It did. And it made him reconsider Ericson. The man might be strange, but he had an acute mind.

'Thank you, sir.'

'You look as if that was useful,' Ethel Kidson said as they waited at the hackney stand by Woodhouse Moor.

'It was. Thank you for taking me there.'

'He didn't seem to say that much.'

'Mr Ericson's given me another line to pursue.' When you were clutching at straws, even the slimmest thing could look like a haystack.

Harper helped her up into the cab, raised his hat, and strode back into town.

* * *

247

'Check the register at the Leeds Club,' he told Fowler. 'Make a note of all the men signed in as guests between April and . . .' Early summer, Ericson had said. 'August. And the members who brought them.'

'Yes, sir.'

'How much good will that do us?' Ash asked after a moment. 'They're just names, sir. They don't mean anything by themselves.'

'True,' Harper agreed. 'But it's information. We know he was there. We'll have a list, and he'll be on it. If we come up with another list of names and look at them both . . .'

Maybe it was just wishful thinking. But it was police work, deduction. And it might bring them some results. It was definitely better than nothing, he thought.

He looked at his men. They looked drawn, worn down, the effort of the last few weeks apparent on their faces. He needed something very soon, before they lost their sharpness.

'Very good, sir.'

'I questioned a couple of the men arrested at the hustings,' Fowler said. 'They both said it was a middle-aged man with greying hair who shouted. They'd never seen him before among Moody's supporters. He was passing round a hip flask at the meeting.'

Not even a disguise and Harper had missed him. How? He'd been looking for the man, examining all the faces. Did he have some way of making himself invisible in a crowd?

'Excellent work.'

Twenty-Five

'I go down to the Bay quite often,' Millgate said. 'It's a pretty place to spend the day.'

He kept gazing around uncomfortably.

'In the summer, perhaps,' Reed said. 'Rather bleak in the winter, though.'

'Depends what you like, Inspector. I enjoy that.'

'It wouldn't have anything to do with the smuggling there, would it?'

'You keep harping on about me and smuggling. That judge said I was completely innocent—'

'That judge was conned and we both know it.' He leaned forward, his voice low and urgent. 'You weren't even born innocent, Terrier. What are they going to think down in the Bay when word drifts back that you and I were seen together having a pleasant conversation in a tea room?'

'Why would anyone care?' He tried to sound casual, but Reed heard the tremor in the man's voice and saw the thin sheen of sweat on his forehead. Good, he thought. Time to press the advantage a little. Just enough to leave the Terrier dangling and wanting some help.

'You heard what happened to Tom Barker, didn't you?'

'Who?'

'The body they pulled out of the water just after the storm.'

'He drowned, didn't he?' Millgate asked sharply.

'The rumour is that he was informing.'

Suddenly the Terrier looked very uncomfortable in his good clothes, as if the tweed jacket itched uncontrollably against his skin and the leather of his shoes pinched hard against his feet. He seemed like a man with a desire to be back in his second-hand Leeds suit.

'Maybe your friends hadn't told you about him.'

'I don't know what you mean, Mr Reed.' He reached into his waistcoat, brought out his watch and glanced at it carefully. 'I need to go.'

'I'll be seeing you around town,' the inspector told him. 'After all, Whitby's a small place. And Robin Hood's Bay is even smaller.'

He'd baited the hook properly, he thought as he watched Terrier John leave. Now he had to hope his fish would bite. Reed laughed at himself. Fish. Whitby must be burrowing into his soul.

'The list, sir.' Fowler rubbed his knuckles. 'I think I've got cramp from all that writing.'

Seven pages of names. Harper leafed through them, recognizing many. Powerful Leeds figures: factory owners, councillors, men who'd inherited their wealth. He'd even met a few of them at the charity events senior police officers had to attend. Nothing unusual or suspicious. But their killer was in there somewhere.

'Did anything stand out to you?'

'I can't say it did, sir. But then, I've never heard of most of them.'

'We'll see where it takes us. Go back over the case file. Make a note of every name and compare them against these.' He thought for a second. 'It would be easier if these were in alphabetical order.'

'Sir,' Fowler said plaintively. Harper smiled at him.

'Get a bobby to do it. One of the trainees.'

Fowler grinned. 'Gladly, sir. I'll get right on it.'

Was this how they were going to solve the case? Whittling away at names on lists? Not so much a detective as a clerk. It felt wrong. But if it gave them the answer they needed, he wouldn't complain.

Maybe policing was changing. Perhaps they'd all end up at their desks most of the day with endless lists, picking out the guilty from columns of names. He liked the world he knew, sitting with informers in pubs, listening to the broken bits of gossip that slowly built a case against someone. He loved the chase, that feeling like no other when you were after your man and you had him in your sights. At this rate it would be the neat men with ink-stained fingers in command of the divisions, and he'd be back on the beat. He tapped a hand against his belly. A little stouter now. More solid. He'd need a new uniform if he ended up pounding the pavement again.a

'I'm not letting it stop the meeting,' Annabelle said. Her voice was determined. Harper knew better than to argue with her. 'I've been down to see the place.'

'Where will you hold it?' he asked. 'Half the hall has burned down and the rest is unsafe.'

'Outside.' She paced angrily around the room.

251

'It's not raining. Everyone can dress warm. I'm not letting him stop me, Tom. He keeps trying, but it's not going to work.'

'Do you think many will turn up?'

'It doesn't matter,' she shouted in exasperation. 'Can't you see that? I need to show him.'

'That's fine.' He kept his voice calm. She had to do this, and he'd be there with her, watching, although he wasn't certain if he could trust his eyes after the hustings. How could he have missed the man, he asked himself again? How?

She was gathering layers: a shawl over her heavy wool gown, a thick muffler round her throat, a warm cloak, gloves. And finally, the hat. Plum-coloured velvet tonight, decorated with an iridescent peacock feather that glistened in the light from the gas mantle.

'Are you ready?' she asked.

He hadn't even had a chance to remove his overcoat. At least they wouldn't need the Engineers tonight.

'Is Mary with Ellen?'

'She's had her tea. She'll be tucked up in bed by the time we're home.'

He'd seen less of Mary since this campaign began. That was inevitable. If Annabelle was elected, it would continue. She'd have meetings in the evenings, duties, all the demands on her time. They were lucky to have Ellen. Not quite a servant, not quite a governess, almost like another member of the family.

Once this was all over, though, he was going on holiday with his wife and daughter, before Annabelle took office and the madness really

252

began. Christmas in Whitby. He'd write to Billy Reed in the morning and ask Elizabeth to reserve the rooms in the guest house.

They were almost late. On the way, a woman stopped them and began chattering to Annabelle. Harper kept a respectful distance, glancing around for anyone suspicious.

'That was Mrs Carter,' she explained as they hurried along the street. The smoke in Leeds hung low tonight, leaving the air foul. 'Her mother's a widow, doesn't have a penny in savings. She's been told she'll have to go to the workhouse. She's hoping I can stop it.'

'You're not even elected yet.'

'Try telling her that,' Annabelle answered with a shake of her head.

'What did you say to her? Can't the family take her in?'

'They have five children and two rooms,' she said. 'Where would they put her? The old woman has all her wits, she can walk around with a stick. What's the point in putting her in the workhouse? All the people she knows in the world are on her street.' She sighed. 'I received a report in the post today. A woman said that a board of male Guardians spent over an hour discussing whether the clothes of children in the workhouse should have buttons or hooks and eyes on their clothes. An hour.' He could sense her anger rising. Good; there'd be a spark to this meeting, no matter if only one person was listening. 'Do you know what happened at the end?'

'What?'

'The dressmaker decided for herself. It makes

253

me furious, it really does. Aren't there more important things to talk about?'

The smell of charred timber lingered around the wreckage of the hall, acrid in the nostrils and throat. There were more people milling about than he expected, about fifteen of them. Some were curious, others surprised, as if the news of the fire hadn't reached them.

Working people, the men in their caps, women in plain bonnets and worn clothes. They were here, they were ready for something, and Annabelle gave it to them. From the first word she was on the attack.

'This happened because someone is scared of women. Not just as Poor Law Guardians or on School Boards. He's afraid of *women*. Frightened of half the population. What is there to worry him? Do you know? Because I'm blowed if I do. Just three years ago there were fewer than two hundred women as Poor Law Guardians in the whole of England. Two hundred out of a total of thirty thousand. Women aren't exactly taking this over, are they? We want to increase that number here. People believe we should. Important people. The Archbishop of Canterbury, no less, thinks there should be more of us. I'll tell you what the Secretary of State for India said: "No Board of Guardians is properly constituted when it is composed entirely of men. Having regard to the fact that so large a proportion of the population of our workhouses are women and children, it seems vital to me that women should take their part in Poor Law administration." Even the men at the top of government and the church think

we belong. The one who set fire to this place –
to *your* hall – he's swimming against history.
Women are running for the offices they can hold,
and some of them are going to be elected. If not
this time, then next, or the one after. We've started
and we're not going to stop. That tide he's
swimming against, it's going to drown him.'

Harper watched as she looked around the faces,
her breath steaming in the air. She was smiling.

'I'll tell you something else. You vote for me,
and you can help send him packing. More importantly, you'll be electing someone who wants to
help the poor, not punish them. You there, John
Winters, Frank Hepworth, Catherine Simms. You
all know me. You know where I live. Maybe the
Temperance people might not like the landlady
of a public house holding office. Yes,' she told
them with a grin, 'I've heard that grumble. But
you know that when I start something, I do it
properly.' She paused and drew in a breath,
straightening her back so she seemed taller.
'You're ratepayers. You can vote. I'm asking you
to put your X next to my name. Thank you.'

'Where did you find that about the Archbishop
and the Secretary of State?' Harper asked as they
walked home. He could sense her excitement, the
way the street seemed barely able to contain her.

'Miss Ford copied it from the newspaper.
Same way she got those figures.' She stopped and
turned to him. In the gas light he could see her
eyes glistening with pleasure. 'I'm really starting
to believe we can do it, Tom.'

'You will,' he assured her and held her tight.

* * *

255

'He keeps trying, but he hasn't stopped them,' Harper said. 'It's not long to the election. He must be getting desperate.'

'He's always been that, sir,' Walsh said. 'Bombs, murder, arson. Hardly the actions of a sane mind.'

'Twisted,' the superintendent agreed. 'I'm worried he might be reaching the stage where he makes a direct attack on one of the women.'

'We have bobbies on all of them,' Ash pointed out.

'So far they haven't had much to do. Make sure they're all still alert. If they're not, replace them.' He turned to Fowler. 'Have you had any luck comparing that list from the Leeds Club with names in the case file?'

'Not yet, sir. None of the people we've talked to are there.'

'Something will match up, sooner or later.'

'It's sooner we need to worry about,' Ash said. 'Later might be too late.'

'Then we'd better make sure we do things sooner,' he told them. 'That's all, gentlemen. Inspector, a word if I might.'

Once they were alone, Ash stretched out his legs.

'He was the one who incited them at the hustings,' Harper told him. 'I was studying the faces from the moment they all arrived and I never spotted him.'

'We said he was so ordinary that people never noticed him.'

'I know my hearing's gone to pot, but I always thought my sight was sharp.' Harper snorted. 'It

256

makes me wonder how good I am at this any more.'

'We're closer, sir. You know that.'

'Yes.' Inch by inch they were gaining on him. 'I just wonder if we'll catch him before he does something drastic.'

'We're all doing everything we can.'

He could hear the faint resentment in the inspector's voice. Defending his men. The same thing Harper had done so often when he held that rank. It all goes around, he thought wryly. He knew they were doing a fine job. He couldn't ask for anyone better. But from this chair, it was the results that mattered.

'Yes,' he said. 'You are. Please make sure everyone knows that.'

'How's Mrs Harper bearing up? They say she's an odds-on favourite to be elected.'

'She has her ups and downs,' he answered after a moment. 'She's terrified, but she's also determined.'

'I can believe that,' Ash said with a broad grin. 'Women. They're made of tougher stuff than us. What about your little girl? Has she recovered?'

After that single day of crying and sleeping, there'd been no sign of anything, as if it had all passed. He wanted to believe that, but he suspected the truth wouldn't be so easy. Time would tell. But he did know he could kill the man who'd caused it all without a twinge of regret. This was someone who didn't care what damage he caused to families as long as he stopped women.

* * *

257

He was ready to leave for his dinner after a morning spent reading and signing the endless mountain of papers. No sooner had he sent them all off than more arrived; it never ended, just the way Kendall had warned him when he'd taken over the job.

Harper looked up as he sensed a shadow in the doorway. Chief Constable Crossley. He started to rise, but the man waved him back.

'No need, Tom. I had some business at the market and I thought I'd pop in and see how you were progressing. Why don't you tell me while we eat? My stomach's telling me it's time.'

Crossley listened carefully, settling back in his chair and lighting a cigar to go with his coffee. He seemed perfectly at ease in the luxury of Powolny's. The waiter knew him by name and made sure he had a table looking out over Bond Street. Without asking, he brought them each a snifter of brandy to finish the meal.

'Do you have any idea at all who it could be? I'm not asking for proof. Just the merest hint of suspicion.'

'I wish I did, sir. At this point I'd have him in before his feet touched the ground. We have threads, but they seem to lead nowhere at all. He might live in one of the streets around Hyde Park – *if* Walsh saw the right man at that meeting in Hunslet. And he was a guest or a member at the Leeds Club at the beginning of the summer, if this Ericson is correct. Nothing's connected up yet—'

'While the election draws closer every day,'

258

the chief said. 'I know. And you can believe Mr Ericson. I've met him a few times. He's a little strange—' Crossley gave a crooked grin '—but he's quite reliable. An excellent memory.' He studied the tip of the cigar for a few seconds. 'By the way, I owe you an apology, Tom. I threatened you with bringing another officer to handle this.'

'It made perfect sense, sir. A fresh pair of eyes.' He knew he had to swallow his pride and say that, however much the words grated. There had been truth to it, he'd said as much himself.

'I thought about it later. There's far more to gain from your family involvement in this than there is to lose. I'm sorry I ever suggested it. But you have a free hand and my complete backing. I want you to know that.'

That was what this luncheon had been about, Harper decided. Crossley's studied apology. And complete backing might arrive with a smile, but it also had a price. The responsibility was completely his. The message was unstated: fail and it was his head on the block, no one else's.

'Thank you, sir.'

Damn them all, he was going to succeed. He was going to catch this man, relish every day of his trial, and be there the morning they put the noose around his neck in Armley Gaol.

On the way back to Millgarth he bought a copy of the *Mercury*, going through the pages until he found the editorial.

Those wards that have Tory Boards of Guardians have suffered under the most

259

incompetent administration we can recall. They have quarrelled with almost every public body in Leeds, and in almost every case they been shown to be in the wrong. The poor man's vote is now of the same value as the rich man's vote. The Tory Members of Parliament tried to prevent passage of the bill which allowed that by placing every obstacle they could in its way. When the last election for Guardians took place, the Tories published a bill where they said that a new hospital, on which the Liberals proposed to spend £10,000, was absolutely unnecessary. Now the Tories want to spend £12,000 on exactly the same thing. We urge our readers to support the Liberal candidates in this election. As for those women who are standing, our considered feeling is that while ladies fulfil so many invaluable roles in our society, their place is not in the hurly-burly that is politics in our city. We could point out that the unseemly fracas at the hustings in Sheepscar Ward the other evening was caused by the presence of a woman on the podium. This can only be an indication of the deep passions aroused by ladies involving themselves in politics. We urge more decorum in Leeds, and strongly believe that stability and real progress in treatment of the poor can only come from our Liberal male candidates.

Rubbish, Harper thought as he crumpled the newspaper in his fist. Blind bloody tosh. He tossed it in the bin behind a market stall and wiped the ink from his fingers.

Twenty-Six

Reed heard the rattle of the letterbox, then Elizabeth came into the kitchen holding a letter.

'For you, Billy love. It looks like Tom Harper's writing. There's a Leeds postmark.'

He ripped open the envelope and took out the single sheet.

'They're definitely coming for Christmas,' he told her as he read. 'He asked if you could go ahead and book the rooms for them. One for him and Annabelle, another for Mary.'

'Oh, it'll be lovely to see them again,' she said, smiling. Maybe things would be better now, he thought. Maybe he and Harper could become friends again, after a fashion. Time had passed, and there was enough distance between them. Not the way it had been, not as close as their wives. But enough to rub along amiably for a few days. 'A separate room for Mary, though? She must be growing up fast. What else does he say?'

'The election's not far off. They've had a lot of problems, but he doesn't give any details. Just that Annabelle looks likely to win.'

'Poor Law Guardian.' She rolled the words

around, savouring them and shaking her head. 'Well, good for her. But I can't see anything like that happening here. Not women holding office. Not in a place like this.'

He'd listened often enough as she fumed at the men she'd had to deal with about her tea room. Those who wanted to speak to her husband and take their orders from him. Others who refused to listen to her, thinking they knew better. Slowly, though, things were taking shape. No hurry, she insisted on that. She'd open once everything was just right. And she'd make sure people knew all about the place first.

Elizabeth had spent a few afternoons at the Inglenook, talking to Mrs Botham, eager to take advice from someone who knew the town and the tradesmen. She'd met others, too, women who ran their own businesses. Like friends, she said, helping each other, passing on tips and ideas.

He left the letter on the table.

'It's here if you want to read it. I'd better be on my way.'

It was a blustery day, a wind blowing onshore to whip up the waves. The tide was on its way in, the breakers crashing loud and hard as he took the long way to the police station, down the Khyber Pass towards the Coast Guard station. The waters out to sea looked dangerous, but the boats moored by the pier were safe enough, barely bobbing in the harbour.

The fishermen were talking, smoking and drinking tea as they inspected their nets and worked on their vessels. They all looked happy enough. But his eyes were searching for one man. No sign of Terrier John. It was early, but after their meeting the day before he suspected Millgate wasn't sleeping too well.

'Anything to report?' he asked Sergeant Brown at Spring Hill.

'Dead as the grave, sir. Not even a fight or a pocket picked. Leastways, nothing reported to us. Maybe we'll be able to put our feet up for a while.'

'Let's hope, eh?'

Someone had lit the fire in his office, and the room was cosy and warm as he settled behind the desk. He had papers to go through that he'd been putting off for a week. No excuses now. Through the window he could hear the squawk of the gulls over the estuary. The quiet life. That was what he'd wanted, and he certainly had it. Once Terrier John decided which way to turn, it would become livelier for a while. But this suited him, he thought with satisfaction. Away from all the industry and dirty air and madness of Leeds. No danger of burning up or falling when he attended a fire.

Elizabeth would have her business, and they'd build a solid life here. It was a place to stay, with plenty of beauty all around, somewhere to grow old.

A knock on the door and Brown appeared.

'I thought you might fancy a cup of tea, sir. I was just brewing up when you arrived.'

'Thank you, Sergeant. You must have read my mind.'

Brown laughed. 'Now, if only I could do that

with my missus, my life would be grand. Not easy to live with, these Whitby women.'

The piles of wood for the bonfires kept growing on every piece of waste ground, Harper noticed with a smile from the top of the tram. Some tiny, others put together with meticulous care so they'd burn long into Bonfire Night. At least some things never changed. First, the malicious pleasure of Mischief Night, when children took their revenge on every house in the neighbourhood where they'd had a clout or a ticking-off. Then, the evening after, lighting the fire as soon as it was dark. Burnt toffee, parkin, potatoes baked in the embers. A special feast they anticipated for months. The memory would remain on the way to school the next morning, with the smell of the blaze lingering in the air, and the ashes black on the ground.

The soot stung his eyes and he rubbed them with the heels of his hands, blinking them clear. Another day had brought them no closer to the killer. The chief constable might have taken him out to eat, but he'd given his message: solve it.

In his head, Harper could almost hear time ticking away to the election. What was the man going to try next?

How had he hidden himself at the hustings? That was a question that niggled and scraped in the superintendent's mind. He was a detective. He knew how to observe, to see. And the man had slipped right through his fingers. Again. He slammed his hand down hard against the seat, loud enough for a few of the passengers to turn their heads and stare.

No sooner was he through the door then Mary was bounding up to him, holding out a piece of paper, her face brimming with anticipation.

'Look, Da, another star. I got everything right.'

Sums. He'd always been terrible at them. She must have inherited that talent from her mother.

'That's wonderful,' he told her, kissing the top of her head. 'Who knows, maybe you'll end up as prime minister at this rate.'

She frowned. 'No,' she told him seriously. 'I want to run a business and make lots of money.'

'Well, you'd make a better rich woman with clean hands. Look at those. What have you been doing, anyway, rubbing them in mud? Run along and give them a scrub.'

'I heard her,' Annabelle said as he walked into the kitchen. '"Make lots of money." She should be so lucky. If you're scraping along you're doing well these days.'

She was stirring a pot on the range. He put his arms around her waist and held her close.

'How was the campaign today?'

'Delivering leaflets.' She groaned. 'If I'd known it involved so much walking, I'd never have stood for election. All I'll get from this is bunions.'

'No problems?'

'A few arguments on the doorstep. Nothing I can't handle. Having that constable close by helps.'

'Glad I insisted?'

After a brief hesitation, she nodded. 'I suppose it does make me feel safer.'

Her admission felt like a small victory. With no meetings for the next several nights, everyone could rest. It was easier to keep the women candidates safe. And it gave them a breathing space to continue the hunt.

In the end, they were curled up and asleep by nine. No disturbances, Harper hoped. It didn't feel like too much to ask.

'A quiet night,' Walsh said with a yawn. 'My missus was pleased to see me. I think she was, anyway. I was away to the world before there was a chance for anything else.'

'Maybe it'll stay like this for a while,' Fowler said hopefully. Harper glanced at Ash. They knew better. The killer might have had a silent night, but he was planning his next move.

'Let's find him and make sure that happens,' the superintendent told them.

'How, sir?' Fowler pushed the spectacles up his nose. 'We've tried everything. We've been working ourselves ragged. You know that.'

'I do, and I appreciate it.' What could he say to put some spirit in them? They'd explored every avenue, come up with ideas. No coppers could have done more, and they still had no results. 'About all I can say is keep on pushing. I'm as frustrated as you are. I was the one who missed him at the hustings.'

'We're doing it all by the book and beyond,' Ash said. 'But there might be two more things we might try, sir.'

'Go on.' At this stage he'd entertain any idea.

'That sketch we have of him – why not give

it to the newspapers after all and see what comes in? And since Walsh thinks he went to Hyde Park, have the bobbies there go round with copies of it and ask people if they know him.'

'Yes,' Harper agreed after a moment. He hadn't wanted to involve the papers, to make their failure so public. It was an admission of defeat. But perhaps it was time. The man had been too smart for them. 'I'll let you take care of it.'

'Yes, sir.'

They were still hammering out their thoughts when Sergeant Tollman knocked on the door.

'Mrs Morgan is here, sir. She's very upset.'

'Bring her through,' he ordered. 'And get her a cup of tea, please.'

Something else had happened. That was the only reason she'd be here. He felt the tension tighten against his forehead and closed his eyes for a moment.

She was with Blythe, the copper who'd been assigned to her. He was holding a small box covered in brown paper. The woman sat in Fowler's chair, trying not to let anything show on her face.

'I'd knocked on the door and said my good mornings,' Blythe began, 'and I was patrolling the street when the postman arrived.' Why did bobbies have to explain everything this way, Harper thought, as if the choice of words made it more official. 'He delivered something to Mrs Morgan. A minute or so later she appeared in the doorway, calling for me. She appeared very distraught.' He held out the package. 'This was on the kitchen table, sir.'

Heavy, Harper thought as the constable handed

it over. He tipped it, and a knife fell on to the desk with a clunk. Reaching into the box, he pulled out a sheet of paper. The familiar writing from the folk song fragments and the first two threatening letters.

Kill yourself or I'll kill you.

And scribbled underneath it:

For young Jimmy was a-fowling, was a-fowling alone,
When he shot his own true-love in the guise of a swan.

He breathed slowly, passing the note around the others. Without a word, Ash left the room. He understood: if she'd received this, the other women candidates had probably been sent exactly the same. Annabelle . . .

'I know it's terrible,' he said. 'He wants to scare you. He wants to make you withdraw from the election. But with Constable Blythe around, he can't hurt you.'

'That's right, missus,' Blythe agreed. 'I'll look after you. You know that.'

She still didn't say a word. Her jaw was set firm as she tried to keep all her feelings inside, not to let any weakness show. He nodded at Walsh. He was good with women, he had the manner to put her at ease, to make her believe they'd keep her safe.

'He won't hurt you,' Harper promised, and hoped it was true.

Out in the corridor, the door closed behind him, he gave Fowler his orders: 'Find out where he bought that knife. Six of them, if he's sent one to all the women. Look at the postmark on the box. Six like that, the clerk at the Post Office should remember that many.'

'Yes, sir.'

'I need to go home for a few minutes.'

Martinson was outside the Victoria. He saluted as the superintendent approached, keeping his position on the corner. A second constable was placed to watch the back yard. Harper took the steps two at a time.

Annabelle was sitting at the table. She'd opened the box, the knife blade shining, the note pressed flat. He put his arms around her shoulders.

'I've been staring at this since I opened it.' Her voice was dull and hopeless. 'He can get to me anywhere, can't he? Even with that copper outside, he . . .' Her voice trailed off, then she lifted her head. 'Did the others get one, too?'

'Mrs Morgan did. She brought it to the station. We're checking on the rest.'

He kneaded her skin softly, but she didn't respond.

'He can come in here, Tom. Right through that door. He can come where we live. And we can't stop him.'

'He's trying to scare you with this.'

Her eyes blazed. 'Then he's doing a good job of it. Mary, the bomb by the back door. Now this.'

'You're safe. I promise, you are. There's

269

Martinson with you every day and I'm here at night.'

Annabelle held up a hand. He could see her trembling. 'If I'm so safe, why am I like this?'

Harper took the knife, with the box and the note. The man knew exactly what he was doing. He understood how to spread fear. Had he planned out his whole campaign in advance?

It hurt him to see his wife like this. She was always so strong, so determined, but this had managed to undermine her defences. Annabelle wouldn't give up, but each morning until election day was going to grow harder and harder for her, not knowing what might come, what was waiting out there for her.

Dear Christ, they had to find him soon. And he hoped the knives and the post office offered them some clues.

'Mrs Morgan said she's decided to retire from the race,' Walsh said. 'She can't take it any more.'

Two down, five left, Harper thought. The man was chipping away at the candidates. They were sitting in the superintendent's office, just the two of them, waiting for the others to return.

'I don't blame her. Anyone would crack under that sort of pressure.'

'How's your wife, sir?'

'Shaken,' he admitted. 'Scared.'

'Will she stay in it, do you think?'

He nodded. However terrified Annabelle might be, she'd never give in to threats now.

'This probably wasn't what you expected when you joined us.'

270

Walsh smiled and lit a cigarette.

'No, but it's different, sir. Might as well be thrown in at the deep end. And we're going to catch him.'

'We are.' But could they do it in time? Forcing another out would only make him push harder on the remaining women.

'My missus reckons he must be petrified of women if he's willing to go to these lengths. Says it makes her wish there was a woman in our ward she could vote for.'

'I think your wife is right.' He was about to say more when Fowler entered, a grim expression on his face.

'Knives from the market, packages sent from the main post office,' he said. 'They remember him in both places. From the descriptions, it's him. But that's all. No names, nothing. He bought the knives two days ago, in the morning. Six of them. Sent them off yesterday afternoon. Sorry, sir.'

'Don't apologize,' Harper told him. 'We're doing all we can. We're just flailing around behind him, that's all.'

'What are they saying?' he asked when Ash returned. 'Mrs Morgan has decided to withdraw. Any others?'

'One who might, sir.' He rubbed his moustache. 'I think she probably will, once she's thought about it a little more. She could hardly speak when I saw her.'

'What about the rest?'

'They'll stick.' He grinned. 'It's made

271

Mrs Pease more determined than ever. But he has them all scared of their own shadows right now.' He hefted a parcel on to the desk. 'I collected all the knives and the notes. Better if they're gone from sight, and we'll need them for evidence later.'

'How do we catch him? We didn't anticipate this. We don't have a clue what he's going to do next.'

'I don't know, sir, I really don't.' The inspector sighed and pursed his lips. 'We can try putting more men on the remaining candidates. But he's like a bloody eel, if you'll pardon my French, sir.'

'Do that. The chief will squawk about money, but we're going to do all we can to keep them safe.'

'Yes, sir.'

'We have two days before meetings start again. If we can get him by then . . .'

'For all it only has two letters, *if* is a very big word, sir.'

'I know.'

'That sketch will be in the papers tomorrow, and the constables around Hyde Park are already showing it to people. Maybe we'll be able to flush him out.'

'Let's hope to God it helps. We follow up on every tip that comes in. Doesn't matter how ridiculous it sounds.'

'Understood, sir.'

Harper glanced at the clock. Almost five.

'Go home,' he said. 'I think we've all had enough for today.'

* * *

272

Harry Pepper smoked his pipe as they walked along the beach. The tide was out, the sand firm under their shoes.

'No one's likely to overhear us out here,' he said. 'Do you really think Millgate will buckle?'

'I don't know,' Reed answered. 'He's definitely worried. I could see it on his face, especially when I mentioned Tom Barker. He thought that was an accident. It seemed to hit him.'

'Then let's hope it keeps pummelling at his brain.'

'Do you know who's behind it in the Bay?'

'The Shaws,' he answered immediately. 'As sure as eggs is eggs. I've just never managed to get the evidence against them. I'd be a very happy man if I could see them convicted.'

'What can you offer Terrier if he turns Queen's evidence?'

'No prison,' Pepper replied after a moment. 'But I want the whole network of them. The people inland as well as those on the coast. Everything he knows.'

'That's asking a great deal, Harry.'

He shrugged. 'That's my offer. Take it or leave it, you can tell him.'

'They'll be watching. People will have seen me talking to him in the tea room yesterday.'

'For his sake, I hope he comes to you before the Shaws kill him, then.' There was no pity in his voice. 'It's up to him. He has to make the next move. You said he has quite a past in Leeds.'

'In and out of jail,' Reed told him. 'But nothing that could mean he'd die.'

'He's a criminal,' Pepper said. 'Nothing more

or less. If he believed you about Barker, he knows what's at stake. As it is, he must have some sort of protection if he's been seen with you and he's still alive.' He turned and looked back towards Whitby, at the ruin of the abbey standing on top of the headland. 'A lifetime here, and I'm still not weary of seeing that. When you're out on the water, it means you're almost home. I love it round here, Billy. I don't like to see people ruin it.'

'Is that what the Shaws are doing?'

'Yes.' There was anger in his voice. 'They're greedy. They want it all, and they'll kill to keep it.' He snorted. 'I don't mind a little bit of smuggling. It's human nature. I used to do it myself when I was on the boats. The odd bottle here and there. They've made an industry of it and they'll hurt anyone who tries to stop them. I want them gone.'

'It would be a big feather in your cap.'

Pepper grinned. 'Goes without saying. I won't deny it. But I'm more concerned with getting rid of the Shaws.'

'We'll see what happens with Terrier. If he's going to come across, it'll be in the next day or so.'

'Either that or we'll be pulling him out of the water.' He looked at his pocket watch. 'We'd better start back. I have to meet someone in half an hour. How are you settling in Whitby, anyway? This is probably more excitement than you wanted.'

'We like it,' Reed replied. He searched for the words. 'It feels right for us.'

274

'Your wife's planning on opening a tea shop, I hear.'

'She used to own a few bakeries.'

'Did she now?' He sounded surprised. 'Quite the businesswoman.'

'She's developed a taste for it.'

'I trust that Her Majesty's servants will receive a discount.'

'I'll suggest it to her,' he said with a grin.

'It might increase her regular custom.'

Reed laughed. 'Is that what life is here? A series of bargains?'

'Isn't it everywhere?' Pepper put the pipe away. 'If you've ever had to make your living by selling the fish you've caught on the dock, you know you always try to get the most you can for them. It's in your blood.'

Twenty-Seven

'The other candidate who was wavering has pulled out, sir,' Ash said. 'Just four of them left now.'

Harper nodded. A shame, but understandable. The candidates wanted to win an election, not fight for their lives. Still, one less woman made it easier to guard the rest. Sending knives and that note . . . Annabelle was right: he could get through the door and into the home.

'Have a word with the Engineers. Make sure they're more thorough than ever.'

'Do you think he'll start using bombs again, sir?'

'I don't know,' the superintendent said. 'He went back to using the post and that's been very effective. I couldn't even guess what he'd try next.'

'We've had the first tips in from running that drawing in the paper,' Fowler said.

'How many so far?'

'Just three, but it's not nine o'clock yet.'

'You know what to do.' He turned to Walsh. 'Any luck with the bobbies in Hyde Park? How have people responded to seeing that sketch?'

'A pair of possibilities, but that's all so far, sir.'

'Compare every name that comes in to that list we have of people who were at the Leeds Club earlier this spring. If any match, focus on those first.' He paused. 'No, pass them to me. I'll go and see them myself.' He looked into their faces. 'We're going to catch him, gentlemen. I can feel it in my water.'

'From your lips to God's ears, sir,' Walsh said with a grin.

'Look into every one of those tips from the sketch yourselves. No relying on the bobbies for this.'

He examined the knives that Ash had collected from the candidates. They were cheap things, poorly put together, the rivets already loose in the wooden handles. Second-quality, the rejects. But the blades were still made from good Sheffield steel, ground sharp as a razor. Damn the man. Damn the bastard to hell.

*　*　*

276

'I'm sorry to intrude, Miss Kidson,' Harper said, 'but I have another query for you and your uncle.'

'Is this connected to the drawing in the news-paper, Superintendent? I saw it this morning.'

'It is, Miss. Sad to say, but it is.'

Frank Kidson looked at the note, then blew his nose, making a show of returning the handker-chief to his pocket.

'This cold,' he explained. 'It's lingering. This is a famous song. *Polly Vaughn*. Sometimes it's *Molly Brawn*.' He turned to Ethel. 'About a man shooting a girl because he mistakes her for a swan.'

He picked up the book by his side and leafed through the contents until he found the page. 'This is it.'

'Have you written about it in your column for the *Mercury*, sir?'

Kidson pursed his lips and stared at his niece. 'Have I? Do you remember?'

'At the start of last year, Uncle,' she replied. 'You talked about the connection to some old legends.'

His eyes widened as he recalled. 'Of course. That piece about the way songs can travel. Does that help, Superintendent?'

'It does, sir. It confirms something, at least. I hope your cold passes quickly.'

At the front door, Miss Kidson asked: 'Does this and what's in the paper relate to one of the women quitting the election?'

'Two now. And I'm afraid it does, Miss.'

'I'm sorry. That's a terrible thing.' A fit of sneezing came from the parlour. 'I'm sorry. I'd

277

better go. I hope you catch him very soon. For everyone's sake.'

'Thank you for your help.'

An odd relationship between Ethel and her uncle, he thought again as he walked to the tram stop. Maybe Kidson was simply one of those men who needed a woman to look after him.

'How many tips have come in?' he asked Sergeant Tollman as he walked into Millgarth.

'Twelve so far, sir. Your men are out following up on them.'

In his office, Harper tried to concentrate on all the papers needing his attention, but it was wasted time. His mind kept straying, wondering how Ash and the others were progressing. He should be out there with them . . . but someone had to run this police station. That was his job now. To go over the budgets and the rotas sitting on the desk. To supervise the men.

It would never sit quite comfortably on his shoulders. He was made for being out there, wearing the soles of his shoes thin and solving cases. But this was his lot. He'd accepted the post. He needed to try harder to make it fit. Maybe he'd lost the knack of being a detective in the last two years. He certainly hadn't managed to crack this case yet. Would the old Tom Harper have had a man under arrest by now? That was a question he couldn't even begin to answer. He wasn't sure he wanted to know. Ash, Fowler, Walsh, they were as good as he'd ever been; maybe better. They worked themselves to the bone, they were clever. The problem lay in him. He needed to trust them completely.

278

But how could he do that when it all came home, with someone threatening to kill Annabelle and trying to snatch Mary?

One by one, the men returned to the station at the end of the day. They looked weary, footsore, each of them shaking his head.

'I had one who seemed like a good fit,' Fowler said. 'Turns out he just returned from London two days ago. He showed me the railway ticket.'

'You came closer than I did,' Walsh complained. 'How anyone can think a bald, seventy-year-old man resembles someone in his forties with greying hair is beyond me.'

'Nothing from the bobbies in Hyde Park, either, sir,' Ash reported. He held up slips of paper. 'We do have more to look at, though.'

'Have something to eat first,' Harper told them. He needed them alert.

Reed had seen the jet workshops dotted around Whitby, but he'd never been in one. The place was empty now, the workers all gone for their dinner. It was a cramped room, far smaller than he'd expected, with barely enough space for men to stand shoulder to shoulder as they carried out their tasks, all the grinding, cutting and shaping of the stones. Dust hung in the air and caught in his throat. Almost as bad as being in the mines, he thought.

The jewellery had been popular since the Queen first wore it when she was in mourning for Prince Albert. Black and sombre, it did possess a deathly beauty. But in this tiny factory there seemed to be little sense of art.

Terrier John stood in the far corner, by a stove that was warming a pan of foul-smelling glue. The inspector hardly had room to edge close to him.

Millgate opened a wooden door, inclined his head, and led the way down a passage. The stone walls were close on either side, and the only light came from the room behind them. Another door, off to the right, took them into a storeroom with a small, high window.

'This is a funny place for a meeting, Terrier,' Reed said. 'You must have something important to say.'

He'd received the note that morning, pushed through the letterbox of his house on Silver Street. No signature, written in a shaky, uneducated hand. Simply an address and a time. And now he was in a small building on Church Lane, upstream from the bridge, near the place they called Abraham's Bosom.

'I know the man who runs this place. He's a friend.'

'Trust him, do you?'

'Yes.' The Terrier paced around, although there wasn't much room. Shelves lined the walls, some holding finished pieces of jet, ready to go on sale in the shops around Whitby, others with stone waiting to be worked.

'Looks like something has you worried.'

Even with no name, he knew who'd sent the note. The man had to be frightened. Just two days since he'd been so desperate to leave their little talk at the Inglenook and he was back. The fish had bitten quickly. Time to reel him in. Reed

280

leaned against the door jamb and lit a cigarette.

'Why don't you stop walking and tell me?' he said.

'I'm scared they're going to do me, and it's your fault.'

'Mine?' Reed raised an eyebrow. He knew what was coming, but he wanted to hear the man say it.

'People have seen me with you. On the pier, then yesterday.' Any pretence of a grand manner had vanished. Now there was just panic. 'I'm scared they're going to do me like Tom Barker.'

'Who will?'

'The people who run the smuggling.' He pulled the watch from his waistcoat. 'We've only got a quarter of an hour before they come back to work.'

'Then you'd better get a move on, hadn't you?'

He let John Millgate sweat a little before he made his deal. Terrier wanted the usual: protection in return for Queen's evidence, and no jail. But Reed was going to exact Harry Pepper's terms. The Excise man would accept nothing less.

'All of them. Not just the Shaws.' Terrier's head jerked up in fear at the name. 'Everyone inland, too.'

'I can't do that, Mr Reed.' His voice was plaintive, his eyes sorrowful.

'It's that or nothing.' The inspector shrugged. 'It's up to you. I'll remind you of this: give them all up and they won't be around to hurt you.'

The room stayed silent for a long time, so quiet

that Reed could hear the soft lapping of the water against the pilings under the noise of the gulls.

'All right,' Terrier agreed finally. It came out like a submission. 'All right.'

He gave it in quick spurts. Contraband arrived all along the coast, from Redcar down to Filey, but most of it from Robin Hood's Bay to Sandsend. The cutters stood offshore, and men would row out in their cobles and take the goods to the beach.

A fair piece of the money to finance it all came from Leeds.

'That's why I'm out here,' Terrier said. 'John Rutherford wanted someone he could trust to keep an eye on things. Watch his investment and work with them here. He'd had someone, but he upped and died. Natural causes,' he added quickly. 'Me and John, we've known each other since we were nippers. He trusts me. He asked if I fancied the job.'

'So you ended up living the high life out here.'

'Until you come along and recognized me. Now them down in the Bay, they're not too happy. You and the Excise people arrested those people down near Sandsend.'

'We arrested you, too. Not even a week ago.'

'Mr Rutherford wanted what we could salvage from when the Excise caught those men. He told me to send someone to get it. I've used Dennison before.'

'We were watching. The way you were pacing up and down the pier waiting for them to come back, you might as well have worn a sandwich board and written "Guilty" on it.'

'Down in the Bay, they're wondering about us talking.'

'What do I get if I help you?'

Millgate swallowed hard. He knew it was going to cost. How much he was willing to pay depended on how much he wanted to stay alive.

'I'll go in court and testify against the smugglers,' he said after a moment.

'That'll be good for the Excise people. They'll like that. But what do *I* get from it?'

'I'll give evidence against John Rutherford, too. He has a big operation. Been doing it for years, and no one has the faintest notion. The Excise in Leeds is a joke, he says.'

'But it isn't here, and you know that. Harry Pepper will be interested in what you have to say.'

'But can he keep me alive, Mr Reed? Can he do that?'

'We're working our way through these tips, sir,' Ash said. 'It takes time, though. You know that.'

He did. Time, and plenty of frustration.

'Nothing remotely worthwhile?'

'They're all worthwhile until they answer the door, sir,' Ash said with a grin. 'Same as ever. None of them could be our man. But we have more left. Those bobbies in Hyde Park finally have one or two addresses for us. Walsh is out looking at them.'

Harper nodded; it made sense to send him. He'd been the one who spotted the man at the meeting in Hunslet and followed him back there; he'd recognize him.

'I feel like the net's closing in.'

'I don't want to put a damper on things, but we've all felt like that before on cases, sir.'

'Yes. Too bloody often.' Harper snorted. 'This time, though . . .'

'Let's hope you're right, sir.'

If he was still an inspector, he'd have been out there himself, looking people in the eye, asking his questions and listening for lies. As a superintendent, he was stuck there. In charge of everything, but at a distance. At least he had men, good men doing the work.

The papers to be read and signed lay in front of him, but after a few sentences his mind kept slipping away. He was grateful when the telephone gave its shrill jangle. Maybe it was news.

'Superintendent Harper.'

'Tom? It's Billy Reed. Can you hear me?'

The line crackled and buzzed, but the words came through. Billy? Had something happened to Elizabeth?

'Yes, yes. What is it?'

'Terrier John. He's given everything to the Excise man here. Do you know John Rutherford?'

Someone had mentioned the name lately, but Harper couldn't recall any criminal with that name. Then it came back. Terrier John's old friend. A distributor of spirits.

'He's the one,' Reed told him. 'Seems that he's behind all this. Harry Pepper – he's in charge of the Excise people here – is planning a big raid tomorrow. He's bringing in men from all over. The Excise in Leeds are going after Rutherford then, too. He has a special place where he hides all the

284

contraband.' Even on a poor line where he missed too many words, he could sense Billy's excitement. 'Could you go along? Pepper thinks the revenue men in Leeds are useless. If you're there, they'll have to do their jobs properly.'

'Yes, of course,' he agreed. 'But we have something going on ourselves . . .'

'This is big, Tom. If Harry nets everyone, it will shut down smuggling all along the Yorkshire coast. But everything has to be co-ordinated. We need to go in everywhere at the same time.'

'I'll be there,' he promised, his heart sinking a little. This couldn't have come at a worse moment.

'They'll have the details in Leeds later. Can you talk to them and arrange everything?'

'I will.'

'I'd have sent you a telegram.' Reed sounded apologetic. 'But it's faster to do it this way, and I can say more.' He hesitated. 'Elizabeth has booked those hotel rooms for you. She's looking forward to seeing Annabelle again.' The line crackled again, then, 'I need to go. If you can keep the Excise people there on the mark, I'd be grateful. We all would.'

'I will. Thank Elizabeth for arranging the hotel, will you? Good luck for tomorrow.'

At least someone was achieving results, the superintendent thought as he replaced the receiver and rubbed his good ear. Terrier John involved in something large. Who would ever have thought that?

Billy was pulling off a coup in his first few months in Whitby, too. That would bring plenty of praise. Harper knew that he ought to feel pleased for him. They'd been through so much together. But that time had passed, they'd gone different ways. The only taste in his mouth, though, was sourness. Envy. He needed his own victory like that. He needed his killer in custody.

Twenty-Eight

Time stretched. Whenever he glanced up at the clock, thinking an hour must have passed, it was no more than five minutes. Still no word from any of the men.

Harper took the slips of paper, all the words from the songs, out of the drawer and set them on his desk. However much he looked, though, they didn't take him any deeper into the killer's mind. Calling cards, Ash and Walsh had said; a signature. A curious one, perhaps, but no mistaking it for anyone else.

Finally, as the hour turned to five and he was about to give up for the day, Tollman came running through to his office.

'Detective Constable Walsh just 'phoned from the Woodhouse Moor station, sir. He knows who your man is. Could you meet him outside the Hyde Park Hotel?'

The jolt was physical. Suddenly Harper was alert. Everything else vanished.

'Call me a hackney,' he said, already reaching for his coat and hat. 'Find Ash and Fowler. Tell them I'll want them, too.'

286

At the door he turned back and took the truncheon from his desk, smiling as he slid it into his pocket.

'Who is it?' he asked as he saw Walsh pacing up and down the pavement. The hackney driver had made good speed, cracking his whip over the horse to keep it moving fast.

'I was going through the addresses the bobbies had given us, sir. This was next to the last. Nobody at home. As soon as the neighbour saw that sketch they said it had to be him—'

'Don't go all round the houses,' Harper snapped. 'What's his name?'

'That's it, sir. As soon as she told me, I remembered him from the Leeds Club list.'

'Who?' He shouted the word.

'Gerald Hotchkiss, sir. The journalist who's written those articles saying everyone should vote for the male candidates.'

For a moment Harper stood, stunned. It all made sense now. Hotchkiss was educated, articulate. He didn't like women in politics. He should have thought of it himself.

'How long ago were you at his house?'

Walsh looked at his pocket watch. 'About three-quarters of an hour, sir. The woman next door said he usually comes home from work about half past five.'

A cab pulled up, the horse snorting and frothing with effort; Ash and Fowler climbed out.

'It's Hotchkiss from the *Post*,' the superintendent told them. 'Walsh has done a good job. I want one of you to go to his office. Search his desk. Ask who his friends are, where he goes. The other to the Leeds Club, in case he's there. If you find him, don't be gentle.'

'Yes, sir,' Ash replied. Fowler smiled with relish. They were back in the hackney before it could pull away.

'Now,' Harper said to the detective constable, 'let's see where he lives.'

Nobody answered his knock at the door. It was a neat terraced villa, three storeys, anonymous among all the other houses on a quiet street off Victoria Road. A ginnel at the back. Harper opened the gate. A tiny back garden, a brick privy standing in the corner, two small flower beds dug over for autumn, everything ordered and tidy.

Harper kicked the back door open. It wasn't legal, but he was past caring. This was their man. He wanted to know him, to sense him, to *smell* him in this place.

'You search upstairs,' he told Walsh. 'I'll look around down here.'

The roll-top bureau stood in the front room. He forced the lock with his pocket knife. Some letters, one half-finished. He recognized the handwriting. Exactly the same as the notes the man had left; that put it beyond a shade of a doubt.

Shelves filled with books. His eyes moved over the titles until he spotted Kidson's *Traditional Tunes*. Next to it, newspaper clippings tied together with string. He pulled them out: a collection of Frank Kidson's folk song columns from the *Leeds Mercury*.

He went through every nook and cranny, hurriedly glancing at things before tossing them on to the floor. Nothing to indicate what Hotchkiss was planning or where he might be. If the neighbour was right, he should have been home by now.

Where was he?

Harper unlocked the front door. Not a soul on the street.

Walsh was still going through the bedroom, thorough and methodical.

'Found anything?'

'He likes to use bay rum on his face after he shaves. That's about it. Some books about politics by his bed. Nothing useful.'

'When you've finished up here, look downstairs again. He has to come home sometime. I want you on hand to arrest him.'

'Don't you worry, sir. This one will be a pleasure.'

'I need to get back to Millgarth and see if the others have him yet.'

'He doesn't often go to the Leeds Club.' Fowler peered down through his spectacles at his notebook and blinked. 'The last visit was a fortnight ago. He usually signs in as a guest of someone called Winchester, but the staff say he's in London.'

'We can rule that place out, then,' Harper replied.

'The people at the paper were helpful,' Ash said. 'Bent over backwards once I told them what their writer has been doing. He had another of his columns written for tomorrow's edition. I saw it; the same vote for men tripe. They've pulled

289

it. I came away with a few names of friends. The bobbies have gone visiting to see if he's with any of them. Evidently he sometimes likes a drink at Whitelock's after work. I stopped in there, but no sign of him.'

He told them what he'd found at the house.

'Pass the word to the coppers guarding the candidates.' He gave a grim smile. 'Now we hunt him, gentlemen. He's around somewhere. Let's find him.'

First, though, a swift trip out to Sheepscar. Annabelle deserved to know.

'Gerald Hotchkiss?' she asked in disbelief. 'That journalist?'

'Him.'

'I never . . .' she said slowly. 'I suppose it's obvious once you think about it, isn't it?'

'Yes.' One name and all the pieces tumbled into place. He should have come up with it earlier, he should have investigated after he read the man's articles. But Hotchkiss was a writer. They used words, not weapons. He'd never made the connection. 'I've told Martinson. He'll make sure the night man knows. You'll be safe.'

'You're going to catch him, aren't you?'

'Yes,' he told her, and this time he was certain. 'He can't get away now. So I need to be back at the station.'

She nodded. Before he left, he pulled her close.

Tonight he had to be out there himself, moving around the streets of Leeds. Harper couldn't wait at Millgarth and hope for news. He slipped from one public house to another, up and down Briggate, along the Headrow, standing just inside the doorway, studying all the faces. His mouth was filled with the metallic taste of anticipation.

He looked at the people passing on the street. Heads down, gazing at the pavement in front of them. Men, most of them. A young woman at the entrance to Rockley Court, staring boldly.

Harper rubbed his face. His fingers came away dark, discoloured by the soot in the air. No escaping it here.

By eleven he still had nothing. Wearily, he trudged back along George Street. His feet hurt, he was tired. But at least he'd been doing something. And maybe the men had found Hotchkiss.

As soon as he saw them, the superintendent knew their luck had been as poor as his.

'Nothing,' Ash said flatly. Fowler polished his glasses with a handkerchief, holding them up towards the light from the gas mantle before rubbing them again. 'Walsh is spending the night out in Hyde Park, just in case. My guess is that Hotchkiss knows we're on to him somehow. He's hiding.'

'Are you ready?' Harry Pepper asked.

Reed was wearing his old suit, prepared for anything the morning might bring. The old hum of excitement flowed through him: action ahead, when the senses sharpened, and every moment seemed important.

'Ready and willing.'

'Have you used a rifle before?'

291

'I was in Kabul for the Afghanistan War,' he replied. 'Served with the West Yorkshires.'

Pepper nodded his approval. 'You know what you're doing, then.' He unlocked a cupboard and took out a weapon. 'One of those new Lee Enfields.'

Reed weighed it in his hands and checked the ammunition before sighting along the barrel.

'Do you think they'll fire at us?'

'I'll be astonished if they don't.' The Excise men checked his pocket watch. 'Let's go. I've had people in position since before first light.'

It was a fast, bumpy ride down to Robin Hood's Bay; they left the wagon out of sight at the top of the hill. One of Pepper's men was waiting for them.

'We're just waiting for the signal, sir,' he said. Reed could see the look in his eyes, the glow of eagerness for the operation to begin.

'I'll blow the whistle twice to start things. Your man Millgate gave us the locations of the caves where they hide things. The Coast Guard will go in and secure those. We arrest the men.' Pepper stared at the policeman. 'Stay alert,' he warned. 'And be ready to fire.'

The streets, barely wide enough for two people, veered sharply off the twisting hill. It had always seemed put together with no rhyme or reason, Reed thought, a maze. But the Excise man knew exactly where he was going.

By one of the cottages he stopped, took a breath, then two sharp blasts from his whistle cut through the sound of the seagulls and the waves on the shore. Pepper brought a pistol from his coat and

292

kicked at the door, bringing his foot down three times until the lock gave. Billy Reed followed into the darkness.

Somewhere in the distance four shots sounded.

'You might as well give up, Solomon Shaw,' the Excise man shouted. 'I'm shutting it all down.'

There was hardly time to notice the detail of the room. The rocking chair, a bright rag rug, the fire prepared and unlit in the grate. A single dried flower in a vase on the mantelpiece. Then he was through to the kitchen, rifle at the ready. His heart was beating fast, thumping in his chest.

A movement caught the corner of his eye. Without thinking, Reed ducked as his old training kicked in. The shot from the musket went over his head and he fired. Once, twice. The clatter of metal and the sound of a body slumping to the ground.

'He'll live,' Pepper said. 'But it's a good job you were quick. He'd have killed you.'

They stood and watched the eight men and three women being escorted to the wagon in irons. Reed smoked cigarettes, one after another, as the thrill of the action started to drain out of his body.

'Pleased with the way it went?' he asked.

'Very.' The man was beaming. 'We got them all, and what they'd brought in. There are probably one or two more holes that Millgate didn't know about, but I'm happy with this haul. I'd say we have something to celebrate.' He surveyed the men who were under arrest. 'Quite a few who won't be going out fishing for several years. Just think: if you hadn't recognized that man from Leeds . . .'

'Hotchkiss never came home last night, sir,' Walsh said. 'I kept watch from a bedroom window. He didn't come near the place, as far as I can tell. I left a bobby guarding the house.'

'Somehow, he knows we're after him.' Fowler lit a cigarette.

'We have a man on the newspaper office,' Ash said. 'But I don't think he'll be going to work today.'

Harper nodded. The man was going to be desperate, and desperate men did dangerous things. He'd glanced at the list Walsh had made of items in Hotchkiss's house. In the cellar he had everything he needed to make more bombs. But he was cut off from all that now. Cut off from everything.

He rubbed at his face. He'd been out early with Captain Burt and the Leeds Excise men, arresting John Rutherford and raiding the secret warehouse where he kept his contraband. Everything straightforward and over in just a few minutes, but he begrudged the time he'd had to spend away from finding Hotchkiss. Rutherford had accepted his arrest with resignation, as if he'd known all good things must eventually end.

'Breaks up the tedium,' Burt said as he watched his men inventory the store. How much of that would end up in their homes? Harper wondered. 'Of course, Whitby will come away with all the glory.'

'They did the work, didn't they?'

294

'We've done our share here.' The captain bristled. 'This is an excellent little haul. And there are actions going on in Newcastle and York. They'll come out of it smelling like roses.'

As soon as he could, the superintendent returned to Millgarth. Billy would take much of the credit for ending the smuggling operation, and he deserved it. But as soon as he stepped on to the pavement, Harper's thoughts were elsewhere.

He wanted Hotchkiss.

'Go after all his friends,' he ordered. 'See if they've heard from him, if he asked for a bed for the night. You know what to do. I want a very tight guard on all the women running for election. There's no knowing what he'll try. He might decide he wants to have his little blaze of glory.'

'Yes, sir,' Ash said. 'What about you? Where will you be?'

He had work needing attention on his desk. But it could wait until all this was over. The fever was in his blood now. He needed to be out there, to be doing something. He wanted to be there when it ended.

'I'll be spending the day guarding my wife,' he answered with relish.

'Stop fretting, Tom,' Annabelle told him. 'You're worse than an old woman.'

She was out delivering leaflets and knocking on doors along the roads off Sheepscar Street. Harper stayed a few yards away, constantly

295

looking around, aware of who was walking, who was standing on the corner. Martinson was a little further back, just as alert.

The superintendent was looking after his wife, and he had a very sound reason. Hotchkiss had aimed much of his venom at Annabelle. It seemed a fair guess that he'd try to do something to her before he was caught.

He fingered the truncheon in his pocket, feeling the reassurance of the polished wood in his hand. He was ready if Hotchkiss came. And he was out here somewhere, in the thick, dirty air, the harsh smell of the chemical plant drifting across from Meanwood Road.

By dinnertime there was no sign of the man, no word sent from Millgarth. Hotchkiss was still evading the law. But not for much longer.

In the café, Annabelle sat with her volunteers, making a plan for the afternoon. Harper and the constable took the table by the door. If the man tried to storm his way in, they'd be ready to stop him.

'Is he mad, do you reckon, sir?' Martinson asked. 'Barmy, I mean.'

'Probably. He's obsessed, that's for certain.'

'I heard at the station that he had all the malarkey for making bombs in his cellar.'

'That's right.'

He shuddered. 'I don't know how anyone could sleep with all that around. I'd be scared stiff it would all go up during the night.'

'We have it under lock and key,' Harper told him. 'It can't hurt anyone now.'

'I don't mind a bit of a scrap,' Martinson said.

'It's a good way to clear the head. But something like that, it gives me the willies, sir.'

Harper thought of the explosion at St Clement's and seeing the body of the caretaker.

'It does the same to me. The women are ready to leave. You watch them, I'll settle the bill.'

'Very generous of you, sir. Thank you.'

The afternoon was a repeat of the morning. How did she do it? Smiling at everyone, listening to their problems, going from one door to the next and asking for their votes. On her feet all day. He'd forgotten what that was like, although he'd walked a beat for years. His mind began to drift. He wondered what success the others were having, how Billy's big raid with the Excise in Whitby had gone. As soon as he found himself wandering, he dragged his mind back, forcing himself to pay attention.

At a quarter to four she packed the leaflets away in her basket and walked over to him.

'That's me done,' Annabelle announced. 'We've just enough time to walk over to school and collect Mary. She'll be surprised to see the pair of us.'

'Where's Ellen?'

'She had something to do in town so I said I'd see to it.' She put her arm through his and smiled sweetly. 'Two men watching over me. I feel like the Queen.'

'Was it worthwhile today?'

'It's all worth the time,' she answered as they walked back through the streets towards Roundhay Road. 'I might convince one or two more people. If they're ratepayers, I want them casting their ballots. No point in having a vote if you don't use it, is there?'

Harper could hear Martinson ten yards behind them. He looked around. Nobody who resembled Hotchkiss. Very few men at all; they'd still be at work until the day shift ended at six. A couple of women stopped to say hello to Annabelle and told her they'd be supporting her in the election. Her gratitude was real, unfeigned.

'Of course I'm glad,' she told him. 'It means a lot to me every time someone says that. They believe in what I'm doing.'

'What will you do if you win?'

'I don't know.' She chuckled. 'I haven't thought that far ahead yet. I daren't. I might lose. Maybe no one will vote for me.'

'They will,' he assured her. 'They all know you round here.'

'Doesn't mean they like me. I've put some backs up in my time.'

It was a board school, built twenty years before. Long enough for the red of the bricks to be lost beneath a layer of soot. A pair of small gravel playgrounds at the front of the building, one for girls, the other for boys, divided by a low wall. Martinson kept a discreet distance as they waited, rocking gently from foot to foot in the old copper's stance.

As soon as the bell rang, the place seemed to erupt. Children poured out in a welter of noise, laughing, happy, as if they'd just been released from a stretch in prison. It brought memories jarring back into his mind of the joy he felt when each day at Gower Street Primary ended.

Most of the boys and girls had already vanished when Miss Mobley, Mary's teacher, escorted her out.

'She came top in spelling again today. Every word was correct, wasn't it?'

'Yes, Miss,' Mary said, beaming.

'It's all we can do to keep up with her,' Miss Mobley said. Her face flushed. 'Now you go off with your mam and dad. I'll see you in the morning.' She turned to Annabelle. 'I just wanted to wish you good luck in the election, Mrs Harper. I can't vote, but if I could, you'd have mine.'

'Thank you.'

They turned for home, their daughter chattering away, the words coming too fast for Harper to catch them all. The Victoria stood tall on the corner, just a hop, skip and a jump away. A tram slowed for the junction, brakes squealing, steel on steel. Mary looked up and began to scream.

He jerked his head around. There. Not even ten yards away. He'd never seen the man in the flesh but he knew who it was.

Gerald Hotchkiss. A knife in his hand.

'Get back to the school.'

Behind him, Martinson was running. Mary couldn't stop screaming.

Hotchkiss was backing away, already starting to run. But Harper was close. This time he wasn't going to get away. People were moving aside; he saw the fear on their faces as he passed.

By the time they reached Manor Street,

Hotchkiss was only five yards ahead. He turned the corner, feet sliding on the pavement.

Another yard gained. Harper could hear the roaring in his skull.

Just three yards between them now. His fists were clenched and ready.

Near the high back gate of the Victoria he launched himself at Hotchkiss. For a moment he thought it was too soon. But he caught the man's jacket, pulling hard. The fabric began to rip. He held on, bunching it in his fingers, and Hotchkiss fell on to the cobbles.

One blow. Another, then another, and the knife clattered on to the ground.

Harper took hold of the man's head and started beating it against the stone. Pull it up, hammer it down. As if he might be able to take away every memory of his life.

A pair of hands grabbed his arms and dragged him away.

'I think he's probably subdued enough now, sir,' Martinson said gently. 'I'll get the cuffs on him and whistle up some help.'

'Yes, yes.' He stood, dazed, gazing around, not even certain where he was for a few seconds. 'Thank you.'

'We don't want you going down for murder. He was resisting arrest. I saw it with my own eyes. You did what you had to do. And he was armed. There are twenty people who'll testify to that.'

'Annabelle?' he asked. 'Mary?'

'They're safe at the school, sir.' Martinson smiled. 'Why don't you go down and see them? I'll take care of things here.'

Harper nodded dully. At the corner he stopped. 'Tell them at Millgarth that we've got him, will you?'

'Gladly, sir.'

Just two hundred yards, but it felt like five miles. He put one heavy foot in front of the other, slowly surfacing like a man coming out of deep water. How could something be over so quickly? After all the searching, all the hopes that had come to nothing, it was done, just like that.

He'd have killed Hotchkiss if Martinson hadn't arrived. Done it and not felt a moment's remorse. What was he becoming?

He squatted in front of Mary, put a finger under her chin and lifted her head.

'It's fine now,' he told her. 'He won't bother you ever again. He's going to prison.'

'I saw him and . . .' She shook her head and bit down on her lip. He could see the tracks of tears on her cheeks.

'I know. But he's gone now. Everything's going to be all right.'

Fine words. If only they were true. Who knew when it might be over inside her mind? And what about the daughter of Mr Harkness the caretaker, or Harry Cain's wife? It would never end for them.

He held his daughter close, then picked her up. 'Piggy back?' he asked.

Solemnly she nodded, and he lifted her on to his shoulders.

'Watch your head as we go out.'

'Is it really done, Tom?' Annabelle asked as they walked.

'It is,' he told her. 'It really is.'

Twenty-Nine

'I talked to Hotchkiss after he came to last night,' Ash said. 'PC Martinson says he put up quite a bit of resistance to arrest. You did a thorough job, sir.' He smiled. Harper didn't say a word. Safer to keep his mouth shut.

There were so many answers he could give: he was catching someone who'd killed twice, once in cold blood. A bomber, a child snatcher. It would all be true. But it wasn't the real reason. He wanted his revenge on the man who'd gone after his wife and daughter. He would have carried on until the man's brains were spread across the cobbles.

He might not like it, he might keep silent about it, but that was the heart of the matter.

'Seems he saw you and Walsh by his house, and he thought he'd better scarper,' Ash continued. 'He hadn't expected to see you with your wife and daughter. That startled him, he said.'

'What did he plan to do?' His voice was a dry croak. He sipped at a cup of tea. Cold, but it wet his throat.

'He was going to kill Mrs Harper, sir. That was his aim. It's a good job you were there.'

'Yes.' He wanted to let it go, not think about

302

it any more, but it wouldn't move from the front of his mind. 'Did he say why he used those bits of folk songs?'

'He wanted to scare. To terrify. And he wanted us to be certain it was him.'

As if there could have been any doubt.

The superintendent turned to the other men. 'You've done an excellent job. All of you.'

'Hotchkiss will be fine to face a jury and hang once he's recovered, sir,' Ash finished.

'It's over.' Harper leaned back in his chair. 'Finally. Now we just have Mischief Night and the election ahead.' He exhaled slowly. 'Thank the Engineers, please, and tell them we won't be needing them again.' He brought his palms down on the desk. 'Right, what else is there?'

Later, alone in his office, he slit open a letter from Billy Reed.

Dear Tom,
I hear everything went smoothly with the Excise raid in Leeds yesterday. Harry Pepper, the chap in charge here, wanted you along because he thought his people there might be on the take from Rutherford. With the police attending they had to stay honest.

We netted the whole ring. One of Pepper's men was wounded, but it was nothing serious. I had to shoot the ringleader of the smuggling family, but I only winged him. With the arrest, Harry thinks he might have shut down most of the smuggling on the

303

coast for a generation, if it can ever start again.

We gave Terrier John ten pounds from funds and sent him on his way. It wouldn't be safe for him round here now. I told him to steer clear of Leeds, but you know what he's like. Don't be surprised if you see him there. Funny, isn't it, we'd have never had this success if I hadn't come across him before and wondered what he was up to here. Small world.

Give Annabelle our best hopes for the election. We'll see you on December 23rd.

Sincerely,

Billy

The blaze crackled and roared. You could probably see it for a mile or more, Harper thought. One woman was going round selling bonfire toffee, another with parkin. He bought some for Mary, more for Annabelle.

The little girl was transfixed by the fire, watching the flames shoot up, gasping at the creak of wood as part of it collapsed, sending the crowd dancing back with shrieks and laughter, and applause as flames licked at the Guy at the top of the pile and it started to burn.

It was a neighbourhood do, on the waste ground beyond the rhubarb fields. A boy in a cap that was too big for him was being chased by some others, until a hand reached out and clipped one of them on the head; that put an end to things.

Harper glanced at his wife. She was smiling, but her mind was elsewhere. Of course. Another two hours and they'd announce the election result. Since Hotchkiss's arrest she'd been out every day, throwing herself into meetings, as if the sense of relief had sparked her even higher. Very soon she'd know if all the work had paid off. He reached across and squeezed her hand. She turned, but she wasn't really there.

'Come on,' he said to Mary, 'isn't that Maisie Taylor over there? Why don't we see what she's been doing?'

He'd watched his daughter carefully since the day he'd caught Hotchkiss; they both had. But she'd carried on as if the moment had passed, and it hadn't affected her. Maybe they'd be lucky and it would all flow over her. But a part of him had lived too long and knew too much to believe that.

Ten o'clock. The church hall was full. Mary sat on the chair next to his, leaning her head against his chest, fast asleep. All the candidates milled around, unable to settle, talking with their supporters.

Annabelle had a small crowd around her, almost twenty, most of them women. Sergeant Buckley from the Engineers was there in his dress uniform, enjoying all the attention the ladies were giving him. But Harper could tell that Annabelle was barely listening to what everyone said. Her hands fidgeted with her reticule, her gloves, the handkerchief she pulled from her sleeve.

They'd gone home after the bonfire, just long enough for her to change into her favourite plum-coloured gown. No bustle, a high neck, the leg-of-mutton sleeves plumped out. A black

305

velvet hat pinned in place, a deep breath and she was ready.

Tonight was a special night; Mary could stay up late.

'Let her see how it works, Tom,' Annabelle said. 'Even if I don't win, she'll know that I tried.'

He'd wake the girl for the results. Victory or defeat, she'd see what was possible for a woman now. Then who knew what she'd do in the future?

The returning officer climbed on to the platform and waved at the candidates to join him. They stood in a line, two with their heads held high, Oldroyd and Wilkinson staring down at their feet as if their polished shoes were the most interesting thing in the room. Harper nudged Mary until she was awake, and sat her on his lap.

'This is it,' he whispered. 'We'll see if your mam's won.'

'The votes in the election for Poor Law Guardians for Sheepscar Ward have all been counted,' the officer said. 'I would like to remind you that the two candidates with the most votes will serve for the next three years.' He coughed and looked out at the expectant audience. 'Mr Courtney Wilkinson, Conservative, twenty-eight votes.' A few hands clapped. Someone giggled loudly. No surprise, Harper thought. The Tories were always going to be on a losing wicket here. 'Michael Oldroyd, Labour, one hundred and twenty-three votes.' The applause was louder. Relief on the young man's face. Defeat, but not disgrace. 'William Moody, Liberal, two hundred and eighteen votes.' His supporters cheered loudly. 'Mrs Annabelle Harper, Independent, four hundred and seventeen votes.'

The women yelled and cheered at the top of their voices. Harper leapt to his feet, waving his hat and grinning as Mary danced around, beaming with pleasure. 'I declare Mrs Harper and Mr Moody to be the Poor Law Guardians for Sheepscar Ward.' He turned to the candidates, who were shaking hands with each other. 'As the overall winner, Mrs Harper, would you care to say a few words?'

It seemed to catch her by surprise, but she moved to the edge of the platform, trying to keep her grin in check.

'I'm flattered,' she said. 'Honest, I am. Thank you, and I'll do the best job I can, I hope you know that. It's been a very difficult time for all the women who've run. Sad for some, too. But thank you to the police, who've done so well, to the soldiers—' she gave a quick nod to Buckley '—and everyone who volunteered to help me. All of you made it possible. But the biggest thanks of all go to my daughter, Mary. She's not seen much of me during the campaign.' She paused for a second, peering through the crowd. 'There she is. I ran to be a Poor Law Guardian to try and help people. But I also did it to let girls like my daughter know that the world is changing and they'll be able to do much more. Having her gave me the desire to do that.' Annabelle took a deep breath. 'I think we need a celebration. Tomorrow night come round to the Victoria and have a drink. Thank you.'

'She's done it, hasn't she, Da?'

'She has,' he agreed. 'But we never doubted that, did we?'

Annabelle looked out of the carriage window at the North Yorkshire Moors. All the strain of the election had vanished from her face, and a smile played across her lips.

'This was a very good idea,' she said. 'I'm glad you came up with it.' Playfully, she tapped him on the arm. 'I just wish you'd told me more than three days ago. I barely had time to pack, let alone buy anything.'

'They have shops in Whitby, don't they?' Harper said.

She looked at him and shook her head. 'Men.'

Mary knelt on her seat, nose pressed against the glass, taking it all in. It was the farthest she'd ever been from Leeds. He'd had to trace the route for her on the map, revelling in her wonder at the distance.

'We didn't do too badly, did we, Tom?' Annabelle asked with satisfaction. 'Me and Mrs Pease elected, another woman just squeezed into third place. It's a decent start.'

'See how you feel after you start the job in February.'

'I'll love it, and you know it.'

'You'll be busy.'

'Nothing wrong with that,' she told him.

The train slowed along the valley and stopped at Whitby station with a final thick hiss of steam. Harper climbed on to the platform, then helped Mary and Annabelle down the step. Five days off, all of Christmas away from Leeds. Far from Millgarth and the police.

He looked around, and saw a figure waving as she hurried down the platform. Elizabeth, looking plumper and happier than ever. The sea air must agree with her. And following, hands clasped behind his back, Billy Reed.

The women embraced, happy to see each other again, and Harper shook hands with Billy.

'You're looking well.'

'So are you, Tom. Being a super seems to agree with you.'

Harper patted his stomach. 'Not every part of it. Not enough exercise. I heard you received a commendation for that work on arresting the smugglers.'

Reed shrugged. 'Who told you that?'

'Ash, of course. God knows where he hears it all.'

'I'll arrange for your bags to be taken to the guest house. I need to go back to the station, but we can talk more tonight. You know what it's like.'

'Of course.'

Elizabeth took Mary by the hand, leading her outside and into the fresh sea air. Annabelle hung back, sliding her arm through his.

Elizabeth had stopped, pointing up to the headland on the other side of the bay.

'Do you know what that is up there?' she asked Mary.

'It looks like a building,' the girl said suspiciously. 'But it's falling down.'

'It's very, very old. It's been there for hundreds

309

of years. There's a path that goes all the way up to it with one hundred and ninety-nine steps. We can climb it if you like and count them. Can you count that high yet?'

'I don't know,' Mary replied seriously. 'But I'll try.'

'Shall I tell you what else is up there?'

'What?'

'A gravestone with a skull and crossbones on it. Do you know what that means?'

The girl shook her head.

'Pirates,' Elizabeth told her in a loud whisper.

'Really?' Mary's eyes grew wide.

It was going to be a good holiday, Harper decided.

Afterword

I'd like to offer huge thanks to the independent academic, Vine Pemberton Joss, who sparked this book by saying, 'Annabelle should run for office,' then provided me with newspaper articles that became the basis for some quoted here, and gave me plenty of wonderful information. From there the book almost seemed to write itself. Any errors are mine, not hers. The Sheepscar ward is fictional.

Under the law of the time, Annabelle could run for office, to be a member of the School Board or a Poor Law Guardian. Catherine Buckton had been the first woman to hold elected office in Leeds when she was voted on to the School Board in 1873.

Long before women received any national franchise, quite a few could vote in some local elections. It was a long, slow march to some women being able to vote in parliamentary elections in 1918, then the universal franchise in 1928, but after the 1894 Local Government Act, both single and married female ratepayers of all classes could vote in local elections. Around the country, more women were voted on to School Boards and became Poor Law Guardians, often in the face of strident male opposition (and very vocal support from others). It's a sad indictment that over a century later, women in politics, and in life, still face the same misogyny, along with threats of rape and death, and that some have been murdered as they tried to help people.

Frank Kidson was a renowned and respected Leeds folk song collector who produced several books, including his first, *Traditional Tunes*. He was also a historian of Leeds Pottery, and is commemorated with a blue plaque in Chapeltown, where he spent his final years.

I'm very grateful to Kate Lyall Grant, Edwin Buckhalter, and everyone at Severn House for the faith and support they've shown for Tom and Annabelle. Many thanks, too, to my agent, Tina Betts, and my editor, Lynne Patrick, for such excellent work. Also to Leeds Libraries, the Leeds Library, and Leeds Big Bookend for the way they get behind local authors in so many ways. Last, but certainly not least, to Penny, who offers very sound thoughts on the manuscripts as they evolve.

And, of course, thanks to all of you who read these books. I hope you enjoy this one.